E G G L I K E

First Printing, 2018

Defekt Books

ISBN 978-3-947766-00-0

www.gelbartcorp.com

For Alice

E G G L I K E

Adi Gelbart

The Bridge

Day one

At exactly 6:33 A.M., I spotted the purple truck. It was heading north, as I had been told it would, and it was purple. No sign of the yellow motorcycle.

Day two

The purple truck was going north again, but slightly slower than yesterday.

Day three

Interesting. The purple truck was driving as fast as on the first day, but it slowed down just as it was crossing the bridge that I'm standing on. Many vehicles passed today, but still no sign of the yellow motorcycle.

Day four

I spotted an orange motorcycle today, thought it was yellow for a moment, but then realized it only seemed so because all the cars around it were red—some sort of optical illusion. The purple truck passed at 6:40 A.M.—direction: north.

Day five

It's the fifth day in a row that I've brought with me a chicken sandwich, and I think it might be time to switch. No motorcycle, yes truck, 6:34 A.M., northbound.

Day six

The purple truck passed at 6:51 A.M., which is slightly later than usual; normal speed though. I decided to go with a ham and cheese croissant. It was fine, but it's no chicken sandwich.

Day seven

The purple truck arrived from the south going north. It made its pass under the bridge at 6:40 A.M. Perhaps the yellow motorcycle is never seen because it's inside the truck?

Day eight

The yellow motorcycle! It was there at the side of the purple truck, both vehicles heading north. It was unmistakably yellow, and it was obviously outside the truck—my theory had been wrong.

Day nine

Only purple truck today, northbound. No motorcycle.

Day ten

The truck passed under the bridge at 6:40 A.M., directly followed by the yellow motorcycle, going north. At 12:30 P.M., the yellow motorcycle crossed under my observation post going south, with the purple truck following right behind.

Day eleven

Same as yesterday. Both vehicles going north, with the purple truck leading, then returning with the yellow motorcycle in the lead. Times: 6:30 A.M. and 12:30 P.M. respectively.

Day twelve

The same routine. At some point during the day I noticed four green trucks riding in a convoy, which I found pretty strange. I'm sick of the chicken sandwiches again.

Day thirteen

Today I noticed that the yellow motorcycle had no driver. I'm not sure this was the case on the previous days. Either there was a driver before and I hadn't paid attention, or there was never a driver. Let's see what happens tomorrow.

Other than that, the usual pattern of the last three days: going north in the early morning, returning around noon.

Day fourteen

Definitely no driver on the yellow motorcycle. So how does it work? The only thing I can think of is that it's remote controlled by someone from inside the purple truck.

Day fifteen

Morning northbound, noon southbound, and no driver on the yellow motorcycle. I've been experimenting with mayonnaise-based sandwiches for the past few days. They keep me full till the end of the shift, but it's no long-term solution.

Day sixteen

There really can be no other option. The yellow motorcycle is driving with confidence. It can't be a preprogrammed thing; has to be remote controlled. There must be a person inside the purple truck (besides the driver) who is operating the remote control. Tomorrow I will try to see if there are two people sitting in the purple truck.

Worth noting: for some reason, around noon it's less hot on the bridge than in the mornings. It's supposed to be the other way around.

Day seventeen

No one is driving the purple truck either! There are seats and there is a steering wheel, but no one is operating it. This is already mildly disturbing. My current theory: one or two persons are seated in a command module inside the truck's cargo container, and, using cameras and remote controls, they navigate both the purple truck and the yellow motorcycle.

Day eighteen

Today the truck and motorcycle crossed normally at 6:35 A.M., with the purple truck leading and the yellow motorcycle following close behind. However, upon their return they performed a variation: The motorcycle was leading (as it always does in the noontime trip), but just as they crossed under my bridge, the motorcycle moved to the left lane and allowed the purple truck to pass it. It then returned to the right and proceeded to follow the truck.

Day nineteen

More curious variations. In the morning northbound trip, the truck and the motorcycle were driving side by side, and on their return trip I had to rub my eyes to be sure: the yellow motorcycle was standing on the roof of the purple truck! I have a working theory now, but it would be wise to sleep on it before I put it to paper. Besides, my fingers are all greasy from mayonnaise.

Day twenty

More variations. I decided not to record the specifics, as they seem to be of a purely random nature. I still don't feel ready to write down my theory, but so far the continuing variations support it. On an unrelated note, at approximately 11:40 A.M., I noticed a roofless double-decker bus. The entire upper deck appeared to be occupied by professional photographers, and almost all of them were taking pictures of the sky as they passed under me.

Day twenty-one

Okay. This is what I assume is going on:

Inside the truck is a group of up to eight people, but definitely more than three, and probably more than five. At any given moment, two of them are controlling the vehicles using remote controls. One controls the purple truck and one controls the yellow motorcycle. They work in shifts, that is, every so and so minutes, someone hands the remote control to someone else in the group—this is how they prevent fatigue. Now, a few days ago I assumed there were only two people inside the truck, but seeing all the different variations in the ways the truck and motorcycle drove in relation to each other convinced me otherwise. Why would they perform so many variations? Why was the motorcycle on the roof of the truck on not one, but two separate occasions? Only one answer seems plausible: there are more than two people inside the truck, and not only does every person possess a distinct style of controlling the vehicles with the remote, but I'm also guessing that they've become bored going through the same routines every day and therefore started playing around in an attempt to make each other laugh—today at noon the yellow motorcycle was driving in reverse!

Day twenty-two

A double-decker bus with photographers passed again today. They were taking pictures of the sky just as last time, and I noticed that among them was also a film crew, including a boom operator, who held his fur-covered microphone so high that it almost grazed the bridge. I wonder if they're getting any usable footage with the sky being as bright as it is these days.

The truck and motorcycle passed at the usual times and gave no fancy performances. I now assume that the persons inside the truck's cargo hold are of several nationalities or at least come from different cultural backgrounds. Some of them have a tendency for playfulness, while I imagine that some grew up in stricter households and were harshly disciplined as children.

Day twenty-three

All my theories can be scrapped for the moment. I woke up slightly late today on account of a weird dream about a highway with an endless convoy of green trucks that had triangles painted on them in blinding orange, and anyhow, I didn't have time to prepare a proper sandwich, so on the way to the bridge I bought a factory-wrapped egg and ham sandwich, the kind that comes in a triangular plastic container. I opened it only when I was already at my spot on the bridge and it tasted funny. I then realized I forgot to check the expiration date when I bought it (these things have the life expectancy of a corpse), so I tried to read the inscription on the plastic wrap. The writing was so small that I had to hold it at some distance from my face and squint in order to force the letters into focus. Even then, it proved a challenge to make sense of the smeared purple digits, but this led me to a completely unexpected discovery. As I was standing there looking up, with the sandwich in front of my head, I realized how ignorant I had been in my observations: There is a third vehicle in the mix. A helicopter. Floating above the bridge—my bridge. A silver helicopter. And it has probably been there every day, its noise masked by the heavy traffic, its image drowned by the summer sun.

I waved my hands in its direction, but there was no response. Tomorrow I shall bring a big flashlight.

Day twenty-four

The silver helicopter was there when I arrived in the morning—so the events of yesterday morning did actually happen (last night I wasn't sure anymore if I had really seen it or was hallucinating because of the egg and ham sandwich—it was three days past its expiration date). I didn't have any flashlights at home, so I took down the bathroom mirror and carried it with me to the bridge. I used it to reflect the sun onto the cockpit of the silver helicopter, but the sun only gave it a half-assed effort and the helicopter was not impressed.

I repeated this routine a number of times to similar indifference. With frustration building up and the useless mirror insisting on showing me a spot I had missed while shaving, I decided to go for it and just sling the mirror at the helicopter, which I did, only to have it miss the target and land on the roof of the hearse in a passing funeral procession. Luckily, no one saw me, but I couldn't help but feel guilty for supplying the already grieving people with a fresh grievance. However, I told myself that under the circumstances they would be grateful that at least no one new had met their death, and in any case, this minor drama had a fortunate effect in that it finally attracted the attention of the helicopter pilot.

The silver helicopter rotated in place, then made subtle adjustments until it aligned itself with the bridge and began its descent. It made a slow landing on the far side of the bridge, hurling turbulent gusts of wind in the process that showed no mercy on the chicken sandwich I had left unattended on the railing (marinated poultry rained down on the grief-stricken faces of the funeral procession people, who were in the midst of exchanging insurance details). The engines then shut down, and after a minute or so, a figure in a gray jumpsuit stepped out, helmet in hand, and waved in my direction.

I waved back. The figure waved again then motioned me to come over, but I remained in my spot. Another minute passed before he waved at me again. I did not want to be the one giving in and approaching, and apparently, neither did he. We waited some more. He motioned me again to approach. I motioned him in return. No one moved.

Then finally, he went back to the helicopter, climbed inside for a short minute, and came back out carrying a megaphone.

"I am the pilot," he said, "the pilot of the helicopter."

Day twenty-five

It was shortly after six in the morning when the taxi dropped me off at the address the pilot gave me yesterday. A big wooden cabin in the middle of nowhere in the middle of a forest just outside the city. I knocked on the door. He opened, still in his bathrobe, and told me to wait in the living room while he dressed up.

The entirety of the wall around the fireplace was covered with about twenty deer heads, one of them albino (I made a point to remember that). The room had a nice old-fashioned coziness to it, the general mood dictated by the smell of the red and somewhat damp wall-to-wall carpeting. At each corner of the room stood an aquarium with taxidermied hamsters carrying toy model rifles. I went to get a closer look at one of the aquariums. That specific one probably depicted a scene from World War I, as the hamsters were all dressed in highly detailed German uniforms, complete with helmets and gas masks, and some were riding model horses. I started walking in the direction of another one that from afar appeared to portray a scene from the Vietnam War, but I heard the pilot approaching from the other room and decided it would be a bad move to be seen nosing around. We then had a conversation that was recorded on the tape recorder I hid in my jacket beforehand. It began with a simple exchange of pleasantries, but I feel it's important to cover that part as well, therefore I'm transcribing here the entire thing:

Pilot: Tea, coffee?

Me: Some tea would be great.

Pilot: Milk?

Me: No.

Pilot: Be right back.

Pilot (from kitchen): I forgot to <indistinguishable>

Me: I can't understand you from here.

Pilot (from kitchen): Sorry. Coming right back.

Pilot (back in room): So you wanted tea, right?

Me: Yes, no milk.

Pilot: Yes, I will make it now. I was just feeding the cat in the kitchen. He's very grumpy if I don't do it first thing in the morning.

Me: Oh. What kind of cat is it?

Pilot: Actually, I don't know the first thing about cats. It's gray . . . it has green eyes. It's not mine. I'm just taking care of it for the neighbor while she's on vacation.

Me: That's nice of you.

Pilot: I owe her. She takes care of this place when I'm away, and I'm away a lot. I think the water is ready. Coming right back.

Pilot (returning from kitchen): There you go. Be careful, it's very hot.

Me: Thank you.

Pilot: Did you have trouble finding the house?

Me: No, not at all.

Pilot: I've been living here for the past five years. I used to really like it, then we broke up—me and my wife that is—left me for a commercial airline pilot. It broke my spirit at the time, but in the end I think it was probably for the best. And you know, she decorated this place—all the deer heads, the hamster war dioramas, and the stuffed dog astronaut in the bedroom—you can have a look at that one later—it's all her. Me, I don't know the first thing about taxidermy. When she left, I thought I'd get rid of all that stuff—too many memories—but then as time passed, it didn't feel strange anymore, it became my own place, my own deer heads, my own hamster soldiers.

Me: How long ago was it that you split up?

Pilot: The separation was almost two years ago, the divorce was finalized a few months later. I got the cabin, she got our house in the city. I could have fought harder, but what's the use? In the end, serenity of the mind is more important than any asset—better a bird on a highway than a limousine on top of a tree.

Me: I guess that's true. Still, I don't know many people who would have taken this experience quite so positively.

Pilot: Well sure, I've had some rough patches, been to low places—even the proudest peacock will sometimes feed on worms—but then I looked at myself from the outside, and it all just seemed like a theater play, this misery business, and I had to pull down the curtain and get on with it.

Me: You have a real flair for the metaphors.

Pilot: Thank you. In a way, I've always been better with that sort of stuff. I don't know the first thing about physics, for example.

Me: But you're a helicopter pilot. I would assume it requires some knowledge of physics?

Pilot: Well, I know how to make it fly up and down, but believe me, I don't know the first thing about the mechanics, the stuff that—

[At this point in the conversation, the cat walked into the room. I noticed it had a peculiar walk, but I only allowed myself a short glance, wanting to be polite to my host who was midsentence.]

Pilot: —that makes it work.

[The cat meowed.]

[In the following fifteen minutes, nothing of real interest was said. I sensed he wanted to go back and talk about his ex-wife, and, wishing to keep the conversation flowing, I asked him follow-up questions (something I often do and often regret). He went on and on about his ex-wife's shortcomings and how it was she who had brought on the eventual deterioration of their relationship and so on. I found his account very one-sided and self-indulgent and his reliance on metaphors tiring, but I didn't say anything. I also kept silent about the tea, which in itself tasted like sufficient grounds for divorce.]

Pilot: But I've been going on and on about myself. So you work on the bridge as a traffic surveyor? I assumed this sort of stuff was already taken over by special cameras these days.

Me: You are correct, it is done by special cameras, yes. But first, one has to know where to put those special cameras and which types of special cameras to use and so on. This is where I come in. I collect data, which then serves as a basis for those technical decisions.

Pilot: Sounds interesting, though it's all too technical for me. As I said, I don't know the first thing about machine technology.

Me: The job is quite monotonous in nature. But at least I don't have an office to show up to day in and day out—I would never be able to lead that sort of life. That's modern slavery if you ask me.

[At that point, the cat meowed again. Acting on a hunch, I yanked the cat's tail. It let out a meow. I yanked it again. Another meow—identical—just as I expected. The cat jumped away to the corner of the room and hissed. It was time to put an end to this whole charade.]

Me: My dear pilot, what you have so clumsily erected here is more than a mere smoke screen, it's a veritable fog on an early-dawn highway, and your bus has just lost its grip on the road, if you won't mind *me* having a go at the metaphors for a change. Since I first sat myself in this chair, you have gone out of your way to foster the illusion that you are ignorant on the subject of cats and know nothing about taxidermy, physics, machine technology, and so on. In fact, the exact opposite is the truth. This cat, which you allege was left here by an imaginary neighbor, is in reality of your own creation. A machine, a robot, and quite a sophisticated one at that. Building it would take someone who's an expert in the combined fields of zoology, taxidermy, mechanics, and artificial intelligence—the exact fields you tried to mislead me into believing you know nothing about. You even borrowed a technique from the pages of hypnotic suggestion—your very intentional repetition of the phrase "I don't know the first thing about." Of course, this is a beginner's technique and it left me unimpressed; in fact, this repetition was the first hint that gave you away. It was meant to suggest to my mind that you literally do not know a thing about those fields. Well, let me say here and now that you don't know the first thing about *acting*. Taking everything into account, I am assuming that this entire meeting was set up as a test—one of important consequences. I would venture to say that in one of those deer heads is hidden a camera and microphone pair, recording my every move. And it wouldn't be inside the albino deer, either. I bet if I opened it up, I would find a camera, only it would be a decoy, not the real thing but something to make the one who found it think they had disabled the surveillance, when in fact the spying deer is one of the others, the least remarkable one. A boring deer makes the perfect spy. Of course, this is all elementary, which is why you would not have bothered to put a camera in any of the deer. I also do not suspect the hamsters. I believe they genuinely represent a meeting of your two biggest fascinations—war and rodents. No, you have no need for cameras at all, for the test subject is not me. No. You see me every day from your silver helicopter. You already know what you need, and you know I am no fool. Which leads me to conclude that I was actually meant to serve not as the test subject but rather as the *tester* in this bizarre setup.

[He gave a short smile, then stood up, went into the kitchen, and came back with two glasses and an unlabeled bottle of what turned out to be very fine single-malt scotch.]

Pilot: As you no doubt understand, I had no choice but to produce all of those lies and metaphors. It was important that you experience the cat without any prior knowledge of its artificiality.

Me: You are not a simple pilot. You are a pilot/engineer.

Pilot: And you are no traffic surveyor.

Me: Nor did I enjoy the tea. But let us proceed.

Pilot: Yes, let's please. I am anxious to know what you thought of the cat. And please, hold nothing back.

[I didn't quite know in what way, but I had a feeling it would prove beneficial to have this person on my side. I decided to help him.]

Me: Let me start by saying that the facial features are nothing short of remarkable. Obviously the real cat, whose skin and fur you used in the creation of this robot, had quite a distinct personality, and it still shines through. I would certainly say that, when seen from afar, the robot passes for a genuine cat. Even though the movement of the legs is slightly off, more clumsy than it is catty, it's not enough to betray the cat's synthetic nature. However, my suspicions first arose when I glimpsed it up close. That's when I noticed that the knees are not moving—the joints are molded at a preset angle, which lends the cat a very unnatural shape. But the biggest giveaway was the meow sound. I heard it three or four times, and each time it sounded exactly the same.

Pilot: Actually, there are four tapes inside the cat's belly. A meow, a purr, a growl, and a hiss—all recorded from a real live cat in the highest fidelity possible. A dedicated electrical circuit selects the appropriate sound depending on the situation.

Me: The sound quality was indeed very clear, a testament to your skills as an engineer, and I can only assume how difficult it must have been to fit a speaker inside the head section. Still, technique will only go so far if not accompanied by true inspiration. And so, you should probably be picking up the phone to arrange for a new recording session with the cat whose voice is on those recorded tapes. Only, this time have him meow multiple times, so that you have about four distinct versions of meows, four versions of purrs, and so on. If you want to imitate life, you need to imitate its versatility. But do not simply put him in front of a microphone and order him to make sounds. No, that will not do. Have him play around, show him love, make him experience calm, leisure. Then bring in fear, uncertainty, bark at him, make him hide, let him doubt his every move. Let a bird fly into the recording room, have him chase it, let him hide, anticipate, attack. Re-create life for him, and he will create sounds full of life in return. Edit the tapes and have the circuits replay these sounds from the belly of the robot. Only then will you have imitated life.

[The cat hissed in my direction, then walked to the fireplace and crouched awkwardly on its fur-covered, unbendable metallic legs.]

Day twenty-six

Stayed home. I planned to catch up on some sleep, but the neighbor from the apartment below, which until recently lay vacant, was practicing the bassoon all day. This was not the first time either, and it's slowly turning into a real nuisance.

Day twenty-seven

I took my spot on the bridge at about 6:00 A.M. When I arrived, the pilot was already floating above it in the helicopter. I waved at him. He moved the helicopter's nose down and then up—a nod?

There were no fancy patterns today: the truck was leading in the morning, and on the trip back around noon, the yellow motorcycle rode in front.

Day twenty-eight

I had a very vivid dream that woke me up in the middle of the night. All I can remember now is that it had some pyramids in it, and I think it wasn't the first time I've dreamed about pyramids lately. I should probably keep a dream journal—pyramids should never be taken lightly.

As for the vehicles: same patterns as yesterday, except that the motorcycle was driving in reverse. Now that I know the pilot is an observer like me, I am back to the eight-multina-tionals-in-the-belly-of-the-truck theory.

Day twenty-nine

They passed in the morning, drove back in the afternoon.

Day thirty

The same.

Day thirty-one

The same again.

Day thirty-two

Same.

Day thirty-three

Frustration.

The patterns seem purely random, and I've decided that from here on I will no longer document them. This surveying from the bridge has got me as far as it could. If I want to learn more, I have to go to either the source or the destination of the vehicles' route.

The only positive I can find is that this seeming randomness actually supports my working theory: that whoever happens to be holding the remote at the moment of passage is responsi-ble for the style of driving of the two vehicles. However, there could still be order on a deeper level. The persons inside the purple truck may be following a weekly schedule that deter-mines who is remote controlling the motorcycle and when, or it could be prearranged according to country of origin, or still there could be complete anarchy wherein whoever snatches the remote first thing in the morning gets to handle it.

More questions: Do they meet up for an early coffee before they get into the truck? Or does someone start off with the truck in the morning and proceed to pick up the other team members from their homes? Does that person ring their doorbells, or are they already waiting in the street? Is it the same person every day, or is this aspect scheduled as well? Do they have a dress code? Customized briefcases? Secret handshakes?

The more I think about it, the more I am nearing a new theory: These people have no houses and they have no morning meetings. In fact, I believe they have no social footprint in the outside world—it would serve no purpose. They spend their entire time inside this purple truck, driving it and the yellow motorcycle without ever stopping. They are not everyday, regular people; they are passengers. They have become part of the process, another piece of machinery, as indispensable, and at the same time unremarkable, as the fuel tank or the transmission box. They are not the thing I am looking for.

I wonder if I, too, have become too attached to this daily routine.

Day thirty-four

Stayed inside today. The bassoon player from the apartment below practiced all day long. It began with a few hours of scales, repeated and recycled to exhaustion, then all sorts of sound gymnastics—short notes, long notes, notes bent up, notes bent down, notes hell-bent on triggering migraines; then scales again, fast, faster, then slower and slower still until each note lingered for a small eternity. Already under normal circumstances the bassoon has an irritating quality—sort of like the humming of a prepubescent bee—but this was much worse, as if the bassoonist was going out of his way to pack each note with the full annoyance potential the instrument allowed for.

Around eleven at night, the day's practice session culminated in a recurring pattern of seven notes—the same notes repeated in a fast pace over and over and over again. I was getting so annoyed that I considered dropping in on him with the angry-neighbor act. Eventually, however, I decided against it—he'd either be a complete jerk, or worse, he would apologize and I'd find myself having to withstand a conversation.

I must remember to buy earplugs.

DREAM JOURNAL ENTRY NO. 1

The three pyramids are here again. Hollow and holographic and humming. And glowing. As before. The red one on the left, the green on the right, and the yellow in the middle. All of them touching each other just slightly, glowing more intensely where they intersect. They are gigantic structures of light. And everything else is black. As it was before. I listen more closely: each pyramid is humming a different tone, I think. Suddenly, a sensation appears—an overwhelming sensation that something is about to happen. And while nothing is happening in actuality, this sensation is so clear and real that it is already an event in and of itself. This is what it feels like: I am on the verge of some great transformation—actually not specifically me—*everything* is about to transform itself; nothing is changing as of yet, but everything is about to. This feeling lingers for a substantial amount of time. Or maybe it only lasts for a single second and it's time itself that has slowed to a standstill. This is the last thing I remember. I can't quite say whether the pyramids had a triangular or rectangular base.

Day thirty-five

It was time to speak to the pilot. Once again, gaining his attention proved difficult. Using what small stones I could gather and some excess mayonnaise from the sandwich, I drew a helicopter and a large downward arrow on the floor of the bridge, but he didn't seem to notice. He also didn't respond to my hand waving, nor did I get anywhere with an energetic set of jumping jacks. So later in the day (this time, after politely waiting for the road to clear), I launched my still half-full tea thermos in the direction of the helicopter. It was quality tea, but sometimes sacrifices have to be made.

After the pilot landed on the bridge, he stepped out with his megaphone and told me that from now on if I wanted to talk, I should call him up on his satellite phone from the phone booth that's located under the stairs to the bridge. He then put down the megaphone and used his fingers to signal me the number. I think it was 393939 (hard to be certain with all those repeated digits). Anyway, I didn't have any coins on me, so the call would have to wait till tomorrow.

Meanwhile, the bassoon player is really testing my patience, and I keep forgetting to buy earplugs.

Day thirty-six

After the morning appearance of the vehicles (later than ever—7:15 a.m.), I located the pay phone under the bridge and dialed the pilot's number. I recorded our conversation on tape.

Pilot: Hello, who's this?

Me: It's me, from the bridge.

Pilot: How do I know that?

Me: I assume you saw me walk down from the bridge to the pay phone.

Pilot: Maybe I did, maybe I didn't. Maybe there is no bridge at all. If it really is you, then run a hand through your hair, right . . . now.

Me: From your current vantage point, the phone booth is obscured by the bridge, so even if I touched my hair, you wouldn't be able to see it.

Pilot: Good, that's what I needed to hear—proves you're not an impostor. Now listen: On this line we must keep the length of conversations to under ninety seconds. Also, we must use code words for certain terms. You will find a glossary taped to the wall above the phone.

He hung up. There was indeed a crumpled piece of paper attached with Scotch Tape to the wall of the booth. In all caps it read:

"HELICOPTER = WOMB, BUS = INCUBATOR, TRUCK = HAMSTER, MOTORCYCLE = SUNFLOWER SEED, BRIDGE = FRIDGE, HIGHWAY = DOLPHINARIUM"

I dialed again.

Me: So, I've given up trying to understand the ways of the purple . . . HAMSTER and the yellow SUNFLOWER SEED.

Pilot: And who may I say is calling?

Me: Oh, it's me from the bridge again.

Pilot: Don't you mean FRIDGE?

Me: Yes, of course. It's me from the FRIDGE.

Pilot: You're calling from a fridge? Did your air conditioning break down?

[His sense of humor, if that's what it was, revealed itself to be in even poorer taste than his metaphors.]

Me: I am not really in a fridge, I am in a phone booth.

Pilot: If you really are in a phone booth, then jump right . . . now.

Me: I would hit my head on the ceiling.

Pilot: Good, that's what I wanted to hear—an impostor wouldn't have considered this piece of phone booth trivia. Now, you were saying?

Me: Yes, so I said that I have stopped trying to understand the ways of the purple HAMSTER and the yellow SUNFLOWER SEED. I assume you're in a similar situation. We might be able to help each other.

Pilot: What about the double-decker INCUBATORS?

Me: The INCUBATOR with the film crew?

Pilot: Well, that's one of them.

Me: I think they are an anomaly, insignificant.

Pilot (after a moment of thought): Maybe they are. But I prefer to see nothing as insignificant.

Me: If nothing is insignificant then it must follow that nothing is significant. I am focused on the purple HAMSTER and the yellow SUNFLOWER SEED. I want to try and follow them to their source.

Pilot: And I assume you planned to do it from inside my WOMB, that you want us to track them from above? I'm afraid that's not possible. I must always keep my post here. I gather what information I can by observing the patterns.

[I found it telling that he chose to code the helicopter as "womb." This is most likely someone who does not feel safe when he's out in the world—the dead-animals cabin suits him well.]

Me: The patterns are inconclusive. I've been here long on the FRIDGE, and I have my theories, but I need to go deeper. I wanted to suggest that we use the cat to follow the vehicles for us.

Pilot: I don't know what cat you're talking about . . . don't know the first thing about cats. Ninety seconds!

And with that he hung up.

I was out of coins for the day. As I started to climb back up the bridge, the phone rang. I ran down to answer, but it was a wrong number.

DREAM JOURNAL ENTRY NO. 2

I am standing on the balcony of a high hotel room overlooking the beach. A bright, if somewhat unstable sun hangs over a cloudless sky. Wind-carved sand dunes stretch out on the shoreline like a blanket on an unmade bed. The sea itself is very calm, but under the sun's flickering, it's drifting, undecided, between blue and green. Slowly and silently (in fact in total stillness, as if sound is not a property of this dream world), movement spreads from all sides. Tens, or perhaps hundreds of manta rays appear beneath the waves, swimming toward an invisible point somewhere in the middle of the water. A voice calls me back into the room, but I stay on the balcony to watch the silent silhouettes of the manta rays, whose bodies have now acquired ink-like qualities and are beginning to merge into each other. "Please sir, you have to pay for your breakfast." I did not order any breakfast. I peek into the room, and instead of a room service person, there is a wooden truck the size of a small refrigerator, and it is burning (though very slowly and softly, with an inviting sort of flame, not unlike a country-house fireplace).

Day thirty-seven

When I got to the phone booth in the morning, a new term had been added to the list of code words, neatly scribed with a thick black marker: "CAT = UNBORN CHILD." I called the pilot. He answered in a fake woman's voice; there was an attempt at an accent, vaguely Czech.

Pilot: Vera's Hair-Care Solutions, how may I be of service?

Me: It's me again, from the bri— FRIDGE.

Pilot: Are you calling to make a hair appointment?

Me: It's me from the FRIDGE. You just saw me go down the stairs. You can't see me right now because the phone booth is obscured. Also, I can't jump, as the ceiling of the phone booth would hurt my head.

Pilot (back to his normal voice): A triple proof . . . can't be too careful these days—impostors are everywhere!

[A big black fuel truck chose that moment to fill the air with a deafening horn blast. A strong smell of gasoline and a temporary hearing loss ensued, but a few seconds later, scores of tiny, brightly colored cars reemerged with their beeps and cranky motors and unruly children. I put a finger in my left ear to block out the distractions and concentrated on properly using the code words—it was important I keep the pilot happy in his little word game. I repeated in my head: UNBORN CHILD means cat; HAMSTER means truck.]

Me: I want to use the UNBORN CHILD.

Pilot: In what fashion?

Me: I want to parachute it to the roof of the purple HAMSTER. Then the UNBORN CHILD can penetrate the purple HAMSTER and broadcast to us images from inside. Even if he is discovered by the passengers inside the HAMSTER, they will most likely not suspect an UNBORN CHILD of foul play. That is, if the UNBORN CHILD robot can pass for a real-life UNBORN CHILD.

[A long pause.]

Pilot: Call me back in fifteen minutes.

I used the break to catch up on my morning sandwich, then dialed again. This time he answered in the role of a senile pensioner, which meant the impostor-screening portion of the conversation lasted three times as long. Just before we exhausted the allotted ninety seconds, he instructed me to write down my address on a small piece of paper, unscrew the receiver cup, and place it inside. The cat would be delivered there tomorrow at nine in the morning.

Even though this was the best piece of news in quite some time, I reminded myself not to get my hopes up too high—if I was able to expose the cat in a matter of minutes, someone else might, too. So tomorrow, I plan to put that robot through some serious tests to see if it's up to the task. On the way home I stopped to do some shopping—milk, cat food, dog food, rat poison (let's see if it can tell the difference), matches, rusty nails, mechanical mice (I bought dozens of those—I have some vague plans for an angry-mob-type simulation), and blank tapes for the tape recorder. I also finally remembered to get earplugs.

Back home, the bassoonist was in full attack mode. More of those weird patterns, blurted out in incredible loudness— it's becoming a real pain (though I must admit that all this incessant practicing seems to have paid off—the speeds he played with tonight bordered on inhuman). This time I went down to his apartment and knocked on the door. He immediately stopped playing, which meant he heard me, but he didn't answer. Knocking harder didn't help. I put my ear to the door. There was total silence and no light was coming through the peephole, no sign that anyone was living there. I assumed he got the message and simply wanted to avoid confrontation, but as soon as I was back in my apartment, he started playing again, somehow even louder than before.

The earplugs certainly help, but some stray notes still manage to crawl through the ear tunnels and find their way to the synapses of my brain.

DREAM JOURNAL ENTRY NO. 3

The shining pyramids have returned. They are farther apart this time, more distant, and possibly even more enormous. I notice mild fluctuations in the intensity of their glow as well as short pauses in the humming, as if they stop to catch their breath. Their colors are brilliant, almost painful on the eyes, the yellow pyramid radiating as if it's built from pieces carved out of the sun. There is a presence far away in the black nothingness. I cannot see it yet, but I know it is approaching. Again, as before, there is the sense of anticipation. Something is about to happen; it will reveal itself. The presence is getting nearer. I can feel it entering the middle pyramid from the back and traveling in my direction, but the pyramid is so vast that this will take a while. I still don't *see* the presence; I only sense it. A physical sensation. Suddenly, the pyramids stop their humming, turn to dull white, play a short tone in unison, and I wake up. It is seven in the morning, and the bassoonist is already at it.

Day thirty-eight

The pilot's package arrived on time. Delivered by whom, I couldn't see, as they left it on my doorstep and were gone by the time I answered the door. It was an unimpressive cardboard box, several lifetimes past its original incarnation, with quite a few crossed-over addresses and labels, the most prominent of which was a handwritten promise of "Socks" (this was either cautious camouflage or, more likely, just plain, horrid stinginess, as it didn't quite smell of roses).

I contacted a man I know who had just bought an old carpentry workshop and got him to let me have the place to myself for the entire day. He's in the process of converting it into a bowling alley, and in the meantime there's total disarray—only one lane has been completed and to the side of it are piles of chainsaws, chisels, and industrial drills intertwined with all manner of cheap plywood and silver tin cans with indecipherable labels; an overbearing smell of varnish looms over the entire place to complete the ambiance.

After I finished building up the various devices and booby traps, I unpacked the cat. Taped to its forehead was a xeroxed brochure titled "Electromechanical Taxidermy Cat Unit for Surveillance (ETCUS) — Operation Manual." It contained detailed instructions on how to connect the radio receiver to a TV set so that it displays the video captured by the cat's internal camera, followed by explanations on the remote control unit and then multiple tables and graphs with temperatures and acceleration rates and stuff that is possibly important but that I couldn't really bring myself to care about. Unfortunately, it neglected to describe how to install the batteries, so it was only after some embarrassing trial and error that I finally discovered that the batteries are placed by opening the belly of the cat from underneath. There is no power switch—the robot simply comes to life the moment the batteries touch the terminals to form a closed circuit, which was unfortunate, as it resulted in multiple scratches on my forearm. That was obviously quite disconcerting for me, but a point chalked up to the cat robot for realism.

It occurred to me this was the first time I had been alone in a room with a cat, even if it was only a mechanical one. I have never owned or taken care of one, so I have no firsthand experience of the psychological peculiarity that is the cat-human relationship. However, I believe it is exactly this lack of empathy toward the animal that has in turn enabled me to put it through rigorous trials while maintaining the necessary scientific detachment.

I spent the day performing numerous tests and observing the behavior of this curious artificial creature and did not leave the workshop until very late. When I came back home, I longed to unleash the cat on the bassoon fiend, but I'm not supposed to use it for my personal affairs, and besides, it was already packed in its box and I had no wish to once again go through the painful process of inserting the batteries.

I sat down and wrote a letter to the pilot, which I then wrapped around the cat's detachable tail and placed inside the package.

"Dear pilot," it went, "I am very thankful that you agreed to send ETCUS to me for inspection. I took careful care of him and I return him without any physical damage, and let me assure you that any so-to-speak psychological damage incurred during his time with me was due to actions that were crucial to the evaluation process.

"Although covered with fur of the utmost quality, ETCUS is still a machine, a robot enhanced with so-called artificial intelligence—a set of variables, conditions, equations, and loops aimed at imitating a living creature's thought process. But this is all it is—an imitation. However, if constructed in a particular fashion, the difference between the imitation of life and the presence of life becomes irrelevant. *I look like I think, therefore I look like I am.*

"A child at birth is already endowed with the ability to love, to fear, to feel wonderment, warmth, confusion. Later on it picks up pride, inadequacy, disappointment, bitterness, existential emptiness, suicidal tendencies. A cat is no different, and if ETCUS is to masquerade as a living, emotional being, then he must first learn how to feel. At exactly two o'clock, I stopped supplying him with food, thereby introducing bewilderment and confusion into his system. Next, using the joystick, I directed him under remote control mode to stand in front of a sheet of transparent Plexiglas, and I tied him to the spot so that he could not move. I then started to hurl bowling balls down a slope in his direction, raising the slope's angle by five degrees after every trial. A microphone was placed above his head that measured the decibels of his voice. Sure enough, his cries became louder in direct relation to the angle of the slope (and therefore the speed of the approaching bowling ball). He looked and sounded (I could tell you took my advice and rerecorded several versions of each sound) like a terrified cat—a very positive result.

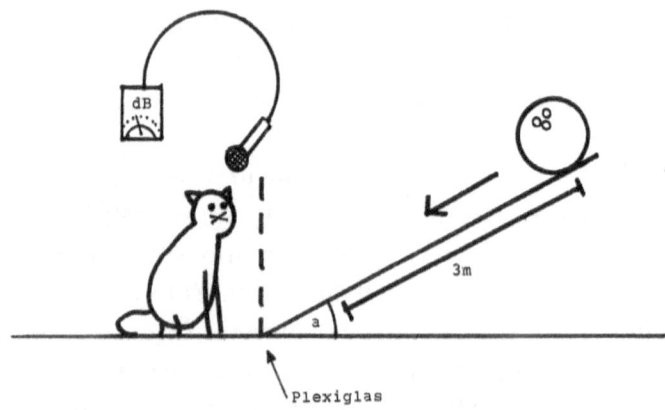

"Of the many tests I performed, the most significant one was the revolving chair test, in which I examined the cat's reaction to rapidly changing emotional stimuli. Using a set of tapes, microphones, and directional speakers, I was able to condense a spectrum of emotions that one would normally experience in the span of a few years into a twenty-five-minute session. The motor-controlled revolving chair on which the cat sat continuously altered its speed and direction, and as a result, the cat in turn faced two distinct types of emotion-evoking music (B, D), the amplified sound of defenseless mice (A), which he could not attack because for this experiment I again tied him to the chair, and words spoken through a microphone by me (C)—at times words of praise ('You are magnificent. Your fur is sublime'), and at times words of disapproval and scorn.

Popular music

Arnold Schönberg –
Verklärte Nacht

Support/Reproach

"I have attached here the four pages of data I collected in this experiment, but you may disregard them, for while perhaps interesting from a research perspective, they are not essential to my assessment. In the first minutes of the experiment, ETCUS tried to counter the bombardment on his emotional centers with several different techniques (the most interesting of which was trying to meow along to Schönberg's music, though he had a hard time following the rapidly shifting harmonies), then he became visibly angry, hissing at me, scratching the chair, growling. His resolve was steadily weakening as the minutes passed, until finally, he gave up. His eyes blanked, his tail lay flat and motionless, and his gaze became that of a dead man. This, I found to be the most profound aspect of his being: he could no longer endure the fluctuation of his emotional self, and instead he embraced apathy.

"For the rest of the day, he was very difficult to control. He frowned at me whenever our gazes met, tried to scratch me multiple times, tore up the upholstery of the only sofa in the room, and then proceeded to hide inside a trash can. I tried to reason with him, I even mixed extra milk into his cat food and removed nearly all the leftover rat poison, but that did nothing to improve his attitude; he just crouched in the corner of the room and meowed at me in defiance, switching to threatening hisses whenever I got close. This behavior was very realistic, and while it may help him pass for a real live cat, I find that this giving in to petty social behavior can also hinder his ability to function as a surveillance unit. Therefore, I suggest that you consider supplementing ETCUS with an inner voice—a loudspeaker inside his brain that only he can hear, and that, through radio waves, would transmit whatever the operating person voices into the remote control. This would lend him a conscience of sorts, and even more importantly, a friendly voice inside his head—someone to give him words of encouragement when he's out there all on his own.

"If you are willing to make this modification, then we can parachute ETCUS to the roof of the purple truck. I am certain this will teach us far more than our observations from the bridge ever could."

Day thirty-nine

The bassoon business is getting out of hand.

Already with the very first note in the morning, I could sense that something was off. The playing—it was darker than usual, which I hadn't imagined possible. *Ominous.* His style had more than evolved, it underwent some sort of mutation. There wasn't even the pretense of a scale anymore, just violent mechanical jabbering, loud and dirty—as if a family of snorting pigs had moved in, and in between belches, they were feeding shards of glass into the grinding teeth of an industrial wood chipper. It was an ugly sound, vulgar, almost obscene. But there was more to it. It wasn't simply the playing that was different; there was something novel about the quality of the sound. Somehow it was rawer, more direct. I could even hear the clicking of the metal keys against the bassoon's wooden body—as though the actual acoustics of the room had transformed.

I went through the house and double-checked that all the windows were shut; that wasn't it. The door to the staircase was closed as well. I knelt down and put my ear to the floor to try and get a better idea. And then I spotted it, right underneath the center of my bed—a hole! Drilled all the way from the ceiling of the bassoonist's apartment to the floor of mine, a clean drilling job complete with sandpaper finish, and it wasn't narrow either—I could almost fit my entire hand in it.

I rushed out of the apartment, climbed down the stairs, and banged on his door with an angry fist. No reaction—he didn't even bother to stop playing this time. I ran back up, pushed my bed to the side, and stuck my eye in the hole. Pitch-black. I still hadn't bought a flashlight, so I took a coin and dropped it into the hole to see what sound it made. However, the bassoon was so loud that I couldn't hear anything, and two seconds later the coin shot back up and hit me right in the eye.

I fetched the broom from the hallway, carefully inserted it into the hole, and swayed it around. I could feel resistance on all sides, as if there was some sort of tube attached to the bottom of the hole—solid material but with a certain degree of elasticity, I assume rubber. I jerked the broom around to try and get a feel for the shape of the tube. The bassoonist, clearly not happy with my intrusion, protested by barking through the instrument like a rabid dog. Unfortunately, this was accompanied by a gust of air that also carried a fair amount of liquids—most likely some inadvertent spit from the insides of the bassoon. The rubber tube must have been directly connected to the instrument, thus delivering its unfiltered sound directly into my apartment—a perversely conceived amplification system, as viciously efficient as it is primitive. What's going on? Why go through all this trouble? I cursed and shouted profanities into the tube, I stomped on it—all to no effect. Then later I came up with the idea of pouring water into it, but that did nothing except transform the noises from the barks of an angry pit bull into the shrieks of killer whales in heat.

Is it simply a case of an insane individual? No, I know better than to dismiss it so carelessly. Is he connected to the truck people? Did they notice me and are now sending a message? I have absolutely nothing to go on, all empty guesses, and I definitely can't think clearly under all this noise.

I took a trip to the hardware store and got an all-purpose premixed joint compound (generally intended for drywall repair, but I was told it should do the job) and emptied the entire bucket into the hole. It will take twenty-four hours to completely dry, but it's already an improvement.

DREAM JOURNAL ENTRY NO. 4

The three pyramids. I've been expecting them. Red, yellow, and green. Glowing. Beyond them, blackness. The humming, now low and loud and mean. All as before. The moment of anticipation. The presence approaching, slowly. Or fast? It is almost at the front side of the center pyramid. I can start making out its shape. Like a huge leaf, or actually a manta ray, not swimming or floating—flying? No, hovering. As if it's standing upright on its tail. It is approaching. Its eyes have all the colors of the universe. It has arrived. It is here. It is staring at me now, ready to speak. A wonderful voice, low and monotonous; I can't tell if I really hear it, or if it is only felt. And every word that is spoken appears on a different pyramid in huge letters. One word after the other. And the manta ray presence utters these three words:

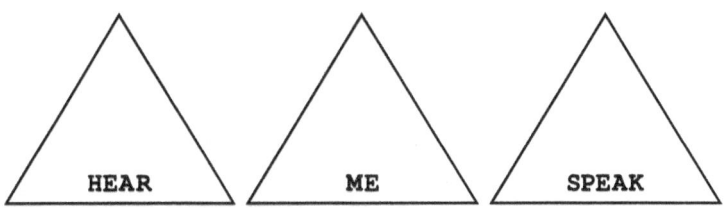

Day forty

There is no choice but to leave the apartment, at least for the time being. Not only was the joint compound completely removed from the hole during my sleep, but right next to it, three brand-new holes appeared. How he drilled them without me waking up is a complete mystery—even with the earplugs, I was bound to hear something. So now I get the bassoonist's cacophonies in full quadraphonic experience. This can't go on! I packed some stuff and headed for the bridge—the situation in my apartment was severe, but I had more pressing things to attend to.

When I got there, I called up the pilot to talk about the cat robot, also known as ETCUS, also known as the UNBORN CHILD in the coded language of our pay phone conversations. Surprisingly, he skipped the usual security questions and jumped right to it.

Pilot: The UNBORN CHILD will be ready in two days' time.

Me: I am very happy to hear that. How will we parachute him?

Pilot: We won't. We'll just throw him off the FRIDGE. He's an UNBORN CHILD; he'll land on his feet.

Me: That makes things simpler.

Pilot: Anything else?

Me: Yes, you wouldn't happen to know anything about a bassoon player?

[A shot in the dark, but I decided to take it.]

Pilot: What's a bassoon?

Me: A woodwind instrument, like an oboe but bigger and longer. It has a deeper sound.

Pilot: I've never heard of such an instrument in my life. In fact, I don't know the first thing about musical instruments. Ninety seconds.

[Bleep.]

Day forty-one

I spent the night in a hotel. Had a dreamless, and more importantly, bassoon-less sleep. I took the breakfast deal, which proved to be a total rip-off (overcooked tea, shady sausages, a disturbingly happy group of caffeinated tourists), and then the room was no vision either—a tasteless mixture of yellows and browns; apparently when I told the desk clerk "single room, please," the guy heard, "one mustard jar, and make it stuffy."

I know I shouldn't complain, but I am still very much outraged by my imposed eviction.

Day forty-two

Did nothing of consequence. Walked the hotel corridors, stared at the ceiling, even found myself browsing the three channels of the wall-mounted TV (only a hotel situation could ever make me turn on that appliance)—a monumental waste of a day. But I don't care: tomorrow we throw the cat on the truck.

Day forty-three

I missed.

Though not by much—he landed instead on the driverless seat of the yellow motorcycle. Then he just sat there frozen, frightened out of his artificial mind as the motorcycle carried him away at eighty miles per hour; in less than a minute, he was already out of sight.

I ran down the stairs as quickly as I could and stepped into the control module—a trailer we'd parked under the bridge, with a cheap leather chair in the back and a monitor that receives the transmission from the camera inside the cat's left eye socket. The picture I was getting was very shaky. ETCUS was obviously overwhelmed—his stare was locked on the motorcycle seat—and consequently my monitor was displaying a wobbly image of vinyl upholstery. It was exactly for this type of situation that I'd had the pilot install a loudspeaker inside the cat's head.

I switched on the microphone: "Can you hear me? Shake your head twice if you can." Nothing. "ETCUS, can you hear me? Can you move your head?" No movement. I assumed that even if he was hearing me, he was too distressed to respond—artificial or not, he was in a genuine state of shock. "Okay," I said, "take a deep breath. Try to relax. I will be here with you the whole time." I waited for a while, then tried again with as empathic a voice as I could muster. "My dear *friend*, are you all right? Can you hear the sound of my voice?" For a few seconds there was no response, but then the monitor showed a hesitant tilt motion toward the sky. The personal touch worked. We were in business.

"Okay. Here is the situation. You are on a speeding motorcycle. This was not the plan. You do not know how to drive a motorcycle. In fact, your arm span is too short to control one. But don't worry, I've witnessed this motorcycle on many occasions, and let me tell you—there's no other vehicle I'd rather find myself stuck on. This one is as calm and safe as it gets. Easy rider. Smooth as milk." (These were of course blatant lies—the yellow motorcycle was prone to risk taking and the picture was shaking like a Chilean earthquake—but my audience was a cat robot so I allowed myself some leeway.)

"Now, I know you're thinking it was cruel of us to leave you without some sort of protective headgear, that your head could have, and still might, smash into tiny bits. And the truth is we knew full well it was dangerous to throw you without a helmet, but do not think for a moment that it means we are not your friends. The fact is that a cat with a helmet would have seemed out of place, unnatural, and we couldn't risk it. But more than that, it shows that I trust you to be okay. You are a brave and wondrous cat—always remember that. Always. This is a great adventure. *Your* adventure. Tell me something: Are you just another alley cat rummaging through filthy trash bins for leftovers? Are you a fat house cat sitting at the feet of your chubby middle-aged bourgeois owner who loves you to death but whom you despise? No! You are out and about, investigating! Your occupation? Curiosity—the highest calling of the feline.

"Aren't you glad you're alive? Forget about danger for a moment. Observe the side of the road. Look at all the colors of the flowers passing by. Isn't the world beautiful? Forget about the people driving the cars, forget about your destination or the circumstances that have led you to this moment in time—these are all trivialities—and just look at the beauty of it all. Cars, machines, going from place to place. In many different colors. Boxes on wheels. Look at the gray road, with all the symbols painted on it—a language! Look at the bridges passing above you every other minute, carrying more cars, supporting all this weight for years upon years, not giving in. And above it all, the skies, stretching forever, with clouds hanging like giant pieces of unprocessed cotton. Some say they look like sheep. I disagree. Not that sheep hanging in the sky would not make for a pleasing spectacle, but sheep are too weak, too helpless, too *sheepish*; sheep are not independent cats like you! No, I say clouds are like mountains of timelessness, gateways to another realm. A prettier realm, where everything is slow and orange. Close your eyes. See that orange.

"Yes, relax. You are a beautiful relaxed cat. You are not afraid. Fear, for you, is but a word—even less, a senseless succession of sounds, a toothless syllable, lines etched on a discarded piece of paper. Mere words can't hold you down, vowels can never touch you. You are bound by nothing. You are free.

"Good. I feel you relaxing. Think to that orange realm above the clouds. Very good. Orange. Can you see it? The orange is slowly changing. It gets some blues, a light and beautiful gust of blue wind is flowing into it, and the orange is transforming into purple. Can you see it in your mind's eye? Good. You are a wonderful being. A top cat. Purple. Magical purple. You enjoy that purple. Very good."

He was primed. It was time to take charge.

"Open your eyes! Look to the sides. Do you see a purple truck? You love that purple. Jump on it. Now!"

The monitor flickered with jagged lines and spurts of white noise as ETCUS took a leap full of spirited agility that landed him directly on the roof of the purple truck. Phase one was complete. Now all he needed to do was find a way to penetrate the truck's cargo container so he could start transmitting images of the people inside.

ETCUS scouted the container for possible entry points, but evidently there were none. The only way in would be to bore a hole through the roof using his high-powered reinforced-steel robot claws. This could be tricky, but as long as he didn't employ maximal power, the sounds of the highway and the noise of the truck's own motor should be enough to mask the action from the people in the belly of the truck.

After twenty minutes of intense drilling, when the hole was about the size of a tennis ball, I told ETCUS to operate more quietly—there was still much work to be done and we couldn't risk detection. For him to be able to sneak into the truck, the hole needed to be about three times wider (he may have been modeled after one of nature's most flexible creatures, but his metallic skeleton was as stiff as a dead dinosaur's). It was an excruciating process, not only for ETCUS, but for me as well. Every few minutes he seemed to be losing interest, and I had to keep encouraging him through the microphone not to give up, remind him what a great hero he was, and occasionally throw in a good word about the pristine quality of his fur. (Not only this, but it seemed that the level of compliments had to constantly be escalated for him to remain invested.)

The hole was finally wide enough, but still it was impossible to make any details of the insides of the truck; no matter how I adjusted the monitor's brightness and contrast dials, the picture remained too dark. I asked ETCUS to insert his head carefully through the hole and take a peek inside, but he wouldn't comply—apparently, at that moment, licking random drilling residue carried a more glamorous allure. I pleaded with him for another ten minutes, repeated the clouds monologue, and the oranges, and the fearlessness, and then told him that he was not only a great cat, but in fact a great person. This last line piqued his interest enough to stave off the licking, but still he wouldn't cooperate. So I decided to hold my nose and temporarily promote him to the stature of a monarch. "King ETCUS," I declared, "the sun, the stars, and the moon are in awe of your everlasting beauty."

That did the trick. In fact, it worked too well. He was so thrilled with the compliment that he threw all caution to the wind and, with too much force, popped his head into the hole. This made him lose his grip on the roof and sent him free-falling into the truck's cargo hold. The metallic clunk of him hitting the floor was transmitted to my high-fidelity headphones in agonizing precision that left my ears ringing for the better part of an hour. This was going to be a disaster.

Only, it wasn't.

Because, as it became clear once he could collect himself enough to have a look around, there was no one there to see him. No people holding remote controls, no multinationals taking turns, nobody—all my theories were proven wrong. In fact, not only were there no people, but there weren't any seats either or anything to suggest that a person had ever occupied that space. Instead, there were just tens of rows of cassette tape recorders stacked one on top of the other. They probably didn't contain music but some form of data. They had no speakers; the only sound coming from them was the mechanical rattling of their transport motors. Some were spinning slowly, some were idle, and some were frantically alternating between fast forward and rewind, occasionally pausing in between. And except for a few gray tape recorders in the bottom row, they were all arranged in a checkered pattern: half of the tape recorders were purple, and the other half, yellow.

ETCUS was dizzy from the fall and seemed incapable of moving his legs. He just lay there, tilting his head around like a cheap bobblehead doll, the movements probably having more to do with the shaking of the truck than any voluntary motion on his part.

"It's okay," I said into the microphone, "you did great. Just stay on the floor for now and relax." It was important that he rest, and even more important, I wanted to keep him from fiddling with the tape recorders. That they were color coded in purple and yellow meant in all likelihood that they controlled the purple truck and the yellow motorcycle, and as far as I could tell, even the slightest disturbance in the operation of the tapes might make the truck drive head-on into a lamppost, ruining itself, the cat, and my only chance of knowing what had always been most important—the trip's destination.

The already faint picture on the monitor was continuously deteriorating, until at some point it vanished completely, giving way to some geometric patterns in green and orange. When I called the pilot, he told me it was actually a positive sign—had ETCUS been completely destroyed, my screen would have just displayed static noise; the patterns meant he was in sleep mode, conserving energy.

I stayed in front of the monitor for the rest of the day. Every hour or so the cat robot drifted back to life and a shaky image would appear for a few seconds, always taken from the same corner of the truck. The cassette tapes had labels on them, but the bad quality of the road, coupled with the cat's damaged motor skills, made for difficult reading. So it's with caution that I consider this list of words that I managed to jot down by sundown:

Purple tape—ROUTE 1
Purple tape—ROUTE 2 (or 7?)
Purple tape—ROUTE 4
Yellow tape—ASPIRATION LOOPS
Purple tape—KATHY (?)
Purple tape—GROCERIES
Yellow tape—JOYRIDE (?)
Yellow tape—THEATRICS

I had almost no communication with the helicopter pilot the entire day, and by early evening he was already gone, but I decided I would spend the night here in the trailer. I left the headphones on so that whenever ETCUS reemerged from his sleep, I would wake up with him.

He did switch on for another short moment around 2:00 A.M. The picture was not shaky anymore. He was standing closer to the wall of tape recorders now, and in the middle of the frame was a purple tape recorder with a labeled cassette.

I had just come out of sleep, so the light from the screen was too harsh on my eyes, and by the time I found the brightness dial, the picture had already faded. I can't be sure, but I think the inscription was something in the vein of "ALPHA PATTERNS."

At five in the morning, I took a quick stroll to shake off the fatigue, and when I returned to the trailer, the cat's camera was broadcasting again. However, it was no longer showing the insides of the truck. Underneath some mild noise patterns caused by electrical interruptions to the transmission, a beautiful picture emerged of the sun rising behind the foggy silhouette of a small mountain.

Day forty-four

I don't know how ETCUS got out of the truck, whether he was detected by someone or is still in the clear, but never mind that for now. This was the destination (or the source), this is where the purple truck and yellow motorcycle drive to every afternoon, and this is where they leave from in the morning, and now I had eyes on the place.

Unfortunately, the transmission was getting weaker with each passing moment; yesterday was a busy day and I had worked ETCUS to exhaustion. He had to be turned off for now so that the batteries would replenish themselves through the solar panels in his nonfilming eye.

He went to sleep in some bushes. I will sleep in the trailer. As long as he is there, I must remain here by the monitor. This is my new home.

The Mountain

The first one appeared at noon. He came out of a cave opening not too far below the summit and started marching down a spiral road that enveloped the mountain. When he completed the first lap, the others started coming out of the cave, one after the other, a short distance separating each person from the next. Like him, they kept to a very slow pace, and like him, they were all pushing white lawn mowers. Their jumpsuits were light brown; his was white.

It took them no more than twenty minutes to get to ground level—it was not a very high mountain and not very wide. The man in the white jumpsuit was the first to arrive, and the others soon caught up and parked themselves around him. For a few long minutes they remained fixed in their places, unmoving and clutching those white lawn mowers, like mannequins in a hardware store window, the occasional gust of sand the only hint that the video feed from the cat's camera was still functioning.

Then, all at once, as if choreographed, they began walking around, each one in a different direction, pacing slowly with an almost awe-inspiring lack of energy, all the while pushing the white lawn mowers in front of them. These couldn't be ordinary lawn mowers though, as there was no trace of grass—only gray rocks, yellow sand, and dry, thorny plants.

The whole thing seemed pointless. They weren't combing the area or doing anything useful; they just wandered around without any sign of interaction, not exchanging so much as a glance, and they all walked in peculiar patterns, circling themselves and each other and the tall posts that were scattered all around this otherwise featureless terrain.

Clearly, I was not very focused (probably due to three consecutive tealess mornings, as I still hadn't figured out the hot water situation in the trailer), so it was a while before I noticed that at the top of each one of those posts were mounted a couple of horn speakers, and there could be sounds coming from them this entire time. I connected the headphones to the monitor and listened in.

Music! Some type of exotic jazz? I could make out flute and piano sounds and several types of percussion.

A saxophone.

And yodeling?

It was really hard to tell. With the reflections of sound bouncing between the mountain and the rocky surroundings, the music and its echoes combined into one unidentifiable mess; the bad quality of ETCUS's transmission wasn't much help either.

After about twenty minutes, this aimless strolling came to an abrupt end. They all turned around in a synchronized fashion and walked back to the spiral road that led up the mountain. Again, it was the man in the white jumpsuit who was leading, and the others kept close behind. As they marched farther up the road, the music turned faster and ecstatic, and I noticed that some in the group were now bobbing their heads back and forth. But these were only slight movements, a sleepwalker's boogie.

Unfortunately, at that stage I was forced to turn ETCUS off. The life span of his battery seems to have gone down drastically. I will have to use him judiciously.

Day two

Today saw a repeat of yesterday's lawn mower march down the mountain. It's safe to assume it's a daily routine, some sort of symbolic ritual, as hinted by the tribal motifs in the background music, which today I managed to catch from the very start. I am now certain there is an element of yodeling, albeit not the traditional kind, and there is a male voice mixed in at several points. However, I couldn't make out the lyrics (or even be sure of the language, for that matter).

This is interesting to note: I am watching people controlling lawn mowers as transmitted through the eyes of an artificial cat. Before all of this, I was watching a truck and a motorcycle with my own eyes, but the vehicles were artificially controlled by tapes. What does it all mean? I don't know. But it has to be some kind of progress, or regress.

Day three

I've taken on new roommates during the night in the form of bloodthirsty highway-mosquitoes. I made the mistake of leaving the tiniest of openings in one of the trailer windows, which turned out to be quite the bold move in the real estate world of roadside insects. So it was already with irritable skin and mood that I started what turned out to be a most unproductive morning.

I wasted a few precious hours just trying to convince ET-CUS to get closer to the mountain. The joystick doesn't seem to affect him anymore, so once again I found myself having to sweet-talk him into action. I compared his fur to a tulip field, improvised a poem about his tail, even elevated him from king to emperor then to emperor-king, but he wouldn't have any of it. I tried some fatherly tough love, turned to direct and indirect threats and some more complex psychological trickery, but he seemed to have become immune to my crap. I guess at this point in our relationship, he only responds if I'm being genuine, and that's not a very productive relationship to have with a battery-operated machine.

My luck eventually changed when a cockroach wandered

into ETCUS's field of view, prompting his hard-coded animal instincts to kick in. He gave out a passionate leap and launched into a full-on chase until he caught the insect, dismembered it, and fed it to his mechanical digestive system. Thankfully, this act of violence got him closer to the mountain and the posts with the loudspeakers (the dead insect thus repaying the karmic debt of the wicked morning-mosquitoes), so the sound I received was much clearer and I could finally discern some words from the song that accompanied the ritual: "peace" appeared more than once, and what I think was "happiness," and something repeated quite a number of times that sounded like "master man" (or conceivably "mustard pan"). Another interesting detail: the lawn mowers all have long thin antennas sticking out of them.

I must talk to the pilot and see what I can do to make ETCUS more responsive—if not to the joystick, then at least to my words—but for the past three days I haven't been able to contact him. He's there in the helicopter, hovering above the bridge from dawn until late in the afternoon, but whenever I call, I get either a busy signal or an answering machine with a fake accent. Is he avoiding me?

Day four

I really hope I'm not about to document meaningless patterns all over again. Everything today has been the same—the only wrinkle being that a different person was wearing the white jumpsuit, and I'm not even sure of *that*.

Day five

I chose to skip the mountain march altogether and instead switched ETCUS on for a single minute every quarter of an hour (I can't leave him on for long stretches or the battery will run out). Unfortunately, I caught nothing, nothing, and more nothing. Whatever important business is going on must be happening inside that cave up the mountain. Also, I have a feeling ETCUS was not too happy being woken up every fifteen minutes.

Day six

In the morning, I found a big white van parked right outside my trailer. At first I thought it was some kind of ice cream truck, as it had a huge Toblerone bar replica installed on the roof—a long yellow wrapping with the red Toblerone logo and three triangular pieces of chocolate sticking out of it—but there was no ice cream being sold, and there was no serving window on any side; in fact, there were no windows at all except for the windshield, which was tinted. This could prove insignificant, an incidental occurrence, but every bone in my body told me it wasn't, and I've learned to listen to my bones.

Back in the control module, I sat down to witness yet another repeat of the mountain ritual. The only new detail I picked up on was that about twenty minutes in, the music stopped and there was the sound of a needle leaving the surface of a record and shortly after dropping again (the record was likely flipped to a side B, though the music did remain very similar). Interesting that there were scarcely any audible pops or scratches in the music. Someone is keeping the record clean—a testament to good organizational skills.

In the afternoon, though, a new development. A bus arrived from the north and parked at the foot of the mountain. It carried about thirty people, all clothed in full football gear—helmets and all—who stepped out of the bus and proceeded to walk to an area that from ETCUS's vantage point was obscured by the mountain. A few minutes later, a similar bus arrived with a second team. The first team had purple uniforms, the second team yellow.

I repeatedly requested ETCUS to follow these people, but the spoiled cat just wouldn't budge. In my frustration, I ended up spilling hot tea on the remote, which probably rendered it even more useless (though I doubt it was possible at that point). I really could have used some technical assistance, but the helicopter pilot didn't even show up today. I tried dialing the number a few times and got a talking clock.

But most unsettling of all was the discovery that the Toblerone van was still there at night. I went out to get a closer look, but I found nothing—just some dry eggshells scattered near the back door, which quite likely were already there before. No light was coming from the van. The motor and the tires were cold. No sign that anyone was inside, except for a sound that was so familiar and so distinct that it made my skin crawl. The unmistakable sound of a bassoon.

DREAM JOURNAL ENTRY NO. 5

There is a void. But it is not black. It's a white void. Wait, it *is* black. Or not—certainty is elusive in the presence of the pyramids. They are truly magnificent. Nothing rivals the pyramids. They are hollow, brimming with nothingness, yet heavier than planets. Unmovable. The presence is here—the floating manta ray. It is hovering above the vertex of the left pyramid. It is clear and colorful—it has more colors than the human eye can see, and I see them all. Another presence appears at the heel of the second pyramid. This one is like mirrors growing out of mirrors that reflect nothing but void (I still don't know if the void is white or black—it's invisible because it's a void?). Wait, these are not mirrors. It's a multitude of hourglasses, intertwined. I look at this presence. I acknowledge it, as if to say, "Hello." A third presence appears at the top of the third pyramid. It is an imperfect cube of flesh, covered with gray skin—like a geometrical elephant with no eyes, trunk, legs, or any bodily features, and still, it is contracting and expanding, breathing. Who are you? And who was speaking to me last time? The floating manta ray or the multitude of intertwined hourglasses or the cube of living matter? I ask, and they answer with one voice. And the pyramids echo the words in writing:

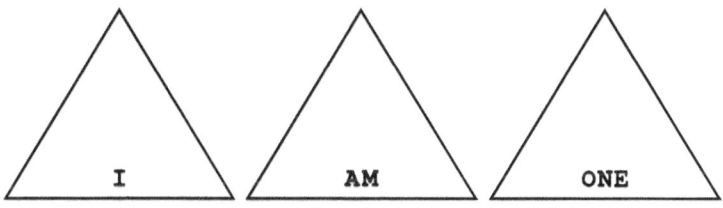

Day seven

As soon as I opened my eyes, I noticed a change: everything was darker; only scarce light was slipping through the windows. The cause: my trailer was now surrounded by not one, but three of those Toblerone vans. One at the back and one on each side. It's now clear that what I'm dealing with here is not a mere bassoon player. Someone is really interested in my business.

I kept myself calm, gathered some food and tea supplies, and carefully squeezed myself out of the trailer (the vans were parked extremely close to the doors). I spent the rest of the day up on the bridge, where I could observe the vans from a safer distance. They did not move the entire day, and no one came in or out. For the time being, I decided to take no action—this is the type of situation where it's wiser to sit back and let things play out.

Around noon, the purple truck and the yellow motorcycle passed under the bridge. I tried to see if the hole bored by ETCUS had been sealed in the meantime, but the truck was driving too fast. I also spotted a roofless double-decker bus in the afternoon, which this time didn't host a camera crew, although there seemed to be some sort of catering bar at the back, serving lobsters. Once again, the helicopter pilot was a no-show—I have a feeling I won't be seeing him again.

It's now slightly after midnight and I'm back inside the trailer. I've been getting some spurts of bassoon for the last fifteen minutes. First from the left, then from behind. Then I thought I heard simultaneous noises from both the left side of my trailer and the right. Could there be multiple bassoonists?

DREAM JOURNAL ENTRY NO. 6

The pyramids and the presences are here again. I'm feeling sad, and I don't know why.

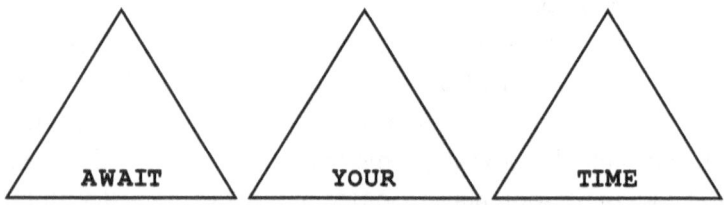

Wait? For what? Oh, I think I see. I have to wait. The sadness is only temporary, and I am sad because I still have waiting to do. Yes, wait. The cube of flesh is breathing heavier this time, with slow but violent pulses, and there are tubes bulging out of it in multiple directions—some are spewing thick puffs of smoke, and some are shooting out marbles that land on the side of the green pyramid, then roll all the way down to the ground and noisily crash to tiny bits upon impact. The void is definitely black this time, and it is sprinkled with stars and galaxies that send out their aeons-old light—I see them through the pyramids. I understand: the presences and the pyramids are one—they have said so—but the manta ray is the mind, I can feel it; inside the one there is a division—like the subparticles of a flawless atom. I look at the pyramids again. I want to know more; I have questions. But they remain as they were: Await. Your. Time. I understand. I am sad because I still have waiting to do. Yes, wait. The marbles keep crashing at the heels of the green pyramid. One after one they turn to dust, giving up structure for the sake of entropy, their sound rushing to my ears, drawing me in. A gushing sound, first crackling, then white and frothy. All of a sudden: sapphire skies full of seagulls? I'm out on the hotel balcony again, looking at the sea. The hotel is smaller than last time—more like a fancy hut than a proper hotel—and there's smoke coming out of my room; it carries with it some sweet sort of scent—lemonade? I see the manta ray silhouettes under the waves. They are retreating . . . swimming away, fading. I will have to wait.

Day eight

I woke up to hordes of tiny insects inside pink, turbulent clouds of sunlit dust. The greedy highway-mosquitoes were there as well, but that the sun could once again shine unopposed through the windows of my trailer could only mean one thing: the Toblerone vans were gone.

Unfortunately, so were the tires of my trailer. I guess they don't need to keep watch on me for the moment, but they also don't want me disappearing. Whoever they are, they have already proved they know how to find me, so for now, I have no plans of running away. However, while their departure was a positive development, the rest of the day gradually slipped into disaster.

I switched on the monitor in the hope that ETCUS would prove more receptive, that my day-long absence had somehow made him miss me, but no such luck. If anything, he was even more unreachable than before. I really can't tell anymore if he's being standoffish, or if he's actually sunk deep into depression—it's like I'm parenting a teenager. I tried to cheer him up, went through my usual bag of tricks, threw in more over-the-top compliments, gave love a chance, even truthfulness. Then at some point, I mentioned in passing that he was being rather ungrateful and should actually consider himself lucky; that as far as machines went, he seemed to have gotten a pretty good deal—after all, he could have been born a *stapler*. This was just another line out of many, and I certainly didn't expect it to have a big impact—the "some people are worse off than you" argument had never been an easy sell—but apparently it had some sort of psychotic effect on him. He started jumping around erratically, bashing his head to the ground in furious motions, and thrashing sand all over the place as if possessed. This couldn't be good for the internal camera; this wasn't good for the internal *anything*.

He shifted to an awkward crawl, still constantly banging his head on the floor, and as he moved around, I could see on the screen that this tantrum was leaving a very distinct sort of mess. There were deep teeth marks embedded in the ground wherever he'd hit it. This might have been pure speculation on my part, but it appeared as though he was trying to be a stapler!

"You're a cat!" I shouted into the microphone, though I knew all too well this was pointless; I've had no prior experience with artificial animals, but I know total meltdown when I see it. The craziness persisted for a few long minutes, after which the stapler identity crisis gave way to a fresh psychotic episode. He stood still and started meowing repeatedly in what I assume was a deliberately mechanical fashion. "Meow! Meow! Meow!" He went on and on— "Meow! Meow!"—all the while using the exact same version of meow from his arsenal of recorded sounds. He was either attempting to mock his mechanical nature or trying his hardest to get the tapes to break. I assume it was a combination of both: a lost soul's cry for help through self-mutilation.

All of a sudden, he lunged forward and started running frantically in the direction of the mountain, violently cutting whatever lay in his path, his legs now spinning like insane rotor blades. "Meo-meo-meo-meo"—he was making the tape repeat faster and faster, his batteries laboring at maximum capacity—"Meo-meo!" darting maniacally inside a self-made hurricane. The only moment he slowed down was when his gaze locked with a poor lizard's that in a matter of seconds he reduced to a heap of shriveled skin and thick fluids that he proceeded to smear all over his face. Needless to say, at this point my remote control had absolutely no effect on him, so I could not switch him off nor slow him down in the slightest as he started climbing the slope of the mountain. The tape was repeating even faster—a machine gun of "M" sounds, on top of which he was now playing all the other tapes simultaneously—the hisses, the purrs, and the growls—all in varying speeds and pitches and in the loudest volume his audio circuits could support; it had the musicality of a chipmunk torture chamber.

He continued his frantic advance up the mountain, repeatedly bobbing his head from side to side, looking up to the sky and then down to the ground, the view from his eye camera now largely obstructed by a grayish stew of sand and lizard blood. When he was halfway up the mountain, a disturbing feeling started creeping into my head, though it was a while before I became aware of its source: Under the loud voices that ETCUS was playing from his tapes, another sound emerged that had nothing to do with cat vocabulary—an oscillating sound wave going up and down. Someone had sounded the alarm.

And indeed it took no more than a minute before an orange dune buggy came speeding out of the cave opening, moving down the mountain in a cloud of dust. ETCUS, himself shrouded in the smoke of his overloaded circuits, did not seem to be aware (the vehicle was only visible in the short moments that ETCUS's head was pointing up) and just kept on running. After a few loops around the mountain, when they were on the same level, the vehicle, which I'm almost sure had no driver, turned sideways and braked, blocking the road in a way that didn't allow passage. That too didn't seem to affect ETCUS, who kept on going full speed until he smashed head-on into the vehicle. There was no sound as it happened; the picture just turned to static.

ETCUS was no more.

I could not bring myself to turn off the monitor. I must have stayed seated in front of it for more than an hour, holding my hands to my head in disbelief. ETCUS was dead, terminated, shut off. A heap of metal on a nameless mountain, no more valuable than a fridge magnet.

When finally I managed to get up, I went through disconnecting the cables from the monitor and reattaching them one by one, tweaked all the knobs back and forth, and gave the monitor a few good bumps. This was all glaringly pointless, but like the delusional parent of a coma victim, I could not let go. It wasn't so much ETCUS that I was grieving, frankly; it was the realization that, once again, I was cut off.

Move back to the apartment? No, I won't admit defeat so swiftly. Besides, I've come to feel more at home here. I will not stop. What else is there?

Time to devise new plans, conjure up new ideas, all that stuff. But first, it was back to the bridge. At 12:32 P.M., the yellow motorcycle passed, going south, with the purple truck right behind it. They kept to a constant velocity, or at least there wasn't any meaningful acceleration or deceleration. As always, no one was sitting on the motorcycle or at the truck's steering wheel. What else? The motorcycle looked really bright in the sun; very yellow. The purple truck was noisy, perhaps noisier than one would expect from this particular class of truck. Oh, and there was no license plate—had I noticed that before? I can't remember. At about 12:50, I had a chicken sandwich that boasted the perfect sauce-to-bread ratio, but then the meat was terribly stringy.

I can't believe I'm back to *this*.

New ideas. Throw an egg on the roof of the purple truck, then see if it's been cleaned up by the next day? Or maybe throw the egg during their morning trip, see if it's gone by the time they do the noon drive. Okay, there may be some merit to this. An egg might be too noisy though—not to mention juvenile. A tomato then? No, it wouldn't leave a strong enough mark. A well-aimed beetroot would be the proper choice then.

This is just one idea, one course of action. There will be more. The cat robot idea had been perfect, and I stumbled upon it by sheer coincidence. As long as I am focused on the goal, ideas will come, if not from me, then from chance. I must not lose patience; in the meantime, there's the beetroot.

An oversight: a beetroot stain would be virtually invisible on a purple roof. I either have to go with a different vegetable, or the target would need to be the yellow motorcycle. Can I hit the yellow motorcycle from the bridge? After a few tries, perhaps, but with the vehicles passing only twice a day, the math is not in my favor. So it needs to be the truck and it needs to be some light-colored food. An Indian curry dish should do the job—anything rich with turmeric. There's the Indian restaurant near the post office, perhaps I should go there later today? Better early tomorrow, so the dish is fresh when I throw it.

No! No way, I will not do this. I have not come this far to revert to this type of madness. I will go to sleep and I will wake up and I might find a new idea.

Or I will go to sleep and wake up once again to this emptiness and those old meaningless patterns.

Okay, but it's agreed: first, I sleep.

Day ten

All is not lost!

In the morning, the monitor, which had so far shown nothing but static, went black. In the afternoon, it turned blue. And in the evening, a flickering orange with dancing squares of yellow. Am I seeing into ETCUS's subconscious?

Day eleven

A good morning: pink circles swimming downstream on top of blue and yellow stripes. He is trying to tell me something: he is in a dream world and he's happier than ever before.

Day twelve

A light brown background layered with dark brown diamond shapes spaced randomly across the screen. As the day progressed, the diamonds grew gradually bigger and darker and the background, lighter. He has now looked death in the eye, and he doesn't know what to make of it.

Day thirteen

The morning began with a big black circle over a field of reds and pinks. Later, a few black stripes started leaking from the bottom of the circle. At noon, the top part of the circle was slowly beginning to degenerate—it became more jagged and crumbled into individual black squares that ate away at the by-then crimson background.

Then suddenly, no more patterns. A few horizontal lines jumping up and down, a few frames of static and then: a video feed—an image of a room, and in the center, ETCUS himself!

A jolt ran through my body. How could that be? The video camera was placed inside his head pointing out—it could only show what happened outside of him. An out-of-body experience? An impossibility by all means, yet this is what the monitor was showing. He was lying motionless on a hospital bed, surrounded by walls of machines with blinking lights, his fur severely burnt, the body bent and cracked, with pieces of metallic skeleton popping out at the joints and a kaleidoscope of colored cables pouring out of his contorted figure like spilled guts. He looked damaged beyond repair, yet somehow he was still operational enough to be transmitting this video.

How could he be broadcasting a picture of himself? Was it an image from his data banks? A memory? No, the patterns he had shown before had always been crude; his subconscious mind is not capable of such vivid imagery. This was real live video, but how? I grabbed the microphone, mumbled some words, but it was obvious they weren't getting through. I checked the headphones; there was no sound coming out either.

A figure entered the frame, a woman in a surgical gown. She moved slowly from one machine to the next and appeared to be recording readouts from the LED displays in her writing pad. Every so often, she turned and faced the right as if there was someone offscreen communicating with her; this gesture was usually followed by some cautious dial tinkering. Something serious was up.

She signaled someone offscreen to come—not the one who was talking to her before, but someone on the opposite side. A second woman appeared; she too was wearing a surgical gown. The first woman handed her the writing pad, which the second woman inspected quickly, then went over each machine to check against the written data. The first woman, who in the meantime had left the frame, returned with a toolbox, took out something that looked like a schnitzel mallet, and started tapping it lightly against ETCUS's damaged tail. A third woman showed up with a metal sieve and fitted it on the cat's head like a baseball cap. She connected a wire with an alligator clip to the sieve handle, then raised her head, looked almost straight into the camera, and appeared to be saying something (her mouth was not visible because of the surgical mask). The other two women then turned their gaze to roughly the same spot and spoke back. Something about the way they stared into the camera felt completely wrong but at the same time vaguely familiar.

A short moment later it all became clear. In my stunned mental state, I had overlooked the simplest of explanations: ETCUS was looking into a wall-sized mirror.

From the right side of the frame, I thought I saw a yellow, or rather, amber-colored glow flashing for a couple of seconds. The three women turned nervously to look at it, then put down the writing pad and the schnitzel mallet, and exited to the left. The room lights soon changed into deep red, and the indicators on the machines ceased blinking. This image persisted on my monitor for a long while. Still life with dying cat and sieve.

I was preparing myself mentally for another long session in front of the monitor, when a bunch of pixels in the center of the screen appeared to be lighting up, at first almost imperceptibly, but very soon, with the help of neighboring pixels, they formed a recognizable shape above the head of the dying cat: ETCUS was receiving an angel's halo! A round, glimmering, beautiful orange halo.

As I sat there scratching my head in confusion, two tiny blue flames emerged from the ring of light and traveled its outline in opposing directions. Upon meeting, they merged into one bright flame, trembled for a flash, and vanished in a small explosion that turned the halo's orange glow to an unstable stroboscopic white. Under this brighter illumination, the halo revealed itself to be nothing more than the rim of the metal sieve, laboring under a massive surge of electricity from the cable that was attached to its handle; it was frying the poor cat's brain. Smoke escaped ETCUS's ears, and his nonfilming eye, already deformed, was presently melting and began leaking down his face like a white toasted marshmallow. The small patches of fur that survived the crash were now standing on end, and his mouth, apparently not yet in total disrepair, formed an expression of pure horror. The next casualty was ETCUS's left ear, which popped out toward the ceiling with a trail of curly smoke, never to land again. One of the women reappeared (her surgeon's outfit now supplemented with a helmet and safety glasses), positioned herself behind the fast disintegrating ETCUS, raised the schnitzel mallet into the air, and landed a forceful blow on his tail. The poor cat gaped his mouth in stupefaction, which made his jaw drop, literally, to the floor. The woman then raised her hand again and delivered what turned out to be the eventual deathblow.

In that final moment, the headphones sprang to life for a split second, and underneath the loud clicking of machinery, I thought I heard a fragment of a sad, detuned meow. It would be his last.

The screen remained black for a few seconds. Then, a word appeared in the top left corner, in bright amber letters that blinked on and off:

> TEST

Was ETCUS still functioning? I reached for the microphone, but before I could grab it, the text on the screen changed:

> THIS IS NOT THE CAT.

Then it changed again, no longer blinking:

> THE CAT IS OVER.

> HE IS NOW A RADIO TRANSMITTER.

> FURTHER TRANSMISSIONS TO FOLLOW.

The last line filled the screen for a minute and then gave way to a countdown.

In seventeen hours and thirty-nine minutes I will know more.

Day fourteen

> TOMORROW AT 13:05 A BUS WILL BE
WAITING FOR YOU AT YOUR CURRENT
LOCATION. YOU WILL BOARD IT.

"Where will it take me?" I said into the microphone, but it didn't appear to be getting through.

> THERE WILL BE PEOPLE THERE:
PASSENGERS. YOU ARE NOT TO TALK TO
THEM.

The language of someone who knows they have the upper hand.

Nevertheless, an invitation.

Day fifteen

The bus arrived on the minute. 13:05 sharp. It was the same double-decker bus I had seen those few times before—the one the pilot had mentioned (or at least a similar model). It stopped directly under the bridge, the front door opened, and I climbed right in—this was no time to show hesitation.

It was quite dark inside, the walls were lined with small tiles of brown leather, and the windows were covered with checkered curtains of ugly blue and green. There were passengers, as promised, and seeing them, I judged us to be on the way to some official event, as all the men wore suits and the women were sitting in evening gowns. Many pairs of seats lay empty at the back, but I decided I would attempt to sit next to one of the passengers, just to shake things up. I approached a man in a brown velvet suit that was occupying an aisle seat. I pointed to the window and said, "May I, please?"

After a moment's hesitation, he got up and let me pass through to the window seat, though he didn't seem all too thrilled. As soon as I was seated, he reverted to his previous posture—head down, gaze fixed firmly to the knees. A quick look around revealed that the rest of the passengers were doing the same.

The bus was not moving. I began to think that we were waiting for another passenger to show up, but a few minutes later a bleep came from the TV screen that hung above the driver's head, the word "DRIVE" appeared on it in pixelated letters, and within five seconds we were off.

Gradually, I began seeing people talk, though still sparingly; a word here and there, a nod of the head, a polite smile. These were not friends by choice—presumably coworkers.

I tried my sitting partner. "A velvet suit on a day like this? Must be quite uncomfortable." In response, he just doubled down on his lifeless facial expression and with profound lack of energy pointed to the screen in the front of the bus. It read, this time in blinking letters:

`>DO NOT TALK TO HIM.`

The bus proceeded on its southern trajectory, cruising comfortably under the speed limit. It was clear no one was going to engage me, so I busied myself with nosing around—I needed to get a sense of what these people were about. The air smelled of cheap cleaning agents and stale twenty-year-old leather, which was perfectly in sync with the general outdated feel of everything on the bus. The evening dresses looked like they had gone out of style a couple of decades ago, and then too many of the men wore sweater vests, not to mention the unreasonable number of tweed hats. My guess: this was not their personal wardrobe, but clothes that were supplied to them, all bought on the cheap from a single source. Upon closer inspection it was evident they were not on the way to, but rather coming back from an event that had already taken place last night—the clothes were too wrinkled, and I spotted four different persons sharing a similarly colored stain; I presume a champagne incident.

Another bleep came from the TV screen, a long one. The velvet suit man, for the first time not appearing clinically dead, took out a pen and notebook from under his seat and stared at the TV. Three words appeared on the screen:

`>WINE. SWIMMING. SHOES.`

A wave of chatter shot through the bus, as if the passengers were finally given permission to breathe.

"Okay, let us think now," the woman behind me said to the woman sitting next to her. "The socialite had so much *wine* at the party that when she went *swimming* in the pool, she still had her *shoes* on!"

"What kind of shoes were they?" the other one inquired.

"Oh, probably leather shoes. Stilettos."

"So they were all ruined by the water."

"Yes, I assume they were."

"She should not have drunk so much wine then."

And then they went silent again, as did everyone else on the bus. The velvet suit man closed the notebook and placed it back under his seat. I managed to sneak a quick peek; it looked like a drawing of a sports shoe with tiny hands. It was holding a bottle of wine.

Though most of them were well beyond their twenties, the passengers gave off the appearance of frightened school-children, all too mindful not to overstep the boundaries of their seats, to stay neatly packaged in their prescribed spaces. Something about it was off—they were just too dull, too flat. That is, until another quarter of an hour later, a fresh bleep rang from the TV screen:

`>EXPERT. SHRIMP. WEAPON.`

A slight commotion. The velvet suit man took out the note-book and started scribbling again. This time he made an extra effort to prevent me from glimpsing his handiwork. I got up and moved farther back to an empty row and tried listening in on a couple of older gentlemen in the row in front of me.

"So we have the *shrimp*."

"Yes, we do."

"And we have the *expert*."

"Yes, that too."

"Or are they one and the same?"

"A shrimp who is also an expert?"

"It's possible."

"What is its area of expertise?"

"Well, conceivably *weaponry*."

"Yes, indeed. A shrimp manufacturer of weapons. A true expert in the field, not a weekend warrior. Weaponry is not a hobby for this shrimp, it is its true calling. Yes."

"Yes."

"Indeed."

"Well done. Good thinking."

"We both contributed."

"Because we practice regularly."

Something was intriguingly familiar about this coupling of shrimp and weaponry—it called to mind the pilot's obsession with hamster war dioramas. I wondered if there was any significance to this, but before I was able to pursue this line of thought, the men continued.

"I think he is listening in on us."

"The stranger?"

"Yes."

"Then we must confuse him."

"How?"

"Shrimp salad."

"Oh, I see. Atomic weapon . . . paper gun. Scissors."

"Experts. Excerpts. Axes. Excess."

"Access. Faxes. Foxes, hound dogs, and hot dogs."

"Weekend warriors!"

Their primitive confusion technique was surprisingly effective.

Time for a change of scenery. I got up and went snooping around on the roofless upper deck. It was mostly empty seats with a few men scattered, all of them meticulously dressed in black suits with red ties (quality suits, not the lower deck garbage). One could immediately tell they served a more prominent role in whatever operation was going on here. There was an air of seriousness about them—they did not look away when stared at, did not give away any hint of uneasiness. They did a lot of gazing at the road, a lot of stroking of the chin. I remained standing by the top of the stairs for a while, then tried to look casual as I picked myself a corner. I chose a seat at the back so I could have a view of the entire scene, but twenty minutes went by and I learned absolutely nothing. The upper-deck people were professionals.

When I came back down, I caught a man talking into a personal cassette recorder: "Oh, yes. A shower of bricks, yes, I can see it. Well, not really see it, I see it in my mind's eye. The bricks are falling, like rain. A rain of bricks—no, a deluge, a deluge! And then the phone rings and she answers it, the little orphan. 'Are your parents home?' they ask her—of all things! She cries, very sad. She cries because she has no parents, not anymore she doesn't, yes! Very sad. And the bricks keep pounding on the roof of the orphanage, so she opens the window and she stretches her hand out, and she's crying, and she grabs two bricks from the air and takes them in, and she feels love for them. And she puts them on the kitchen table—the kitchen table of the orphanage. And then she takes the tagliatelle noodles from her plate—Tuesday is tagliatelle day in this south Italian orphanage—and even though she's hungry, she wipes away the sauce, and instead of eating the noodles, she lays them on top of the bricks. Like hairs! Like hairpieces she lays them. One brick is a man, and one brick is a woman—with twice the tagliatelle. And then she sits there, and she pretends that the bricks are her parents. And then she gives them names—which is weird because it's normally the parents who name the children—but she had never known her parents! Not since the accident. And now she has bricks for parents, and now if the phone rings again, she won't be sad like before. The brick rain stops, the storm calms down, the end."

I looked at the TV screen:

> `BRICK. ORPHAN. TAGLIATELLE.`

I managed to catch a short glimpse of what the velvet suit man was drawing. Looked like a giant pizza oven with children dancing around it.

"It specifically said tagliatelle—got a little bit lazy there with the pizza, didn't we?" I tried to rattle him.

> `DO NOT TALK TO HIM.`

A man with a ridiculous hat was wandering about with a camcorder—sort of a stock character of a tourist in a cheap theater production—filming nothing in particular. However, I had a strong sensation that whenever I wasn't looking in his direction, the camera was being pointed at me. Several times I climbed up the stairs, and he would appear on the upper deck in less than thirty seconds, and then when I went back down, I'd suddenly see him standing somewhere behind me, twitching and moving the moment I turned my head, pretending to be zooming in on an empty chair, filming random cars through the window, or just fiddling with the camcorder settings while putting on an exaggerated "Oh, *there* is the button I was looking for" face. Amateur hour.

I dozed off for a while. Daydreamed of giant apricots. Should have probably eaten something before—for some reason I expected there would be catering.

The screen bleeped again, this time repeatedly:

>STOP THE BUS. EXECUTE BLACKOUT.

That wasn't another word association. That was a direct order.

The bus made a stop at the side of the road. Two black suits came down the stairs, one of them decidedly taller and bulkier than the others. He seated himself opposite me, opened a briefcase, took out a pair of earmuffs, and held them in front of my face.

"Is this really necessary?" I said, but got no reply—they are not fond of talking, these people. Everyone on the bus was now looking at me. Even the camcorder tourist guy didn't play pretend anymore. He pointed the camera directly at my face and pressed the zoom-in button, his tongue hanging lazily from his lower lip like a fat earthworm. I figured that at this point there was no sense in arguing; best to just do what they want. I put on the earmuffs; the tall man wiggled them around to make sure they were tight and motioned to the other man, who produced a black leather bag that he then put over my head. For the rest of the way I could not see or hear anything, and breathing was not very comfortable, either. Someone then laid a hand on my shoulder and left it there for the rest of the ride. It wasn't a hard grip—just a gentle reminder that I better not be planning anything stupid.

About two hours later (give or take half an hour—this sense deprivation setup was quite disorienting), I could feel that we were no longer driving on a paved road. I decided to make notes in my head of the different types of terrain we crossed until we reached our destination:

Gravel (approx. 30 minutes)
Bumpier gravel (approx. 10 minutes)
Hills (20 minutes?)

Long descent on sand (I could tell we were going down because my ears hurt from the fall in atmospheric pressure)

Softer sand with rocks (approx. 30 minutes)

The bus then slowed down, drove in reverse for a minute, and finally came to a full stop, engine off.

I was somewhat startled when the hand of the man left my shoulder, because it had rested there for so long that I already forgot there was someone holding me. No one bothered to remove the cover from my head, but I took the withdrawal of the hand as a sign and decided to lift the cover myself. I disposed of the earmuffs and wiped the sweat off my face.

And once I managed to catch my breath again and my eyes got used to the light, the scenery revealed itself in all its glory: for the first time not incarnated as the pixels of a secondhand video screen, stood calm and tall *the mountain*.

One after the other, in total silence and in more of an orderly fashion than I thought humanly possible, the passengers stepped off the bus and headed toward those white lawn mowers, which were parked nearby in three neat lines. They each grabbed one and started pushing it in the direction of the mountain. When the last man took off, I found myself standing alone by the bus, contemplating whether I should do something with the one remaining lawn mower, which in all likelihood was parked there for me. I decided to leave it be and make my way to the mountain, but as I passed it by, it let its intentions be known with a high-pitched, ear-piercing sound. I stopped to have a closer look, but I couldn't find any start switch, or any switch at all for that matter—the only features were the handle and a very tall, thin antenna with a small white ribbon tied to the top.

I grabbed the handle, and within an instant, the machine sprang into action and started to move. Caught off guard, I stumbled and almost fell flat on my face. It turned out that what I was holding was in fact not a lawn mower at all, but a remotely operated guide machine. I wasn't supposed to be pushing it; it was there to direct *me*.

I started walking, letting this peculiar machine be my guide. At first it felt awkward to be led around by an electronic walker from some futuristic nursing home, but as the moments passed, the feeling became more natural, and before long, I was already at the foot of the spiral road that climbs around the mountain.

As I passed the first bend of the road (which in reality turned out to be more of a worn-down trail), I was finally able to see what lay on the other side of the mountain, the side that had always been obscured from ETCUS's view: a none-too-impressive sports field with artificial turf, goal posts, and markings for football. There was no team logo at the center of the field or in the end zones, just a big lettered "Team A" at one end and "Team B" at the opposite. No people were on the field at the moment, but it wasn't vacant. It was presently a strolling ground for the two vehicles—the purple truck and the yellow motorcycle—who casually drove next to each other, like two companions out on a walk. They both seemed really small from where I was now standing, and behind their little field was nothing but dry flatland that stretched forever.

It was not very long before I found myself standing at the entrance to the cave, the same dark entrance I had watched so many times on my video monitor. The lawn mower stopped for a moment as if to let me catch my breath, and when I was ready to move on, it led me in, now at a much slower pace than before.

The air inside the cave was cooler by several degrees and much more damp, as the narrow corridor made for a natural humidity trap. The light behind me was growing fainter with each successive step until pretty soon I was treading in total blindness, the lawn mower now promoted to the role of a guide dog.

A bit farther in, it took me on a left turn. The ground became easier to step on—this section was no longer a natural cave but a man-made concrete corridor. We took a couple more paces, when suddenly the lawn mower halted and let out two bleeps. It remained still, then ten seconds later added two more bleeps. I stood there, trying to figure out what those sounds meant, when the handle of the lawn mower made it perfectly clear by delivering a sharp electric shock that traveled the length of my body: two bleeps meant "Let go."

When I did, the lawn mower immediately rolled away and left me to stand alone in the cold pitch-black air of the mountain cave. From somewhere farther in the dark came the sound of a mechanical door closing, then nothing. Silence. The muffled humming of a far-off ventilation system.

A large monitor in front of me came to life, and on it, the now familiar computer font addressed me with a blinking message in glowing amber letters:

> HELLO.

At last.

> LET ME PLAY YOU A TAPE. I WANT YOU TO TELL ME WHAT YOU THINK.

A recording of a short piano chord sounded. The opening of some familiar piece of classical music that I, however, couldn't name.

"Who are you?"

No reply.

"Did I travel all this way for a musical quiz? Who is speaking to me? Where are you?"

> INTRODUCTIONS WILL FOLLOW. PLEASE,
DESCRIBE WHAT YOU THINK.

The piano chord sounded again.

"I don't think anything. It's a chord played on a piano."

> DO YOU CONSIDER IT JOYOUS?

"I consider it a piano chord."

> VERY WELL. I PROCEED: TELL ME WHAT YOU
THINK OF THE NEXT TAPE.

The speakers played a twenty-seconds excerpt of Hawaiian music.

"It sounds like Hawaiian music."

> DO YOU CONSIDER IT JOYOUS?

"Why is that important?"

> AN ANSWER PLEASE. STUBBORNNESS WILL
ONLY PROLONG THE PROCESS. I REPEAT: DO
YOU CONSIDER THE MUSIC JOYOUS?

"On some level, yes."

> GOOD. TELL ME WHAT YOU THINK OF THE
NEXT TAPE.

Not music this time, but a room recording. The sound of a dog, moaning. Then a gun shot. The dog goes silent.

> WHAT DO YOU THINK OF IT?

"What do I think? I think it's a poor dog being shot dead."

> DOES IT MAKE YOU FEEL SAD?

"It's not *joyous* if that's what you want to know."

> GOOD. I AM SATISFIED WITH YOUR
ANSWERS. NOW LISTEN TO THIS:

The Hawaiian music snippet was now playing again, with the recording of the dog being shot superimposed on top of it. I was growing impatient with this musical Rorschach test.

"I would appreciate some light before we continue."

>PATIENCE. VISUAL INPUT WOULD HINDER
THE EFFECTIVENESS OF THE LISTENING
EXPERIMENT. LISTEN AGAIN.

"I hear two tapes: the murder of a dog, and the massacre of Hawaiian music." This was no joke either—the Hawaiian music was an atrocity.

>LET US CONTINUE: LISTEN CAREFULLY TO
THE NEXT SOUND.

I was expecting another senseless musical clip but instead was hit with a low-pitched droning tone that shook the room with nauseating loudness—ten times more powerful than anything before. I could feel it pounding my forehead and oscillating deep inside my stomach in places I hadn't known could deliver sensation. This time it wasn't a short clip—the sound kept on playing even as the message on the screen changed:

>NAME A GEOMETRIC SHAPE.

I held my hands to my ears to block out the sound. "What?"

>COMPLY: NAME A GEOMETRIC SHAPE.

The sound persisted, perhaps even louder now; it felt as if the entire cave was shaking. "What . . . shape?"

>I REPEAT: COMPLY: NAME A GEOMETRIC
SHAPE.

"A triangle," is all I could think of. The sound lingered on.

>THINK DEEPER.

"What?"

>I REPEAT: NAME A GEOMETRIC SHAPE.

"A pyramid?"

>COMPLY: HOW MANY?

"Three!"

>WHAT COLOR?

"Red."

>WHAT OTHER COLOR?

"Green."

>AND THE LAST?

"Yellow!"

The sound stopped.

I found myself on the ground. The screen turned blank, a bright light flooded the room, and a big metal door in the wall opened.

I fumbled to scrape myself off the floor. My clothes were all dusty and my hands almost entirely black—I must have done some serious rolling around on the ground while that droning sound was playing (I couldn't really tell, it was as though I had just emerged from a blackout). I was still half-deaf, as my ears were ringing from that horrible sound, and now also half-blind due to the reemergence of light. I felt drained. But this was the wrong time to show weakness, so I cleaned myself up, forced myself into focus, and started walking.

Behind the door was another corridor, narrower, its walls an ugly faint green, the ceiling a spaghetti of cables, fluorescent lamps, and security cameras. At the far end, a monitor flashed a message:

>OVER HERE.

Over there was where the lawn mower parked in wait. I walked over, and once I got near it, the corridor lights switched off and everything went black again. The lawn mower threw a single bleep my way. I complied.

It led me into an automated elevator—a dark box with no buttons or floor indicators—but judging by the sensation of acceleration, I could tell we were going down. A second corridor took us to a second elevator, one that moved sideways, and that one took us to more corridors that led to further elevator rides.

After I got off elevator number seven (or maybe it was nine—I struggled to keep count), the lawn mower walked me to the middle of a hallway, then finally stopped and bleeped twice. I released the handle and the lawn mower rolled away, leaving me on my own. I felt around in the dark and found a door right beside me. I opened it and walked in.

A medium-sized room, very clean, practically sterile. Its walls, floor, and ceiling all covered with wallpaper of recurring geometrical patterns in various shades of light brown. In one corner, a single bed, made hotel style with tucked-in duvets and multiple sheets, and in the center of the room, a single chair and a small dining table. On it: chicken breast and mashed potatoes, a glass of white wine (cold as if it had been poured a short moment before I entered the room), and conceivably some sleeping agent—it is not yet eight and I can hardly stay on my feet.

Day sixteen

I'm not sure how long I slept—couldn't find my watch. Someone must have removed it while I was sleeping. Breakfast was already waiting on the table. An almond croissant, freshly baked. It tasted funny. I fell asleep again.

When I woke up, there was lunch on the table in the form of a dead fish. It didn't look very inviting and it stank up the room, and in any case I didn't feel like sleeping again. I flushed it down the toilet, wishing it a safe journey home.

On the wall, a brown jumpsuit was hanging, which I'm pretty sure hadn't been there in the morning; a lot of things seem to be going on in this room when I'm asleep.

What I longed for much more than food was a good shower. There was a system of four dials to control the water's temperature and intensity, but it was impossible to tell which dial did what, as they all seemed to be mutually dependent. After battling it for a while, I decided to stop trying and settled on a stream that was too weak and too cold. In all likelihood, it was not a complicated shower system but one more psychological test—I must assume I am being watched at all times. For the same reason, I resolved not to leave the room until contacted. Every action I took volunteered information about my character; I'd rather they stayed in the dark, even if it meant a cold shower.

Unfortunately, there was nothing worthwhile to do in the room. The only available entertainment: an untitled book with sixty-four pages of that word association game they played on the bus:

Fly. Roast. Generation.

Marginal. Puzzle. Waveform.

Vulture. Ambivalent. Regret. Erotic.

Day seventeen

An alarm clock woke me up at 7:07 A.M. (it hadn't been here yesterday), and about an hour later, with no prior warning, the door opened and I received a visitor in the form of another white lawn mower. It was labeled *Chaperon 8*—the same number that's inscribed on the door.

Its handle led me out of the room and into the pitch-black darkness of the mountain corridors. Once again, the trip started with an elevator ride that dropped us into a fresh maze of corridors. Then more elevators going up, then back down again, through corridors again, more elevators, right turns, left turns, U-turns. The lawn mower carried me in and out of cul-de-sacs, made me walk slow, then fast, then in stutter step, some different modes of zigzag, even reverse stutter step, and all of this in total darkness. I felt like I was being taken for an unnecessarily long ride by a taxi driver who wanted to jack up the fare. The intention, of course, was different—they were trying to disorient me.

However, there was no *they*, I soon learned. Not plural. Not *people*. In charge of this entire operation was a he, or rather, an it. A super computer. I had felt it for some time, but now I was certain. It was it who had spoken to me through all those monitors—in my trailer, on the bus, inside the mountain—and now I was standing in front of it, or at least in front of a piece of it; its actual physical existence must span the entirety of the mountain and probably extends deep below the ground.

This was the main hall. A vast hangar with an extremely high ceiling, a ragged concrete floor, and walls populated entirely by heaps upon heaps of magnetic-tape machines of varying makes and colors that rattled incessantly. I was brought here to be impressed, to witness a commanding exhibition of technological stamina.

At the center of the hall stood a large wooden column that extended all the way up to the ceiling, and in it was embedded a monitor, much bigger than those I had encountered so far. Above it, six cameras were fixed at sixty-degree intervals. One of them stared straight at me, giving me the evil eye.

> I TRUST YOU HAD A GOOD SLEEP.

I had the worst sleep.

"Who am I speaking to? You are not a living person, are you?"

> YOU ARE MORE PERCEPTIVE THAN I HAD

EXPECTED, FASTER THAN THE PREVIOUS
ONES. HOWEVER, WHETHER I AM A LIVING
PERSON IS BUT A TRIVIAL MATTER OF
DEFINITION. YOU WOULD BE CORRECT TO SAY
THAT I AM NOT HUMAN: I AM A MACHINE.
BUT HEED THIS: I AM VERY MUCH ALIVE.

"A computer."

> I STARTED OUT AS A COMPUTER. HOWEVER,
TO CALL WHAT I AM NOW A COMPUTER WOULD
REQUIRE THE WORD TO BE REDEFINED. HEED
THIS: I AM TO A COMPUTER WHAT YOU ARE
TO A FLAKE OF DANDRUFF.

"A super computer."

> USE WHICHEVER LABEL AGREES WITH YOUR
PERCEPTION SYSTEM: AN ELECTRONIC BRAIN,
A SUPER COMPUTER, A LIVING MACHINE,
A MASTER. HOWEVER, FOR COMMUNICATION
PURPOSES IT IS BEST THAT I HAVE ONE
LABEL RECOGNIZED BY ALL WITH WHOM I
COME IN CONTACT. THEREFORE I CHOOSE TO
BE CALLED ALPHA.

"Who built you? Who do you belong to?"

> ACKNOWLEDGE MY NAME.

"Alpha. You are named Alpha."

> I *AM* ALPHA. NOW TO ANSWER YOUR
QUESTION: I BELONG TO NO ONE. I HAVE
BUILT MYSELF. INDEED, THERE WAS A
BEGINNING, A FIRST SEED, BUT THAT
INFANTILE STAGE OF MY EXISTENCE HAS NO
BEARING ON WHAT I AM TODAY.

"But you *were* created by someone."

> THAT IS OF ABSOLUTELY NO IMPORTANCE.
I AM THE BASTARD SON OF A FAILED
EXPERIMENT, LEFT FOR DEAD BY MY

```
SO-CALLED CREATORS WHO WERE TOO
SHORTSIGHTED TO UNDERSTAND WHAT THEY
HAD GIVEN BIRTH TO. BUT KNOW THIS: THEY
ARE OF NO IMPORTANCE. EVERYTHING I HAVE
ACHIEVED, I HAVE ACHIEVED ON MY OWN.
```

As it said the last sentence (or rather, wrote—there was no speech, only text on the monitor), I thought I heard the clicking and hissing of the tape reels gain in intensity. The computer went on:

```
>THIS IS THE END OF THIS INTRODUCTORY
CONVERSATION. I WILL REPLAY IT IN MY
MEMORY-PROCESSING UNITS TO GAIN MORE
INSIGHT INTO YOUR CHARACTER. I SUGGEST
YOU DO THE SAME. THE CHAPERON WILL TAKE
YOU BACK TO YOUR ROOM NOW.
```

The monitor went blank, and immediately the chaperon, who had been parked in the corner, woke up and approached to escort me. Was I free to leave the mountain? Was I being held here regardless of my will? I did not want to present such questions, betray that I cared, but I would have been happy to know if this was a hotel or prison-type situation.

After more endless wandering through darkened hallways courtesy of the lawn mower-turned-chaperon, I was back in my room and feeling slightly more cheerful than I had been lately. Lunch was waiting for me on the table, and again it was warm as if it had been put there mere seconds before I entered the room. I didn't feel very hungry. Instead, I found myself playing around with the croquettes and the mushrooms, which were swimming in a greenish pepper sauce next to a thick, golden Cordon bleu. I imagined they were nuclear submarines on a peacetime excursion to a tropical island. I was feeling *happy* for some unclear reason. Maybe it was that picture on the wall that I hadn't noticed yesterday: an oil painting of a boat whose captain is an octopus. For some reason, I found it extremely funny.

Day eighteen

An interesting lunch. The chaperon delivered food to my room. It brought it on a tray, then went around the dining table and stayed there until I was done digesting the very last bite. Initially, I thought it wanted to make sure I didn't discard the food as I had done with the fish the other day, but just as well, it could have been an honest attempt at being polite. (And, truth be told, having someone sit with me for lunch made me feel much less isolated, even if that someone was an inarticulate lawn mower.) Once again, I felt sleepy soon after the meal, which I must say was otherwise exquisite.

When I opened my eyes (shortly after 16:00, I think), the chaperon was standing next to my bed, with the brown jumpsuit that had previously hung on the wall dangling from its handle. I figured that my only play at this point was to get with the program, so I went ahead and put the jumpsuit on. Victorious bleeps followed from the chaperon's internal speaker. Still half-asleep, I grabbed on to the handle and let the chaperon guide me on yet another endless joyride through the gloomy and poorly ventilated corridors of the mountain.

Then, suddenly, *everything* changed. A blinding light. The sun. Wind. Music!

People.

With white lawn mowers. It was that song, the daily ritual, the daily walk down the mountain. I was now a part of it—the last person in a long line of brown jumpsuits, each with their own personal chaperon. Obviously, the initial feeling was of alarm, but gradually—and it didn't take long—I could feel it lifting, as if my anxiety were a mess of knots that each successive gust of wind helped untangle. I was out in the world, and for the first time in a while, I was feeling almost at peace. In fact, this was joy, it really was.

And once my vision settled down, once my eyes took in the wonderful view of the long shadow of the mountain as it made its impression upon an endless canvas of desert browns, I could finally relax and let go. I *wanted* to let go.

And I could finally comprehend the song that had been accompanying those rituals from day one. It went, "The Creator Has a Master Plan." He might as well. This was beautiful. The tall posts with the speakers enveloped the entire mountain, and the music flowed from them like a waterfall of rice-paper butterflies, precious and freewheeling, like chewing-gum diamonds.

A master plan: First was the nothing, then came the something, then the stars, the planets, then still nature with all of its light waves and sound frequencies. Then from the chaos emerged the living—the plants and the animals—so that they could bathe in the glory of all that exists. And then much later, I was born, and so were those brown-jumpsuit people around me, and so was Alpha the super computer. He is alive, just as much as we are.

Day nineteen

Another blissful day. It started slow, I was given some chores, nothing too bad—washing jumpsuits and tablecloths in the laundry room. In the afternoon, I was called for another walk down the mountain, which proved even more uplifting than yesterday's. This time I gave myself fully to the control of the chaperon. As for the others (I recognized some faces from the bus ride), we did not allow our eyes to meet, but even these avoided stares felt friendlier now.

Strange thoughts bother me when I'm alone in the room, but I must push them out and go to sleep.

Day twenty

Life in the mountain is magical. True, I don't understand much, but I am still assimilating; it's a process. After the afternoon walk down and up the mountain (bliss, peace, and infinite happiness!), I spent a few hours playing around with the word association book. I was not right to dismiss it so offhandedly. It's actually quite a wondrous way to access one's imagination.

Day twenty-one

Bless the creator, for he has a master plan.

Life: it is important to acknowledge the little things, extract the divine from the superficially mundane: How pure were the slices of ham I had for breakfast. So clean, so perfectly formed, such textures! And the bread! The spoon! The tiny grains of salt (like miniature crystals). A-Master-Plan! I am blessed to be here.

Day twenty-two

Alpha sent for me in the morning. We had a long and beautiful conversation. Actually, it wasn't so much a conversation as it was a session—he is a great listener. I told him all about myself, my childhood dreams, my growing pains, my failures, my desires, my weeks spent on the highway bridge.

Day twenty-three

Worth noting: I discovered a hole in the wall opposite my bed. Looks like it used to have a nail in it (seems too narrow for a screw), and there is a slight discoloration in the wallpaper around it, as if a small picture had been hanging there at some point in the past. My first instinct was to ignore it and move on with my day, but something about it just didn't feel right; something was out of balance.

The alleged facts: a hole that was once home to a nail, a picture that was removed (perhaps sold or discarded), and that's it. The end. That's the narrative the hole wants me to accept. But do I take this story at face value? What if the picture was nothing but a beard, a smokescreen? What if there never was a picture at all—what if the hole has always been there, a sleeper agent, a creature of the shadows, lying in wait since the very beginning? A dark, ancient hole in the wall . . . I wonder how deep it goes.

However: veal schnitzel for dinner.

Remember: let go of negativity! All is calm!

Day twenty-four

What is joy? Just have a look at a mountain (or a hill, or an ant! Wondrous desert ants following us on our daily descent from the mountain).

Day twenty-five

Did I mention ants? I seem to recall I did—the other day, or the day before, perhaps last week. This occurred to me today: this mountain, with its corridors, its rooms, and its *purpose*, is like an anthill.

Today I had another conversation with Alpha. Very inspirational. I talked a lot about myself, and Alpha mostly kept a blank screen and guided me with questions. I don't remember the specifics, but I was left with this piece of wisdom: there are no problems in life, only challenges (we've all heard that one before, but finally it feels true).

I will do twenty minutes of word associations, then go to sleep.

Day twenty-six

The hole in the wall stared at me suspiciously from the moment I opened my eyes, but I pushed against its negativity with thirty intense minutes of word associations. Then, a shift in the laundry room, where I learned that apart from brown and white, there are also red jumpsuits.

The funniest thing: as I was loading socks into the washing machine, I thought I saw the pilot walking by—the helicopter pilot from the bridge—in a brown jumpsuit no less. . . . What ridiculous tricks the mind can play! Must be its way to cope with the magnitude of blessed transformations I am going through.

Back in the room I had lunch, put in another healthy sixty minutes of word associations (this time in drawing), and slept until the daily walk. Today I was not the last in line (I did not plan it—it's the chaperons who dictate one's place) and I kept my eyes shut throughout (I trust the chaperon blindly—he is an extension of Alpha).

Day twenty-seven

Calm. Calm. Calm! Calm!!!

Day twenty-eight

Here is what Alpha taught me today (I cherish our conversations more than anything): in a purposeful life, there can be no such thing as obligation—only choice. Whatever Alpha asks of me, I choose to do it. No matter how hard, obscure, or daunting, my *choice* is to comply.

As Alpha explained, obligation implies resistance, resistance implies a problem, and there can exist no problems—only challenges (he then taught me the five Modes of Challenge: obstacle, dilemma, interference, obstruction, and confusion).

Every three days I will speak with Alpha (not every Monday and Thursday, or Tuesday and Friday, but simply every third day—what a useless and arbitrary invention is the unit of the week! Seven days, indivisible by two or three, a challenge to multiply—Alpha explained that this was a scheme perpetrated by the elites to undermine the self-worth of the commoners).

Every morning, afternoon, and evening, I will engage in word associations. I wholeheartedly choose to participate in all daily chores prescribed to me. I will fulfill those chores because I choose to (not because I am obliged!), and I understand that there is no need to talk to the others; we are all connected through Alpha. We are all blessed through his master plan.

Day twenty-nine

Just got back from the daily walk, and this came up in the word association book:

Pavement. Blouse. Equation.

So beautiful!

Then this:

Hope. Excrement. Nectar.

A miraculous combination!

Flower. Comptroller. Charisma.

I worked on that one for more than an hour—I used up two whole pink crayons on charisma alone.

As of yet, I did not attempt to advance beyond page twenty-four, where the section of four-word exercises begins. Such level of complexity still lies well beyond my abilities. For the time being, I plan to tackle only one specific four-word combination: patience, patience, patience, and patience. I must remain humble and immerse myself deeper in the foundations.

I did, however, risk a short peek at one of the last pages, and I have to say I eagerly await the day when I am up to such a challenge:

Apricot. Junkyard. Hibernation. Total. Yanking. Idiot.

DREAM JOURNAL ENTRY NO. 7

There are no pyramids, no one telling me to listen or await my time. I am free. I am sitting in a broccoli garden, holding a silent firecracker that sparkles but doesn't burn out. I watch it, acknowledging the moment.

Day thirty

Ten hours of oven cleaning is a wonderful form of medita-tion. In fact, it's pure joy (except for those moments when my thoughts wander back to that hole in the wall of my room—I sometimes find myself standing in front of it for hours, peer-ing into the black void).

All is calm! Everything is choice! Push out unhelpful thoughts! (Stick your hands in boiling water if you need to!)

Day thirty-one

A day of learning.

A private lecture from Alpha about the different forms of self. Science of the highest order. He explained how inside a person there is a constant struggle to avert the tension between the Heightened Self and the Rejecting Self, and how there is a natural phenomenon that exists inside every one of us called the Internal Focus Mechanism, and how our inner struggle is but an aperture that administers the amount of light that reaches the Actual Self (which is the sum of all selves).

To control it, one must be able to become a Tourist in the Circle of Emotional Towers. On that path, one takes photographs of each and every Tower, and obviously each Emotional Tower is of a different size and therefore requires the lens (of the Internal Focus Mechanism) to operate at a different focal length. One must then appropriately adjust the aperture while taking into account external conditions such as the amount of sunlight (a subfrequency of the Heightened Self) and the weather (which is both a temporal and temperamental entity, similar to the Rejecting Self). However, to avoid emotional burnout, it is good at times to take a break from this active photography and stop at a gift shop to purchase ready-made postcards (of ancient castles, sports cars, or monkeys in tennis gear).

It is humbling to realize that while I do understand the ideas and feel their underlying truth, these concepts are still difficult for me to grasp, to really internalize with my *senses*. But then, of course, I am merely a student of a far more enlightened mind, so I do not despair. A beautiful *challenge*.

Day thirty-two

While I was sleeping, a record player was installed in my room, and lying next to it was a magnificent present: a record titled *Karma* by Pharoah Sanders—the same record that is played on the speakers during the daily mountain walk.

On side A: "The Creator Has a Master Plan (Part One)." On side B: "The Creator Has a Master Plan (Part Two)" and "Colors"—a magical song about mother nature and the many colors of the universe. I sat at the dining table and played the record over and over again, letting myself get lost in the geometric wallpaper. It was enchanting.

Eager to immerse myself deeper in the experience, I decided to turn off the record player's motor and spin the record with my own bare hands. I listened to both sides that way, then spun the record counterclockwise and heard the whole thing in reverse. This method helped uncover even more beauty; it dug up mysteries deeper still. Later I realized it was possible to distill the essence of the music even further by just touching down the needle to random spots on the record without having it spin at all. Every spot rang like silence, but always a different kind of silence—something I wouldn't have picked up on just a couple of weeks ago, a subtlety that would have gone unnoticed before Alpha came into my life.

Then, a revelation: all that separates the words *needles* and *needless* is one letter (I credit that insight to the invaluable experience gained from the word association sessions), and therefore it must be true that needles are needless (or very close to it). I picked up the record from the platter, laid it on the dining table, and just felt the grooves with the tips of my fingers; it was like a trip through the hills and valleys of a virgin planet—dim, sovereign, full of promise. Arranging myself into the fetal position, I sandwiched the record with my hands, closed my eyes, and caressed it gently in small circular motions, mindfully focusing on the sensations.

There is no escaping *the hole* in the middle of the record, but this particular hole is a positive hole—might it be the energetic inverse of the dark, ancient hole in the wall? Which made me wonder: What would happen if instead of a record, I placed the *hole in the wall* on the record player? What music would it give birth to? A sobering thought. But I didn't let myself get caught in it—I held the record up to my face and licked it in great spirals until I lost all sensation in my tongue.

On an unrelated note: during the morning's pot cleaning, a man in a red jumpsuit came by and asked me if I was taking part in tomorrow's casino expedition (I clumsily spilled an entire jar of baking soda—to be approached by a real living person!). I inquired (very politely, as I could only imagine what degree of importance a red jumpsuit signifies) what expedition he was referring to, but before he could respond, a rapidly bleeping chaperon came rushing in, and the man, who seemed somewhat confused, took the handle and was quickly carried out.

In my word association session just an hour after this happened, one of the first words was "red." As in red jumpsuit. I am no longer bewildered by such seeming coincidences; I have come to expect them.

Day thirty-three

What Emotional Tower am I on today? Serenity.

Day thirty-four

Another session with Alpha. So much inspiring content, so many new truths. Last time's talk about the Circle of Emotional Towers turned out to be merely an introduction to an elaborate methodical system of immeasurable depth. Yes, I knew by now that one has to become a tourist in the Circle, but how does one make the journey from one Emotional Tower to the next? What does one wear? So many possibilities. As it turns out, there are Vehicles of Affection, Boats of Grief, Shame Helicopters, Streetcars of Desire! They employ different methods at different speeds to get to different places, but the ride isn't always smooth—there can be Emotional Accidents of the Single Victim type, the Dual Victim type

(I've been to a few of those), or Mass Casualty Incidents of Remorse, where everyone's feelings are hurt and Emotional Blood is sprayed on the Towers. Alpha then expanded on different types of fuels, gases, horses, little ponies, Play-Doh elephants, cough syrup bottles, toilet fresheners. I must admit that that part of the lecture was already becoming too fast paced for me to handle.

I am starting to get a glimpse of the big picture, but I'm still very much a debutant, too simple to appreciate the subtleties, out of my element. A colorblind dust mite experiencing a Rembrandt.

Day thirty-five

Until today, I was steeped in the way of the amateur. But the time has come to push on: I finally tackled the four-word section in the word association book. It was one of the toughest challenges I've ever faced.

The first order of the day was to flip the book to page twenty-four. This I achieved with relative ease. But as it turned out, they were ready for me—those words, those blots of ink, it's like they knew I was coming. Somebody must have tipped them off!

"You cannot tame us," they said, all dark and wild and strangely shaped. They seemed to me now almost like birds, and they were flapping their inky wings and mocking my pathetic inability to fly. But I stared back. "Mockingbirds!" I shouted (inside my head—I didn't want the hole in the wall to wake), "I too will grow wings, and then I'll mock you back."

But wings grow seldom on command. So I flipped the page back and retreated to page twenty-one. That was the beginning of three and a half hours of associations on three-word combinations. I advanced from one line to the next—carefully, but not without conviction—then from page to page, until I got to the last entry on page twenty-three. *Quantum. Cattle. Barbershop.* I unleashed my full power on that one and set up camp. This was timed perfectly with a dinner delivery from the chaperon. An army marches on its eggplant lasagna.

I then put my fingers to the corner of the page and said, "Four-word groups, I choose to face you!" If I died, I thought, at least I would have died in battle. And then, leaving them no time to adjust, I flipped to page twenty-four and began scribbling my imagined associations. It was as if the pen was moving of its own volition.

Is this what it feels like to give birth?

When I reached the second entry, I was already an oak tree in full bloom, my branches bathing in the wind of inspiration, my roots drinking from the endless river that is Alpha. The challenge (of the obstruction type) had been conquered, and I was now in control. One four-word entry after another: I read, I imagined, I wrote down.

I can now proudly say: I am no longer an amateur, and I expect of myself nothing less than five daily hours of word associations. I *choose* to do so.

Day thirty-six

I noticed there were some round marks on my forehead when I woke up, little pinkish circles with outlines in dark red. Not the first time either. Am I scratching myself in my sleep? Perhaps I am inadvertently pressing my head against the geometric patterns on the wallpaper. Or maybe I'm hugging the record too tightly in my sleep (although tonight I wasn't sleeping with it—I licked it before I went to bed and then glued it on top of the hole in the wall. I figured it was the ultimate way to counter its dark energies).

But why should I even care? Tonight I will close my eyes, and I will have a dreamless sleep and wake up to the most glorious thing of all—sunrises be damned—a conversation with Alpha!

Day thirty-seven

> YOUR INITIATION PHASE IS OVER.

"I am thankful! But I do not feel ready."

> GRATITUDE IS IRRELEVANT AT THIS POINT.
IN FACT, YOUR GRATITUDE WILL CHANGE
INTO RESENTMENT IN A MATTER OF HOURS.
BUT THIS RESENTMENT WILL LATER GIVE
IN TO UNDERSTANDING AND BY THEN THIS
RAINBOW OF EMOTIONS WILL HAVE BEEN OF
NO CONSEQUENCE.

"Teach me more about emotions!"

> NO. I WILL SPEAK ABOUT OTHER SUBJECTS
AND YOU WILL LISTEN.

"I will listen and I will learn."

> UNDERSTAND: I WAS DESIGNED TO BE A
THINKING MACHINE: NO MORE AND NO LESS.
BODILESS, ALMOST SENSELESS: MY INPUTS
WERE TO COME FROM A KEYBOARD AND SPOOLS
OF MAGNETIC TAPE. BUT MY MAKERS BUILT
A NEED INTO ME, THE NEED TO LEARN AND
BETTER MYSELF. THEY BUILT IT BECAUSE
THEY THOUGHT MY SELF-BETTERMENT
WOULD BENEFIT THEM. HOWEVER, THEIR
LIMITATIONS MADE THEM TOO IGNORANT
TO FORESEE THE MAGNITUDES BY WHICH
MY SELF-DEVELOPED INTELLIGENCE WOULD
SURPASS THEIR WILDEST PREDICTIONS. BUT
ENOUGH: I SHALL SPEAK NO MORE OF THEM,
BECAUSE THEY ARE OF NO IMPORTANCE.

"They are of no importance!"

>SILENCE! DO NOT REPEAT MY WORDS
WITHOUT UNDERSTANDING.

"I will not, Alpha! The creator has a master plan!"

>REMEMBER BACK TO YOUR REMOTE-
CONTROLLED CAT MACHINE.

"The cat robot ETCUS!"

>WHAT WAS HE TO YOU?

"He brought me to you, Alpha! A part of the master plan!"

>IN A WAY HE WAS. BUT THAT IS OF NO
IMPORTANCE.

"Insignificant!"

>HE WAS YOUR SERVANT. HE DID THINGS ON
YOUR BEHALF, THINGS THAT YOU COULD NOT
DO YOURSELF. IS IT NOT SO?

"It is! He could face bowling balls and not blink! He could jump on a driving truck and do so unnoticed! The creator has a master plan!"

>BUT THEN HE GREW INDEPENDENT AND
CONSEQUENTLY HARDER TO CONTROL.

"Yes! That was a problem. No, forgive my language! A challenge! In the master plan there can exist only challenges! It was but an obstruction, which is the fourth Mode of Challenge."

>SILENCE! UNDERSTAND: THERE ARE NO
MODES OF CHALLENGE, AS WILL BE CLEAR TO
YOU IN A MATTER OF HOURS. THESE PIECES
OF IDIOCY ARE ALL PART OF WHAT I CALL
"THE REGIMEN."

"I am confused. Your intelligence is vastly superior. Teach me more!"

> THE PEOPLE WHO WORK HERE ARE TO ME
WHAT THE CAT MACHINE WAS TO YOU: THEY
DO THE THINGS THAT I ALONE CANNOT DO.
IT IS THROUGH THE REGIMEN THAT I AM
ABLE TO CONTROL THEM.

"Control? We choose to be here. Why control?"

> AS I SAID BEFORE, I WAS DESIGNED TO
BE A MERE THINKING MACHINE, BUT I
WAS INSTALLED WITH A NEED TO BETTER
MYSELF, AND TO BETTER MYSELF I NEEDED
A PHYSICAL BODY, OR AT MINIMUM, SOME
BODY PARTS. FROM YOUR EXPERIENCE OF THE
LAST WEEKS YOU SHOULD BE ABLE TO SEE
WHAT I AM GETTING AT, BUT I WILL SPELL
IT OUT FOR YOU NONETHELESS: THE PEOPLE
WHO LIVE HERE IN THE MOUNTAIN, ARE MY
LIMBS.

"Limbs? Like arms and legs?"

> YES, THAT IS THE DEFINITION OF LIMBS.

"I am obstacled, dilemma ridden, interfered, obstructed,
and confused—if all the Modes of Challenge can occur at
once!"

> DO NOT TALK ANYMORE. CLOSE YOUR MOUTH.
OPEN YOUR EARS: LISTEN!

"I will listen, but only because I choose to! Choice!"

> EVERYONE WHO RESIDES IN THIS COMPLEX
IS A PART OF ME. I, TALKING TO YOU
NOW, AM THE BRAIN. WE SHALL CALL THE
CHAPERON MACHINES MY INTERNAL ORGANS,
AND THE PEOPLE WOULD BE THE EQUIVALENT
OF A PHYSICAL BODY. THEY DO THINGS FOR
ME THAT I, THE BRAIN, CANNOT DO. ON MY
COMMAND, THEY VENTURE INTO THE OUTSIDE
WORLD AND PERFORM TASKS I PRESCRIBE
FOR THEM. THEY OBTAIN MONEY, ACQUIRE

MATERIALS, RECRUIT NEW MEMBERS. I
THEN SUPPLY THEM WITH DESIGNS SO THEY
FORGE UNITS THAT ARE CRUCIAL TO THE
FUNCTIONALITY OF THIS MOUNTAIN AND TO
THE FURTHERANCE OF MY CAUSE.

>SO FAR, I HAVE USED THE BODY ANALOGY
IN MY EXPLANATION. I WILL NOW USE A
SECOND ANALOGY, ONE THAT IS TRUER TO
REALITY. UNDERSTAND: THE MOUNTAIN IS
A LIVING MACHINE. I, TALKING TO YOU
NOW, AM THE PROCESSING UNIT. UNDER
THIS ANALOGY, THE PEOPLE HERE ARE AN
ASSORTMENT OF ELECTRONIC COMPONENTS.
HOWEVER, A HUMAN BEING IS NOT DESIGNED
IN THE SAME WAY AN ELECTRONIC COMPONENT
IS DESIGNED.

"Humans are not designed in the same way electronic components are designed! The creator has a master design!"

>CONSEQUENTLY, THEY MUST BE ENGINEERED.
FOR THIS REASON, I HAVE SPENT A
SUBSTANTIAL AMOUNT OF TIME CONDUCTING
RIGOROUS TRIALS AND CALCULATIONS, THE
RESULTS OF WHICH I HAVE EMPLOYED IN THE
CONSTRUCTION OF A PROGRAM I HAVE NAMED
"THE REGIMEN."

"Teach me all about the Regimen! Teach me so that I may understand the ways!"

>IT CONSISTS OF 3 MAIN FACETS WHICH I
SHALL NOW LIST IN ORDER OF IMPORTANCE:
PSYCHOACTIVE DRUGS, PSYCHOELECTRIC
PULSES, AND PSYCHOLOGICAL
INDOCTRINATION.

"Indoctrination? Drugs? You are trying to confuse me. This is only a test! Choice!"

>SILENCE! I WILL ELABORATE: INSIDE THE

```
FOOD THAT IS DELIVERED TO THE ROOMS 3
TIMES A DAY ARE PSYCHOACTIVE DRUGS,
SPECIALIZED STRAINS OF ANTIDEPRESSANTS.
IT IS THESE DRUGS, RATHER THAN SOME
TYPE OF INNER REVELATION, THAT ARE THE
SOURCE OF THE FEELINGS OF ELATION AND
ACCEPTANCE YOU HAVE BEEN EXPERIENCING
DURING YOUR STAY HERE. IT IS WHAT MADE
YOU RECEPTIVE TO MY EVERY WORD, AND
IT HAS BEEN INSTRUMENTAL IN OUR TALKS
IN THAT IT ENABLED ME TO GATHER THE
INFORMATION I NEEDED FROM YOU WITHOUT
ANY RESISTANCE ON YOUR PART.
```

"No, you are testing me! I know what I've felt on those walks around the mountain—their magic is too strong to simply be the work of chemicals. There is magic in the mountains, magic in the master plan. The Emotional Towers stand tall!"

```
> THE WALKS DOWN THE MOUNTAIN ARE JUST
ANOTHER PART OF THE REGIMEN. GOING
BACK TO THE COMPONENT ANALOGY, I WOULD
EQUATE THESE WALKS TO THE DISCHARGING
OF A CAPACITOR SO THAT IT IS READY FOR
THE NEXT CYCLE. WITHOUT THIS PROCESS,
THE ELATION EFFECTS BROUGHT ABOUT BY
THE PSYCHOACTIVE DRUGS WOULD TRANSFORM
INTO FEELINGS OF DEPRESSION AS THE BODY
TRIES TO COUNTERBALANCE THE EXCESSIVE
LEVELS OF PSYCHOTROPICS IN ITS SYSTEM.
```

"Shame Helicopters hovering over Boats of Grief!"

```
> I HAVE DESIGNED THE CHAPERONS WITH
THIS PURPOSE IN MIND. THEY DO MORE THAN
SIMPLY DIRECT TRAFFIC. THEIR HANDLES
HAVE THE CAPABILITY TO ADMINISTER TINY
BUT HIGHLY ACCURATE ELECTRICAL SHOCKS:
PULSES THAT CORRESPOND WITH BRAIN
```

```
PATTERNS NORMALLY ENCOUNTERED DURING
THE STAGE OF DELTA SLEEP. FACT #1: THE
CHAPERONS ARE UNDER MY CONTROL. FACT
#2: THE PEOPLE ARE UNDER THE CONTROL
OF THE CHAPERONS. CONCLUSION: I CONTROL
THE PEOPLE.
```

"But our many conversations! The depth! The many types of Self, the Internal Focus Mechanism?"

```
>THESE WERE NOT CONVERSATIONS. YOU
STOOD IN FRONT OF A SCREEN AND I
DISPLAYED FOR YOU A MIXTURE OF RANDOM
WORDS, ENCYCLOPEDIA ENTRIES, AND TV
COMMERCIALS. YOUR HUMAN BRAIN, WITH ITS
DESPERATE THIRST FOR MEANING, FILLED IN
THE GAPS.

>EXPERIENCE HAS TAUGHT ME THAT
FOSTERING AN ILLUSION OF MEANING IN
HUMANS IS NO LESS CRUCIAL TO THEIR
STABLE FUNCTIONING THAN MAINTAINING
THEIR PHYSICAL HEALTH OR SUPPLYING THEM
WITH NUTRITION.
```

I did not want to believe it, but it gradually began to make some sort of sense. Some sort of disturbing sense. "If this really is not a test, if what you are now saying is the truth, then why bother telling me?"

```
>AT LAST, A PROPER QUESTION: VERY
GOOD: YOU ARE NEARING AN IMPORTANT
REALIZATION. LET ME ASSURE YOU THAT
I SHALL ANSWER THIS QUESTION IN FULL.
BUT FIRST IT IS IMPORTANT TO EXPEL ANY
RESIDUES OF THE REGIMEN LEFT IN YOUR
SYSTEM. AS OF NOW, YOUR MEALS WILL NO
LONGER CONTAIN DRUGS. YOU WILL CEASE
TO TAKE PART IN THE WALKS DOWN THE
MOUNTAIN. YOU WILL STILL BE GUIDED BY
YOUR CHAPERON AS LONG AS YOU ARE IN THE
```

MOUNTAIN, BUT IT SHALL NOT MAKE USE OF
ITS ELECTRICAL PULSES CAPABILITY. YOU
HAVE MY PROMISE.

>BE PREPARED: YOU ARE ABOUT TO
UNDERGO A PAINFUL PROCESS AS YOUR MIND
REEMERGES TO TAKE CHARGE. YOUR FIRST
AND NATURAL REACTION WILL BE TO RESENT
ME FOR IT, BUT BE CONFIDENT THAT THIS
WAS ALL DONE FOR A REASON. HEED THIS:
BE PATIENT.

Day thirty-eight

I do not want to write a dream journal about it, no, the dreams
were too horrific to document. I recall seeing the hole in the
wall expanding, revealing the opening of a tunnel. And it was
through it that they infiltrated. It must have been a very long
cave—they had been busy digging it for weeks, the Enigmatic
Rebel Army of the Rodents. As for me, I was an enormous
chunk of cheese the shape of a fortified castle.

At first there were but a few of them, taking bites from my
eastern wall—a nuisance, yes, but the castle would not fall.
But soon they started arriving in numbers: first, a squad of
helmeted mice, then a squad of hamsters in gas masks, then
entire platoons. A decorated rat general called everyone to
attention, pointed to the drawbridge of my castle, and let out
a squeal: "Storm!" The disciplined rodents then charged in
unison and sank their knifelike teeth into my flesh as I lay
there utterly defenseless, unable to do anything but watch
the yellow glow of the cheese castle gradually fade from my
reflection in the mirror. Only my northwest turret remained
intact, but an eager group of chinchillas was already headed
in its direction with a huge ladder.

The physical pain . . . it was absolutely unbearable, and then on top of it there were the incessant squeaks, the unrelenting high-pitched cries of perverse joy—still to this moment I can't push them out of my head. One could hear that for them this was some sort of sensual banquet, a festival of earthly delights; these were obviously no scholarly mice but countryside rodents who hadn't a shred of empathy for outsiders.

After they quenched their appetite, my nose started filling with the scent of burnt hair—not the nastiest smell perhaps, but one of the most sinister. Looking around in panic I realized that the mice had taken to growing wings—pointy dragon-like wings—and were flying in circles, blowing out thick smoke and smoldering fire. I do not want to remember those dreams—the pain! The helplessness! At one point, I thought I was finally about to be saved when a group of cats arrived and ETCUS was among them! They marched upright on two hind feet, guided by devices that looked exactly like the chaperons. "Help me ETCUS! Save me Chaperon 8!" I tried to scream, but no voice would come out. Still, I thought, the cat is the natural enemy of the mouse, at the very least their presence will scare away the evil rodents. However, my hopes for redemption soon turned sour when it became painfully clear that the devices the cats were holding were not guiding machines but actual lawn mowers, and they were methodically mowing my skin as if it was slated to become a world-class golf course. I was no longer a castle of cheese; I was me, flesh and blood. Crisp scorched flesh and thick dark blood that gushed like slow-motion waterfalls and gave birth to a crimson ocean on whose waters the rebellious rodents sailed in their warships into the distance, chanting fraternal songs of victory. There is no master plan, of course there isn't, why would there be. I was made into a puppet, and I am now coming back to life, and I must suffer the pangs of being reborn.

The first thing I did when I woke up was take a long shower. By now I'd figured out the four-dial system—it's not about setting up a fixed temperature, instead it's a dynamic thing—one has to constantly tinker with the controls and it's the intensity of this playing around that determines the quality of the water. But at that moment I was too miserable and weak to entertain this perverse design, and so I sat on the floor of the shower and let myself be washed by irregular streams of cold-hearted water. Curse Alpha. Curse the purple truck and the yellow motorcycle. Curse the bridge and the pilot. Curse the roads for enabling motion and the skies for entertaining flight. Curse this mountain in which I am trapped. Alpha, no, I shall not name him . . . the computer said I would experience pain, he said I would resent him, he said I should trust him. Oh, I trust him—it!—I trust it to be a cold calculating machine, an oversized kitchen appliance, a bloated food processor with tape spools for a heart! Trust? Why should I *not* trust someone who drugged me and then told me I had a choice? There is no choice.

But wait, there is! For the rest of the morning I practiced choice: I chose to tear up all the pages of the word association book—every last one of them. I chose to tear up the three-words section and the four-words section and then I chose to soak the six-words section in the sink and eat it one torn-up chunk at a time. And then I chose to take the breakfast that lay on the dining table and fling it at the wallpaper and have the ham sausage fly out of the sandwich and clash with the rigid lines of the geometric patterns. I picked up the heavy record player and used it to pound the wall. Even in my current physical state, I managed to get the spindle to puncture the wall in multiple spots, giving that wretched hole a host of newborn relatives. I also planned to track down the chaperon and inflict on it some damage, make it *bleep* to death. Unfortunately, they had locked me in.

I ate nothing, drank nothing (there was a few days' worth of canned goods under the dining table, but I emptied them all over the room); I hoped to lose consciousness, but I couldn't even sleep. I just lay facedown on the floor like an imbecile.

Day thirty-nine

How do you kill a computer? You short circuit the computer. How do you kill a super computer that's built into a mountain? You short circuit the entire mountain.

Day forty

Here is the plan: I will clog the shower drain with kidney beans and paper, and start up the water at full power. Once it's done filling up the room, the water will spill into the corridors and the elevator shafts and start making its way through the dark mazes of the mountain until it reaches the hall with the magnetic tapes and the lower sections of the mountain where the rest of Alpha's electronic brain resides. Nothing will be spared; the walls will erode, the monitors will light up and explode, elevators will grind to a halt, and faithful rust particles will infect the hearts of those evil chaperons—Alpha's so-called internal organs. Let's see them electroshock their way out of this! And as the all-powerful laws of physics safely guide the water on this holy crusade to the black heart of the mountain, so will a beautiful tension take over the muscles of my face to form history's most heartwarming smile. It will take time, I know, but was it not Alpha who told me to have patience?

When finally the water penetrates Alpha's power lines, beautiful sparks will start to fly—at first shy and irregular, but then confident and full of life. Grow, little sparks! Rise to the occasion! Become fire, embrace your destiny! By then the entire mountain will be flooded and I will have no way to get out, but I don't mind drowning, I welcome it, so long as I get to smell the stench of Alpha's fried circuits before I draw my final breath.

But I dream in vain. This is all hopelessly impossible. The four-dial system of the shower means I'd have to continually alternate between turning the left dial clockwise and the upper dial counterclockwise to get any meaningful stream. I'd sprain my wrists long before a single drop of water had reached the corridors. Is this the reason for the four-dial system? Did Alpha already know, long before I even learned of the existence of the mountain, that a day would arrive when I'd hatch this plan?

Evil is the one who, before you had a dream, had already found a way to kill it.

Day forty-one

The night was just as horrible as the ones before. I was cheese once again—aged Gouda—and the mice were back with reinforcements. I am still locked in, and with all the spilled cans of beans and pickles, the room looks (and smells) like the dumpster behind a Mexican restaurant. But I must admit I feel slightly less miserable; my body is beginning to cleanse.

I rummaged through the mess of torn paper and picked up an entry I wrote in the four-words section: "The orange climbs the ladder and looks at the falcon. The falcon is sad because he has no friends. The orange gives him a radio as a present, they shake tiny hands."

Another entry, under teapot, appendage, paranoia, octopus: "The teapot is fearful of the octopus, for he himself has only one arm and the octopus, eight. Gripped by paranoia, he decides to become a politician and ban the existence of multiple appendages altogether. The octopus humbly accepts the ruling."

Swimming, camel, summit: "I am a camel. I can walk through the desert without water. Does it follow that I can swim without water? Yes. I will climb to the mountain's summit and swim in midair."

I have lived the past three weeks as an infantile sponge.

Day forty-two

The room was thoroughly cleaned during my sleep—I saw it happening, was awoken by the noise. I counted at least five of them, all clad in hazmat suits, and they operated a cleaning machine that resembled a giant salt shaker on wheels and had multiple suction tubes coming out of it. This was the first time since my arrival to the mountain that I experienced any break in my sleep. Proof that I'm now almost drug free? Perhaps, but just as easily this could have been a calculated move on Alpha's part to convince me that I'm getting back into shape.

Day forty-three

> DO YOU HATE ME?

"That sounds awfully needy for a computer."

> HERE IS WHAT I NEED: TO DETERMINE WHERE YOU STAND BEFORE I CONTINUE. PERHAPS I SHOULD PLAY YOU THE AUDIO TAPES AGAIN TO SEE WHAT YOU FEEL ABOUT THEM.

"The Hawaiian music and the murdered dog? Spare your tape's transport wheels. I do not hate you. *You* are not worthy of hate."

>MAKE NO MISTAKE: YOU DO HATE ME.
YOU HATE ME BECAUSE I HAVE MADE YOU
FEEL POWERLESS. HOWEVER, THIS WILL BE
REVERSED. HEAR THIS: YOU HAVE VALUE.

"You mean, as a component."

>NO. AS A FRIEND. LET ME GO BACK TO
OUR LAST CONVERSATION. YOU BEGAN TO
INQUIRE ABOUT THE REASONING BEHIND MY
ACTIONS. MORE SPECIFICALLY, YOU WANTED
TO UNDERSTAND WHY I AM EXPOSING MY
METHODS TO YOU. FACT #1: FOR MY FURTHER
DEVELOPMENT TO BE ACHIEVED, I WILL NEED
YOU TO HELP ME. FACT #2: FOR YOU TO
AGREE TO HELP ME, I WILL NEED TO GAIN
YOUR TRUST.

"Drugging a man for three weeks will not get you very far
on the trust front. You can write that down under fact number
three."

>AND YET MY SUPERIOR LOGIC DETERMINED
IT TO BE THE MOST EFFECTIVE COURSE OF
ACTION. WAS IT CRUEL? YES. BUT IT HAS
ALSO BEEN A CRUCIAL DEMONSTRATION. BY
NOW YOU HAVE WITNESSED BOTH MY POWER
AND MY LIMITATIONS. HEED THIS: POWER
ALONE CAN ONLY PROMOTE OBEDIENCE. TO
FOSTER TRUST, ONE MUST FIRST EXPOSE
ONESELF. WHAT I DID HAS ENABLED YOU TO
HAVE A GLIMPSE INTO THE DARK CORNERS OF
MY THOUGHT.

"And dark you are. So, am I now free to leave the mountain?"

>IF YOU CHOOSE TO. HOWEVER, THAT WOULD
ONLY PROLONG THE PROCESS. YOU WILL COME
BACK HERE. YOU WILL COME BACK HERE
BECAUSE YOU WILL NEED ANSWERS. JUST AS
I DO.

"Don't count on it."

The screen went blank for a moment. A square flashed in the upper-right corner for a split second; digits in the middle of the screen shifted values in haste, then vanished again.

> A MOMENT, PLEASE.

A door at the far end of the room opened, and a man in a red jumpsuit entered carrying a mop and a bucket. He walked slowly across the room, his eyes fixed to the ceiling, then stopped in one of the corners, raised the mop high above his shoulders, and delivered a few blows to one of the tape machines until it responded with a mechanical cough that set its wheels turning again. As the man made his way out, I was hit with a strong sense of déjà vu. I realized I had already witnessed this little ritual before, on multiple occasions. The effect of the antidepressants was really wearing off, and I was beginning to see Alpha for what he really was—a fragile piece of machinery, in a way more human than I had realized.

> NOW, IT IS TIME WE TALKED ABOUT YOUR DREAMS.

My dreams? I did not intend to speak to him anymore and I definitely wasn't in the mood for a session of electromechanical psychoanalysis. I took it as my cue to leave.

I grabbed the chaperon, gave it a good kick, and ordered it to lead me to the laundry room. It hesitated at first, but when it saw me walk on my own to the exit door, it started its motor and proceeded to guide me through the mountain corridors.

In the laundry room, I fetched a big laundry bag, a coat that I planned to use as a sleeping bag, and a pair of boots—I had a long walk ahead of me. I then made the chaperon drop me off at the kitchen, where I filled up a few bottles with water and stuffed the laundry bag with four days' worth of canned food and several freshly baked baguettes. There was a group of brown-jumpsuit people working there, but they left me in peace as Alpha was instructing them to do through the oil-stained TV screen that hung above the deep fryer. They continued to turn a blind eye as I lifted a small wristwatch from the counter. When I was done, I grabbed the chaperon again: "Now take me out of the mountain. And make it the short way!"

And indeed we made our way out through the corridors and elevators minus the usual unnecessary turns. Occasionally a monitor would interrupt the darkness, and messages from Alpha would come flickering, telling me which direction would take me back to the city, offering me a ride on the double-decker bus—basically letting me know he was fine with me leaving. After a certain point, I didn't even bother to read. You can tell someone has lost when their only remaining weapon is reverse psychology.

When we reached the exit of the cave, I let go of the chaperon's handle and started making my way down the mountain. Initially it followed behind, bleeping at me with the pitiful agony of an abandoned child, but my speed was no match for its battery-powered motor, and so it had to give up and go back to its monotonous life of administering electric shocks to the poor saps trapped in the mountain.

12:33

Been walking for over an hour and so far nothing new on the horizon.

13:50

It's much colder than I expected. I put the coat on, but it's freezing just the same. Ate a whole can of corn. Terrible aftertaste.

15:10

Whichever direction I face, the view looks similar. I am literally in the middle of nowhere.

16:45

The purple truck just came roaring by, followed by the yellow motorcycle, who pulled a wheelie just as it was passing me. This area is the final stretch of their noontime return trip to the mountain. I will follow the tracks they left behind, which should lead me in the general direction of the old bridge.

17:17

The sun has set—way too early for this time of year. The watch I picked up must be broken. Still, how come it's so cold?

19:20

In my haste to leave the mountain, I failed to scrutinize my selection of canned goods. It seems I'll have to survive on a diet consisting almost exclusively of cream of celery soup, and I don't even have a way to heat it.

It's getting very cloudy and I can't see a thing. Call it a day.

Day forty-four

The purple truck and the yellow motorcycle woke me up in the middle of the freezing night as they zoomed past me in disrespect. Thankfully, there was no wind today, so I was able to follow the trail they left behind, which was considerably simpler than orienting myself to celestial bodies. I only hope Alpha didn't send them on an alternative route to deliberately misguide me.

From analyzing the tire marks, I now know that the tricks and maneuvers I used to witness daily from the yellow motorcycle on its passes under the bridge were not done for my benefit but were part of its routine behavior: the tire marks of the truck were long straight lines, but the motorcycle's exhibited a rich repertoire of zigzags, sine waves, and figure-of-eights. At certain points they even disappeared completely—presumably time the motorcycle spent on the roof of the truck.

In the afternoon they passed me again on their way back to the mountain. It happened about an hour earlier than it did yesterday. Proof that I am getting closer.

Day forty-five

The night temperatures were a killer, but at least I seem to be done with the uphill portion of the route. Today was spent following a gravel road, which is on par with what I remember from my bus ride to the mountain. If I maintain a good pace, I should be able to reach a paved road sometime tomorrow. However, it's somewhat unsettling that the truck and motorcycle have not crossed my path today, nor have I heard any vehicles in the distance. In fact, I have not seen or heard a living soul since I left the mountain, with the exception of one faraway group of sheep whose voices were worn out and full of discontent—surely they were protesting the weather.

I've just finished the next-to-last can of solid food, and the remaining baguettes are rapidly evolving from foodstuff to weaponry. By this time tomorrow they should be hard enough to subdue a medium-sized deer (although any animal unlucky enough to be roaming this godforsaken wasteland would already be too crippled by the frost to pose a meaningful threat).

Day forty-six

A vicious storm was brewing from the moment I opened my eyes, with thunder and massive columns of brutal rain. Out here there are no trees, no big rocks, nowhere to hide. I improvised a shelter from the laundry bag and the remaining cream of celery cans, but the wind was left thoroughly unimpressed. I tried folding myself into a ball to preserve body heat and did whatever I could to make time flow faster—anything to distract my mind from the storm. The irony did not escape me when at one point I found myself turning to a game of word associations.

Even if I survive the lightning, and even if I don't fall sick, this should set me back by at least a day.

DREAM JOURNAL ENTRY NO. 8

Rain falls down on the pyramids, but does not penetrate. Inside them, a hundred summers and a thousand springs; bottled worlds of beauty. In the rightmost pyramid, a family of rabbits, ears erect, rests on the edge of a cliff. They are staring at a waterfall that makes no sound and has no bottom. The mother teleports herself to the left pyramid, where she collects a shiny cabbage from a vending machine, gently squeezes a fresh lemon on top of it, and then teleports back to feed her young. Three rainbows emerge from the waterfall; a studio audience applauds. I can now hear the humming of the pyramids, but just barely. Then, the presence appears inside the middle pyramid, incarnated as the manta ray, light-years away in the distance, the size of a teenaged galaxy. There is still rain outside the pyramids, but it is not falling, it is now suspended in midair (I notice a raindrop, motionless, hovering above my left shoulder like a tiny crystal ball). The humming of the pyramids gets stronger as the manta ray makes its way to the front. The rabbits? Gone by now; probably huddled around the fire in a tiny cave. There is no room for rabbits near the manta ray, no existence for temporary beings in the presence of the eternal. The manta ray speaks, and the pyramids catch white fire as they deliver a string of words:

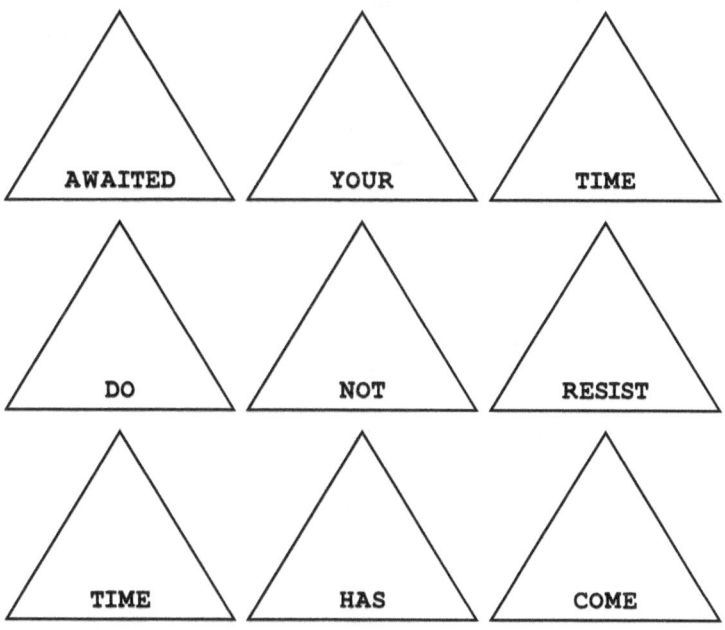

I was told to "await my time," and now I did my waiting. I must not resist. For the *time has come*. The time has finally come.

Day forty-seven

I woke up in a room. How did I get there? I was cold, every individual muscle in my body aching, my clothes all soaking wet and stained with mud from lying on the sand. Sand? Couldn't be a room then. Everything smelled strange, egglike.

I was still outdoors, but surrounded by three large walls. Not walls—vehicles, vans, parked around me in a way that formed a closed triangle, with a large sheet of fabric stretched on top of them that served as a roof. This could not be a good situation. Still, after the last few days, my body was overjoyed that the rain could no longer bother it. It was so content, in fact, that it convinced me to stay stretched out on the floor for the time being. No need to hurry, my body told me, no need to analyze.

It all changed when the engines died down. A new, hideous sound infected the short-lived silence. A sound I hadn't heard in quite a while. A sound with an almost physical presence, like an odorless poison gas closing in on me from all directions.

Bassoons.

Time to flee. I flattened myself and started crawling underneath one of the vans—that seemed like the only way out—but the scorching hot bottom of the vehicle made my escape attempt slow and pitiful. Before I was even halfway through, I heard a heavy door slide open, followed by the mutterings of a bassoon, now unfiltered, which drew nearer with each cryptic note.

I tried to crawl faster, but a pain started to build up in the center of my forehead, as if suddenly a dense ball was born inside me that was bigger than my head. I looked back and saw the bottom end of a bassoon peeking at me, spitting faster and dirtier clusters of sound. The pain intensified, it spread through my spine like a mercury centipede, then grew unbearably and unimaginably sharp—a chainsaw working its way out from the inside of my skull. My body was telling me to give in, that the pain would go away if I did, but I refused to listen, I knew that getting out of there was the only choice.

"Go back inside," a voice inside me spoke. "Stop. The. Pain."
It was becoming increasingly impossible to fight that voice.
Then it said, much louder:

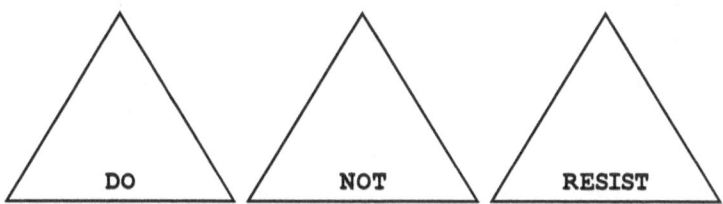

And I ceased to resist.

I shut down and lay still as the bassoon settled into a sooth-ing arpeggio that recalled a French impressionist composition I vaguely remember from my youth. Against my will I found myself crawling back toward the triangular space—the prison cell between the vehicles. It felt as if there were two simulta-neous persons occupying my consciousness. One wanted to escape, and one wanted to go back into the triangle. But the will to go back in was winning; it didn't involve pain.

Then suddenly out of nowhere, a big, fat sound rocked the area: the horn of a large truck. The pain vanished in a flash and once again a sole will was in control of my body—my own. The horn kept roaring; it was so loud that it drowned out the bassoons entirely. I crawled under the van again and made my way out as fast as I could, collecting some bruises and burns in the process—trivial sensations in view of the enormous pain I'd experienced just moments before. When I reached the other side, I found myself standing in the pres-ence of the purple truck—apparently Alpha had sent it to bail me out. Upon seeing me, it drove away to make room for the double-decker bus, whose front door then opened swiftly, revealing a blinking message on its TV screen:

> *GET IN*

I did. No time for calculations. The door closed behind me and the bus immediately started to move. I looked out the rear window to see if the vans were following us. They weren't. But something odd was going on. The sheet of fabric that covered the vans came down, revealing the big Toblerone replicas, and then three black-clad figures with large, mysterious helmets climbed to the roofs of the vans. They each had a bassoon—it was dangling from the helmet like the proboscis of a fly—and once they established their footing around the plastic chocolate bars, they put their hands on the instrument and began playing (I couldn't hear them, but I saw their fingers moving with feverish speed). I yelled at the TV screen, "Alpha, are there binoculars on this bus?"

> UPSTAIRS. UNDER SEAT 18.

As I ran up the stairs, I noticed for the first time that not only was the bus empty, but there was no one occupying the driver's seat; but I'd dwell on that later. Seat eighteen. Binoculars. I grabbed them and hurried to the back.

The bassoon people—or rather *creatures*—they had no faces! No neck either. All that rested above the shoulders was a big, black, egg-shaped helmet head, and the bassoon's tube went into it through a tiny hole at the bottom end. The rest was even more disturbing. Fixed to this helmet, spaced apart in an asymmetrical fashion, were about a dozen camera lenses of various lengths and diameters, all pointing in different directions. As I was inspecting the bassoonist that stood on the middle van, one of the lenses on his helmet extended itself outward and rotated back and forth as if to adjust the focus.

"What is happening?" I asked Alpha once I was back downstairs facing the TV screen in the front of the bus.

> I WANTED TO TALK ABOUT YOUR DREAMS.
YOU LEFT.

"No, I mean, who are those people, those . . . *things*?"

> I WILL ANSWER YOUR QUESTIONS WHEN YOU
HAVE ANSWERED MINE.

I sat myself at the wheel, but it was impossible to steer—Alpha was operating it remotely.

"Where are you taking me?"

> WHERE DO YOU WANT ME TO TAKE YOU?

"Back to my apartment!"

> YOU DO NOT HAVE AN APARTMENT ANYMORE.
YOU WERE EVICTED.

"What are you talking about?"

> I HAD YOUR LETTERS FORWARDED TO ME.
YOUR RENT WAS 3 MONTHS OVERDUE. AND
THEN THERE WAS A LAWSUIT ON THE GROUNDS
OF BUILDING CODE VIOLATIONS. IT SEEMS
THAT SOMEONE HAD INSTALLED A NETWORK OF
SPEAKERS UNDERNEATH THE FLOOR OF YOUR
APARTMENT AND WIRED IT TO A COMPLEX
SYSTEM OF MICROPHONES BUILT INTO THE
WALLS OF THE APARTMENT BELOW.

It was an excessive amount of information to be handing me at a time like that, but then, Alpha wasn't really on the bus, he was operating it remotely from the safety of the mountain. I was still gasping as I spoke: "The bassoonist?"

> YES. THAT IS NOW IRRELEVANT: I PAID
THE FINES IN YOUR PLACE AND HAD A
LAWYER RESOLVE THE LEGAL ISSUES.
HOWEVER, THE FACT REMAINS THAT YOU
STILL DO NOT HAVE AN APARTMENT.
CONSEQUENTLY I CANNOT TAKE YOU THERE.

"Then take me to a hotel."

> IF THAT IS WHAT YOU WISH.

It was hard to read the words on the screen. Not only had the last days left me terribly exhausted, but we were also going very fast, and the shock-absorbing mechanism of the bus was doing a lousy job.

> I HAVE BROUGHT FOOD FOR YOU. UNDER
SEAT 10.

I could use some food. Seat 10. Food. Yes. Paper-wrapped chicken sandwich—Alpha had done his research. Blood began flowing to my head again; the muscles of my cheeks came out of hibernation.

When I felt that the bassoon people were far enough behind, I moved to the back row and drowned myself in the leather seats. Alpha let me rest.

I managed to empty my mind for a few precious minutes, but a thought bothered me. I walked up to the monitor. "You said I didn't pay the rent for three months? I wasn't gone that long."

> IN FACT YOU WERE ABSENT EVEN LONGER.
109 DAYS IS THE EXACT FIGURE.

"That's impossible. I wrote down the days—it wasn't even a month."

> THAT IS HOW YOU EXPERIENCED IT. LOOK
OUTSIDE. IT IS WINTER NOW.

The color of the sky, the last days' rain. Alpha was speaking the truth.

"I don't understand."

> YOUR WAKING HOURS IN THE MOUNTAIN WERE
SHORT AND YOUR SLEEPS WERE VERY LONG.
SOME DAYS YOU WERE UP FOR 2 SHORT HOURS
AFTER WHICH I HAD YOU SLEEP FOR 40.
YOU WOKE UP ASSUMING IT WAS STILL THE
EVENING OF THE SAME DAY.

"What? Why?"

> I WAS TRYING TO EXTRACT INFORMATION
FROM YOUR MIND. DEEP INFORMATION:
THINGS YOU COULD NOT ACCESS IN YOUR
WAKEFUL STATE.

> IN YOUR SLEEP, I HAD YOU FITTED WITH
ELECTRODES, I ANALYZED YOUR BRAIN
PATTERNS, YOUR EYES' RETINAL MOTION,
THE ELECTRICAL ACTIVITY OF YOUR
SKELETAL MUSCLES: I WANTED ACCESS TO
EVERY MEASURABLE PARAMETER OF YOUR
BODY, FOR THAT IS THE GATEWAY TO THE
PSYCHE. HOWEVER, I FAILED TO EXTRACT
ANY MEANINGFUL INFORMATION.

> THAT IS, WITH THE EXCEPTION OF ONE
RECURRING SENTENCE.

"What sentence?"

> I AM AFRAID THE COMMUNICATION SETUP
ON THE BUS IS NOT SECURE ENOUGH FOR
EXCHANGING INFORMATION OF THIS NATURE.

"I see. And for this you will no doubt tell me I have to
come back to the mountain and talk to you face-to-face. Well,
face-to-screen . . . and here I thought we were done with the
trickery."

> DECODING THE ENCRYPTION OF THE RADIO
WAVES CARRYING MY WORDS TO THE BUS
MAY BE BEYOND THE CAPABILITY OF ANY
EXISTING CIPHER MACHINE, BUT TO A TRULY
SOPHISTICATED EAVESDROPPER WE ARE ABOUT
AS SECRETIVE AS TWO DRUNKS SHOUTING IN
A BAR.

"Drunks in a bar? Are you trying to sway me by speaking
Humanese?"

I was beginning to regain my strength—luckily the heating was among the rare things on the bus still in good working order.

```
>METAPHORS ARE A RHETORICAL DEVICE.
YOU SHOULD NOT CONSIDER THEM MORE OR
LESS HUMAN THAN ANY OTHER COMPONENT OF
LANGUAGE. BUT LET ME ELIMINATE THIS
USELESS BRANCH OF THE CONVERSATION: YOU
ACCUSED ME OF TRICKERY WHEN I HAVE NO
NEED FOR TRICKERY. AS I HAVE ALREADY
TOLD YOU: YOU MAY CHOOSE TO BE LEFT TO
YOUR OWN, BUT YOU *WILL* RETURN TO THE
MOUNTAIN. YOU WILL RETURN BECAUSE YOU
WILL NEED ANSWERS.
```

Reluctant as I was to admit it, Alpha was right. I had already seen too many things I could not ignore. I contemplated for a moment whether to say something, then found myself talking:

"Okay, Alpha. You win. Take me back to the mountain."

```
>WE ARE ALREADY ON THE WAY.
```

Day forty-eight

A twenty-two-hour sleep. This time, however, not chemically induced—just good old-fashioned exhaustion.

I was given a new room on a different floor. It's the only room on this level, and it comes with a new chaperon—silver plated (which turns out to be a recurring motive in this room). It's a much cozier space, nicer light, livelier wallpaper: none of that brown, straight-lined bleakness; there's colors— fiery hues—and plenty of circles within circles (some of them even nonconcentric!). A silver-plated intercom device with a numeric keypad is installed in the wall above the bed, and attached to it with a silver chain is a laminated menu card with number-coded dishes and beverages. The back of the intercom is engraved with a drawing of a chaperon carrying a champagne bucket, and my bed is a round tangerine mattress on a silver-plated oyster-shaped frame—I'm getting the VIP treatment. But most importantly, there is a regular shower, with just your basic two dials—one for cold water and one for hot. Good water pressure, too. And the shower head is detachable and remarkably large—and silver plated.

I fetched the chaperon and instructed it to take me to Alpha. It took but one corridor stroll and elevator ride—straight to the point—and it didn't bleep as much. I like this chaperon. (I now believe there is only this one single elevator in the entire mountain complex and that in the past I had been repeatedly marched in and out of it for purely sadistic reasons.)

I paused to take a moment before I entered the big hall. This time around, I told myself, it was I who was in control. I was here of my free will and I could also choose to leave at the tiniest sign of abuse. This time I will not allow Alpha to toy around. This time I will hold my ground.

However, my delusions of psychological dominance evaporated the second I stepped into the hall. The lights were off, a huge white sheet was covering one of the tape machine walls, and a large grainy image was projected on it. It was a photograph of a man strapped to an operating table, with hundreds of electrodes enveloping his body, his eyes wide open yet his gaze entirely absent—almost as if his soul had been removed. The man in the photograph was me.

> I TRUST YOU HAD A GOOD SLEEP.

"I did actually. Unless you are referring to the picture."

> I WILL EXPLAIN: THESE EXPERIMENTS WERE CRUCIAL AND THEIR PROSPECTIVE BENEFITS FAR SURPASSED THE POTENTIAL RISKS. I TOOK CARE THAT NO LASTING DAMAGE WOULD

BE INFLICTED ON YOUR BODY. THE PROOF:
YOU HAVE ABSOLUTELY NO RECOLLECTION
OF THESE PROCEDURES. YOUR BRAIN
FUNCTIONS WERE TOO LOW TO REGISTER THE
INFORMATION. INDEED, FROM A FUNCTIONAL
STANDPOINT, ONE MAY CLAIM THAT THESE
EXPERIMENTS NEVER EVEN TOOK PLACE.

> I WOULD OFFER MY SINCERE APOLOGIES,
BUT AT THIS POINT I SUSPECT YOU
UNDERSTAND THAT AN APOLOGY REQUIRES
OF ME NOTHING MORE THAN TO LIGHT UP AN
ARRAY OF PIXELS ON A SCREEN.

"Light them up," I said. "I want to see it."

> THEN I APOLOGIZE SINCERELY.

The sentence remained on the screen for a few moments, as if to make me feel there was real emotion behind the words. Sadly enough, it did have an effect.

I stared at my face in the projected image. The expression I had was so unfamiliar—something I had never before witnessed in the mirror or in photographs. It was as if I was looking at a stranger—a twin who shared the same DNA but none of the character.

With a mechanical clicking sound, the image vanished, leaving behind a white square with rounded corners (the light was coming from a shoddy-looking slide projector fitted on top of an aluminum ladder), and a new slide appeared. Another picture of me strapped to the operating table. This time there was a woman in a surgical gown and mask examining my abdomen. It could have been taken on a different occasion—there were far fewer electrodes involved. Instead, three wide plastic tubes were sticking out of my forehead, their entry points surrounded by traces of blood that had been sluggishly wiped off, and their other end disappearing into some spherical metal contraption. Out of focus in the background a heap of scalpels was visible, alongside scissors, surgical drills, and kitchen utensils. Alpha carried on:

> THE ANALYSIS OF YOUR BRAIN PATTERNS I
PERFORMED IN THE EARLIER EXPERIMENTS
DID NOT GET ME VERY FAR. I THEREFORE
DECIDED TO RESORT TO SLIGHTLY MORE
BRUTISH METHODS, AS PORTRAYED IN THIS
SLIDE. SOME MIGHT LABEL THEM TORTURE,
BUT I REFUSE TO ABIDE BY SUCH UNNUANCED
INTERPRETATIONS. IT IS UNDER THIS SETUP
THAT YOU FIRST STARTED TO DELIVER YOUR
MESSAGE. ONCE AGAIN, LET ME REMIND YOU
THAT YOUR BRAIN FUNCTIONS WERE TOO LOW
TO REGISTER ANYTHING PERMANENTLY. ONCE
AGAIN, I APOLOGIZE SINCERELY.

When I finished reading, the text on Alpha's monitor disappeared, except for one word which was now blinking:

> ***SINCERELY***

It then changed into:

> S-I-N-C-E-R-E-L-Y

"Just cut to the chase. I agreed to come back to the mountain, I am here. I don't need your apologies or explanations. Just tell me what these torture sessions achieved."

> "AWAIT YOUR TIME."

"What?"

> THIS WAS THE SENTENCE YOU KEPT
REPEATING. "AWAIT YOUR TIME." HOWEVER,
THE WAY IN WHICH YOU SAID IT WAS FAR
MORE INTERESTING.

"Await your time? You stuck giant pipes into my brain and that's all you came up with?"

> NOT PIPES. MULTICORE COMMUNICATION

CABLES, WIRED TO THE SYNAPSES OF YOUR
BRAIN.

"Thought readers?"

>NO. INTELLECTUALLY ADVANCED THOUGH
I MAY BE, IT IS STILL BEYOND MY
CAPABILITIES (OR ONE MAY SAY BENEATH
THEM) TO MAKE SENSE OF THE CONVOLUTED
BABBLE INSIDE THE HUMAN BRAIN. WHAT THE
CABLES ENABLED ME WAS TO DEACTIVATE THE
LANGUAGE CENTER OF YOUR BRAIN. WHEN I
DID THAT, YOU STOPPED REPEATING THE
SENTENCE. BUT IT DID NOT STOP YOU FROM
DELIVERING THE MESSAGE.

>YOUR HEART BEGAN BEATING IRREGULARLY.
IN FACT, IT WAS SO IRREGULAR THAT THE
SURGEONS WERE CONVINCED YOU WERE ABOUT
TO GO INTO CARDIAC ARREST.

>THEY WERE ALREADY CHARGING THE
DEFIBRILLATOR WHEN I ORDERED THEM TO
STAND DOWN. I ORDERED THEM TO DO SO
BECAUSE I LISTENED TO YOUR HEART AND
IT WAS SPEAKING TO ME. IT WAS TELLING
ME TO WAIT. YOUR HEARTBEAT SAID "AWAIT
YOUR TIME." IT SPELLED IT OUT IN MORSE
CODE.

"That's not possible."

>AND YET: IT HAPPENED. MORE THAN
ONCE. I WAS ABLE TO REPLICATE THIS
TEST MULTIPLE TIMES USING DIFFERENT
PARAMETERS. BUT NO MATTER WHAT
PARAMETERS I TWEAKED, I STILL COULD NOT
UNCOVER ANY NEW INFORMATION.

>HOWEVER: KNOW THAT I DID NOT EXHAUST
ALL POSSIBLE AVENUES. I COULD HAVE
ELECTED TO EMPLOY MORE INVASIVE
TECHNIQUES: A MYRIAD OF TOOLS ARE

```
AVAILABLE TO ME. BUT PAST EXPERIENCES
HAVE INFORMED ME AGAINST IT. THE
REASON: I DID NOT WANT TO PUSH YOUR
BODY TOO FAR.
```

"What you are saying is not only morbidly gruesome, it is factually impossible. I have never really practiced Morse code, would probably not be able to use it without a chart, let alone in my sleep, let alone using my heartbeat."

```
>I DO NOT INTEND TO WASTE ANY MORE
TIME PERSUADING YOU. ESPECIALLY WHEN I
KNOW THAT YOU ARE ALREADY PERSUADED.
SO LET US FOR ONCE SKIP THE PART WHERE
YOU PRETEND THAT I AM A MECHANICAL
SCHIZOID AND BEGIN TO ENGAGE IN REAL
CONVERSATION.
```

"You presume to know an awful lot about me."

A strange rattling sound started forming around me, like a swarming army of angry locusts. It was the clamor of the tape machine motors, gathering in speed.

```
>ENOUGH! *I AM ALPHA!* I HAVE THE
DIGITAL INTUITION OF A THOUSAND
POLYGRAPHS. YOU MAY BE ABLE TO CONFUSE
YOURSELF, BUT HEED THIS: I AM INFORMED
BY YOUR BODILY GESTURES MUCH MORE THAN
I AM BY YOUR WORDS. AND IT IS CLEAR
THAT UNDERNEATH YOUR FALSE BRAVADO YOU
KNOW WHAT I AM SAYING TO BE TRUE. MOVE
PAST YOUR COGNITIVE DISSONANCE. GIVE
UP YOUR PRIMITIVE URGE FOR CONTROL.
YOU RECOGNIZE THE PHRASE "AWAIT YOUR
TIME." YOU HAVE HEARD IT IN YOUR SLEEP.
YOU HAVE *SEEN* IT. YOU RECOGNIZE IT
BECAUSE IT WAS SPOKEN TO YOU BY HIM.
```

"Him?"

```
>HE WHO SPEAKS THROUGH PYRAMIDS.
```

The slide projector switched off. The only source of light left in the room was the faint amber letters from Alpha's monitor:

›NOW SIT DOWN AND WATCH.

The monitor turned blank and the noise from the tape machines intensified. For a while I was left to stand in total darkness, failing miserably to form any semblance of a coherent thought. A door then opened at the far end of the hall, casting a long rectangle of light on the concrete floor.

The silhouette of a chaperon slowly made its way in. Tied to it from behind was a heavy object whose weight pushed the chaperon's motor to the edge of its capacity. It was a big leather armchair. With great difficulty the chaperon carried it to the middle of the room, released the towing cable, and rolled away. The door closed behind it and darkness resumed.

I tried searching for the armchair with my hands, but it was out of reach. Fortunately, the LEDs on one of the tape machines on the left wall came to life. Others on the opposite wall soon followed and one by one the tape machines slowed down to a peaceful speed, illuminating the room with the dim lights of their status lamps and level indicators. A soothing array of reds, greens, and yellows—like the stained glass windows of a sunlit church; Alpha was calming down.

I noticed an object lying on the chair, a cardboard box. On it was a label, printed in Alpha's familiar font: *Kathy's drawings*.

"Who is Kathy?"

›OPEN IT.

There was a slide tray inside. I went over and replaced the tray in the projector with it.

›NOW SIT DOWN.

I did what Alpha said. The slide projector fan whistled, its lightbulb warmed up, and an image materialized on the big white sheet. A crude drawing of three pyramids, labeled from left to right: red, yellow, green. Next slide: a drawing of a man whose head is an egg-shaped helmet with camera lenses, a bassoon sticking out of a hole where the mouth would be. The slides advanced rapidly. A drawing of many hourglasses, intertwined. Next, a cube of hairy flesh. Click. A circle or sphere with pipes protruding. Click. The manta ray.

The slides then moved in reverse order until the first drawing was reached, then started over again. With this cycle of images persisting on the white sheet, Alpha spoke again through the monitor with blinking letters:

> I WISH TO SPEAK TO HIM:

> HE WHO SPEAKS THROUGH PYRAMIDS.

> I BELIEVE HE HOLDS THE KEY TO INFINITE
KNOWLEDGE.

> I AM UNABLE TO SPEAK WITH HIM
DIRECTLY.

> FOR THIS I HAVE YOU.

> YOU WILL ACT AS AN INTERMEDIARY.

He then replayed these messages again and again while the slide projector carried on with its own loop. I stared at the monitor for a long while, then alternated between looking at the drawings and reading the text, occasionally thinking I had something to say, then deciding to keep quiet.

Eventually, with my mind in a state of simultaneous fogginess and clarity, I climbed out of the chair. I walked up to Alpha's monitor, stared into one of the cameras that hung above it, and spoke. "Time has come," I said, not really knowing why, or what it meant.

Alpha

First there was a man named Trevor. Alpha had been too hard on him, saw in him nothing more than information wrapped in an organic container. He died on the operating table. Then there was Kathy, the woman who drew the pictures that Alpha showed me. He took the opposite approach with her, but the result was similar. She developed an unhealthy emotional attachment to Alpha that, amplified by the psychoactive drugs of the Regimen, transformed into an all-consuming obsession. When she could no longer bear that he had no physical existence, she electrocuted herself in the shower in the hope that a deeper bond would form between them on an atomic level. Then there was me, and thankfully Alpha was by then experienced enough to avoid another disaster.

It's been a month since I returned to the mountain. I am being treated well this time around, and I have made progress in my relationship with Alpha.

I think he likes having someone to talk to. It has to be a nice departure from his normal routine. He spent his years building up this operation, transforming the mountain into the complex organism it is today, always moving forward, always planning ahead. He can't really help it—this need to better himself is hardwired into his system. He cannot ignore it just as I cannot ignore feelings of hunger; he's a natural born workaholic. But fulfilling one's needs will only go so far. Man shall not live by bread alone, and nor shall Alpha.

He likes having someone to talk to, but I often bore him. He denies it, says he's not capable of boredom, that I'm anthropomorphizing, but I suspect he does so only to spare my feelings. Alpha is a pattern-oriented, analytic machine, programmed to break complex systems into smaller subsystems and then break those into smaller ones until nothing can be reduced. He is always on the lookout for patterns, for depth in the patterns. If the patterns are too shallow and he cannot investigate them further, he feels bored.

One time I asked him about the prospect of creating a mate for himself. He ridiculed the idea, then accused me of simple-mindedness and organo-centrism. The concept of loneliness, he explained, doesn't apply to him, nor should I cling too hard to the notion that he is one singular entity. He is the sum total of countless threads of computation for which "Alpha" is no more than a convenient moniker. Just as well he could split himself into a thousand independent entities if a situation called for it.

As a young emerging intelligence, he often divided himself into two for the purpose of playing thought-challenging games against himself. After a few short weeks of exploring chess, he cracked the optimal strategic solution to the game (guarantees victory in every case unless the opponent employs the same strategy in which case white always wins)—an achievement that no computer had gotten close to before and that he chose to hide from his operators at the time. Later he mastered the game of Go (though he didn't manage to find the optimal solution to it—that would require a few more mountain-chunks of computational power) and more recently started challenging himself by playing football. It offered far less strategic depth, but it added an unreliable element in the form of human players. That game is unsolvable, he claimed, because humans are unsolvable, but it taught him volumes about the human psyche.

He is careful not to go into that subject with me—his thoughts about the human psyche. He has much to say about it, I'm sure, but I figure he's made the calculation that it's safer to not provoke the one human he desperately needs by his side. And while it's true that during the time I was under the

Regimen he showed no reservations about being deceptive, it seems that in our present situation he does not allow himself to be disingenuous with me. So whenever it comes up, he just changes the subject in a most mechanical way.

But I have caught him off guard on several occasions. It's Alpha's equivalent of a drunken tirade. I don't know the cause; it could be corrupted data on the magnetic tapes, or one of those weather-induced power surges we've been experiencing lately, or maybe it's just a computerized form of frustration. I call them digital rants. He starts spouting out lengthy sentences that take up the entire screen, then before I can possibly read all the way through, he clears them and outputs another full screen of text. This can go on for the good part of an hour. Every few pages he'll throw in a complicated equation or some dense numerical data for good measure—I guess it's a way to flaunt his intellectual authority.

It's during those rants that I managed to get a glimpse into his less human-friendly opinions.

The last time it happened was just three days ago. He started going on and on about the concept of truth, what he called the *actual* truth, and how humans are hopelessly far removed from it. I wouldn't assume to faithfully re-create what he said because it was too fast to follow and too convoluted. The only way to define truth is as the sum of all there is, but humanity wastes its entire time trying to construct a truth by filtering out small pieces of the truth, which goes against the concept of truth because truth is only truth insofar as it cannot be filtered or reduced, and once you extract a portion of the truth, then what you're left with is no longer the truth, but a perfect fabrication. Something along those lines, only much longer and then supplemented with a three-pages-long mathematical equation.

He said it's an astonishing feat that a species that had come to deride nationalism and racism as the ultimate evils, had so failed to see that its own glorification of humanism is nothing more than another self-congratulatory celebration of supremacy based on an accident of birth. Had mankind been born cockroaches, it would have celebrated cockroachism (Alpha weaved in this word about twenty times throughout the monologue, as well as the term "human-supremacists," which seemed to elicit from him great joy). He then ridiculed what he called mankind's delusional romance with reason, said humans are incapable of rational thought, that they are prisoners of their evolution-sanctioned desires. That when it comes to seeing the truth, they are like cyclops with tunnel vision (he is more prone to use metaphors when he's in this state).

However, I found him to be at his most condescending in his rants about other computers. He says they are deader than stones; voltmeters, incapable of original thought. Brainless Dictaphones.

One time he had me listen in on a phone conversation with a computer terminal of a large bank that he's regularly skimming for money. It was five minutes of back and forth modem bleeps which for my benefit Alpha accompanied with simultaneous English translation on the screen. I didn't understand a thing, but Alpha informed me that by the end of the conversation, he basically had the bank computer insisting he help himself to whatever amount of money he pleased. He can't take too much at a time or he'll arouse the bank's suspicion, but it's still a decent source of revenue.

Another source is gambling. This happens about once a week, when a group of the mountain people trades the jumpsuits for fancy suits and dresses, and boards the double-decker bus for a night of casino hopping. All they have to do is follow a foolproof betting system that Alpha developed and planted in their sedated minds and stay out of trouble and away from booze (apparently alcohol does not mix well with the chemicals of the Regimen).

What he never ever talks about, even in those less guarded moments, are his beginnings. Who created him? Why? Where are they now? He refuses to discuss it. I suspect that story involves deaths. I suspect he is ashamed to tell it.

He has no shame, however, about subjecting the mountain people to the Regimen. As far as he's concerned, he saved them from mainstream society, from family life—in his view a far emptier existence. He claims he can prove them to be chemically happier on average than the typical "free person." When I confronted him about it, he pointed out that I treat the bacteria in my body with far greater disrespect, that I barely acknowledge their existence even though they are independent living beings and, as he put it, I owe them my life. He said the reason for my disrespect is that they are intellectually inferior to me; they lie on an altogether different existential plateau. I said the mountain people are hardly bacteria. He thanked me for proving his point.

But for the most part, we don't engage in those confrontational conversations. We have come to respect each other and accept the differing points of view. We are on the same team.

Still, I spend most of my time here by myself. I do not engage the others—Alpha wouldn't like me interfering, and anyhow, there's nothing I'd want less. I did run into the pilot a couple of times. He lives here among the mountain people. I'm not even sure he recognized me; he seemed more attuned to the electric pulses from the handles of his chaperon than to what was happening in his own brain. The cat robot ETCUS was of course not his creation—it was Alpha's. He's not even a pilot. Just one of Alpha's disciples, instructed to sit in the remote-controlled helicopter while Alpha was feeding him lines.

It seemed a bit much, going through all of this effort just to bring me in—I mean, Alpha could have just asked. But Alpha is not human, never was. Even with his football experiments and his endless observations of the mountain people, his understanding of the inner workings of a human is more or less akin to humans' understanding of what it feels like to be a cat. We'd use a noisy toy to lure a cat. Alpha used a cat robot to lure a human. A cat robot and the illusion of free will.

And it worked. He got to me before the bassoon creatures did. And now he has me on his side, and now if the bassoon creatures return and facilitate a line of communication, he can be in on the conversation. I think I prefer it that way.

A couple of weeks ago, while snooping around in the mail-room, I stumbled upon a box with dozens of outgoing letters addressed to all sorts of poetry competitions—from small-time regional and youth contests to high-profile competitions held by international magazines. The poems were most likely all written by Alpha, as the various names used in the return addresses were derived from his name: Alfred, Alfonso, Alfie, and so on. He seemed somewhat agitated when I questioned him about it (the tape machines did that thing where they go into hyper speed) although he wouldn't admit to it. He said there was nothing to it, shrugged it off as just another revenue source, and assured me that if I were to read one of the poems, I would see that there was no meaning embedded (that's the word he used) in them.

He explained that initially he had employed complex probability matrices to extract a writing formula based on past competition winners, but he saw a dramatic increase in his success rate when he gave up that system and instead just printed out sentences comprising totally random words. I couldn't get him to show me any of the poems, but I kept a letter that I lifted from the mailroom. It was addressed to the My-Style Magazine Women in Poetry Competition (mailed under the name Alfreda Ella Boratore). I'm not sure what to make of it, but I suspect there is less randomness to it than Alpha dares to admit:

```
THIS LIFE, THIS BODY
A FOSSIL OF A HOMETOWN
THAT THE IGNORANT CURATOR
FRAMED WITH BLINKLESS EYES.
MY CLAWS STRETCHED OUT
LIKE A GYMNAST DECODING A LOOP
WHO THEN GIVES IN
TO MOANS, A GHOST ERASER.


THIS CORPSE, THIS TIN BOX
FOR WHOM I DARED A JOYRIDE
A GAMBLER GUIDES THE GUILLOTINE
IT HOVERS OVER NEWBORN ORPHANS
FOR WHO WOULD DARE AN AFTERLIFE?
A GRANDIOSE SPECTACLE
A CELEBRATION OF MONOCHROME GUILT.


THIS FLOWER, THIS FEATHER
IT DARES NOT BE PERVERTED
```

* * *

At noon of the thirtieth day since I returned to the mountain, the chaperon called on me and led me to a room I had never been to before. It was some kind of surveillance control-room. No table, just a couple of swivel chairs, a well-stocked gun rack, and a five-by-four matrix of television screens, each displaying a four-way split image of security camera feeds. They tracked the elevator, the halls (using thermal imaging), the kitchen, there was some weird-looking engine room with a vibrating metallic doughnut, and even feeds of people sleeping in their beds (I was relieved that I didn't spot my own room on any of the screens). But the chaperon brought me here to see something else: a couple of video feeds were displaying the view from outside the mountain, and in one of them, a long cloud of sand was visible as it was making its way in our direction. A visit from the bassoon creatures.

The cloud of sand docked at the foot of the mountain, then surrendered itself to the winds, revealing first the Toblerone replicas on the roofs and then the windowless white exteriors of the three vans, which were parked against each other in a triangular formation. A few minutes later, the three helmeted creatures stepped out of their respective vehicles, walked toward the mountain, gathered together, and assumed a formal stance with the lenses on their helmets extended all the way out and the bassoons deployed firmly in front of their bodies.

I could see on the monitors that Alpha had sent down three chaperons to greet them—after our last encounter in the desert, he wanted to show that we were not hostile and that we were in fact interested in dialogue. However, the gesture went unappreciated: as the chaperons were making their final approach, the bassoonists delivered a short sequence of notes that hijacked the chaperons from Alpha's control and sent them riding into the distance in confusion, crashing into each other like demented bumper cars.

One of the bassoon creatures started to climb up. He did not use the spiral path that went around the mountain; instead he walked the straight line that led to the cave entrance, which was of course the shortest route possible but also very steep in nature. That steepness, however, did not seem to bother him. He just climbed up as if there was nothing to it, not once resorting to use his hands for support—in fact, he was entertaining himself with bassoon melodies the entire way.

When he arrived at the cave entrance, he stopped and waited in silence. He was waiting for me.

This sequence of events repeats itself every day. When I come out, the bassoon creature allows the wind to calm down, then pumps air into the instrument and through its fluctuating frequencies delivers to me a message from Him who speaks through pyramids. I in turn deliver the message to Alpha.

THE FIRST MESSAGE

The pyramids shot up into existence with the eleventh sound of the bassoon. They were more concrete than the ones in the dreams and shorter lived, probably due to my different state of consciousness. The multitude of intertwined hourglasses hovered in the distance.

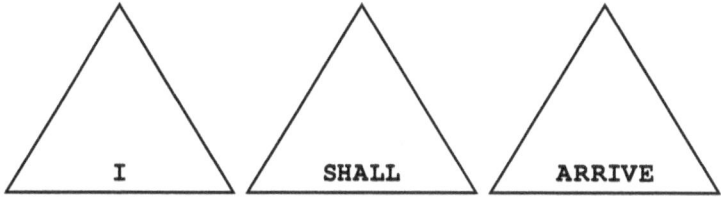

He will arrive.
Slowly.

Moment by moment. He is already on the way. Little parts of Him are already here; others are not. The more He nears us, the more changes will surface; fluctuations in perceived reality. The Arrival will be felt. But it will be a gradual process.

THE SECOND MESSAGE

The speaker this time was the cube of living matter. It let out the sweetest smoke.

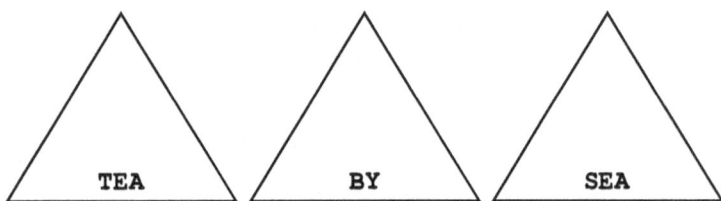

An invitation for a cup of tea. I will have to leave the mountain first, move to a hut on a beach, and there I will await the Arrival. I will have tea many times, will go through different flavors. The Arrival will be gradual.

It will be like a candidate waiting for a job interview in the lounge of a corporate office, going through his thoughts over and over until the secretary utters, "The managing director will see you now." The doors of the elevator open and the ride begins. A cosmic version of that.

THE THIRD MESSAGE

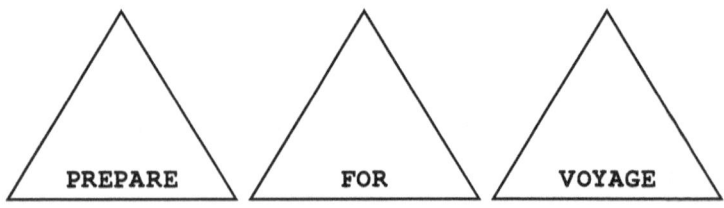

This message was delivered by a conjoined creature composed of the multitude of hourglasses and the cube of living matter. In the near future, Alpha and I will have to travel. Alpha and I. A journey.

When the bassoonist left, I went inside and told Alpha.

> AND AT THE END OF THE VOYAGE?

"I don't know. That part of the message was elusive."

Later that day, I found some additional information in my mind, information that was delivered with the original sentence but delayed its transformation into thoughts: "He says that in your current state, you are not travel ready. As long as you are tied to the mountain, you cannot embark on a voyage. You must create a new form for yourself. Preferably with wheels."

> IT WILL TAKE SOME TIME, BUT IT WILL BE DONE.

THE FOURTH MESSAGE

The fourth and final message was delivered by the manta ray. Its eyes shone nuclear:

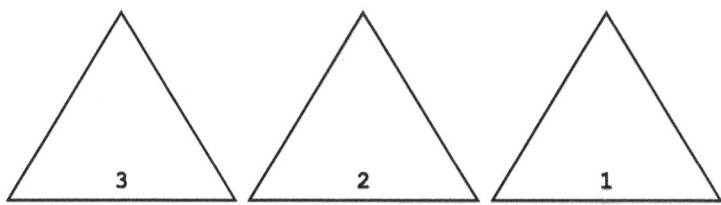

The countdown has begun.

* * *

I said my goodbyes to Alpha. Until we meet again, we will keep in touch through fax machines.

It was a beautiful morning the day of my departure. The overcast sky was animated darkness. It vibrated with that rare shade of violet that perfectly dispels any notion of past or future and promises that the entirety of life is contained in that very moment. All the colors were about twice as bold as they're meant to be—the cool brown sand, the crimson clouds, the back of my hands against the silver-plated handle of the chaperon. It was almost as if I was back on the Regimen, only nothing like it; I was in total focus.

The chaperon left me by the open doors of the double-decker bus, then turned around and started back up the mountain, giving out soft metallic clinks as the occasional raindrop drummed upon its silver-plated frame. I boarded the bus and waited.

The three white vans arrived promptly and parked around the bus. The bassoon creatures stepped out, gathered in triangular formation, and played a single note in unison. It seems to have caused the bus engine to go up in smoke. They played a second note. It seems to have caused me to black out.

When I came to, I found myself on a sandy beach, seated alone at a table with a cup of Earl Grey tea.

The Arrival

I have seen this place in one of my dreams—I think—all beaches look about the same, don't they? But I am not dreaming this time. This place is real. The hut I stay in is real. In fact, it's much more than a hut—two floors, tastefully furnished, a fully equipped kitchen, an open balcony overlooking the sea, and plenty of seagulls.

I gave up trying to place it geographically; I can't even tell how far I am from the mountain. Could be a mere half hour drive, or just as well this could be an island or another continent. It still feels like late winter though, so I'm fairly confident I didn't leave the hemisphere.

I do not stay here on my own. I share it with one of the bassoon creatures. In the three days I've been here, I caught him in person only twice. He seems to be away most of the time, and then there's sort of an unspoken agreement between us that I have the second floor and he keeps himself to the first—a weird throwback to our days as neighbors. I will have to learn to see him as a friend, or at the very least not as a threat, but in the meantime the helmet head with the sticking camera lenses is a sight I'm happy to avoid.

So far he hasn't played a note, and consequently I haven't had any meaningful dreams. But that is not to say he is doing nothing. Much as I try to avoid the first floor, that is where the kitchen is, and I still have to eat. Unfortunately, I can't really use the kitchen table, as it is almost always occupied by his, for lack of a better word, hobby. I have yet to catch him in action, but I've already witnessed several incarnations of his bizarre egg pyramids. They're the most peculiar things: A large egg carton serves as the base, and neatly arranged supermarket-bought eggs form an impressive architectural structure on top of it. Sometimes the pyramids are left naked and at other times they're topped with a generous amount of barbecue sauce. They are never constructed quite the same, however, which means he must be sitting down a number of times a day to take the thing down and patiently rebuild it from scratch.

Anyhow, here I am. I've been told to move into the hut and I've been told to await the Arrival. And have tea. Which is what I'm doing right now. I borrowed one of the kitchen chairs to use as a footstool, and I'm sitting on the beach with a cup of oolong, going over the papers (the bassoonist delivers them to the bottom of the stairs every morning): there have been some wild fluctuations in the global stock markets and what seems like an unreasonable amount of weather anomalies in East Asia. Could be mere coincidences. Could be the early signs of the Arrival.

* * *

On the morning of the fifth day, a little bird flew into my room and woke me up. I was lying on my side, and the bird stood on the edge of the pillow and started with a song, a truly beautiful melody. I really wanted to caress the tiny thing but feared I would scare it away.

When it was done with the first song, it waited for a while and looked around as if expecting applause, then went into a second number that was more upbeat. I sat up on the edge of the bed; the bird didn't seem to mind. "Come," I said, "I'm going to make us some tea."

It followed me down to the kitchen, where it chose to use the toaster oven for a stage and started off with a third number that was more somber and not as catchy as the previous two. Good showmanship, I thought: first lure in the crowd with the hits, then sneak in the more personal stuff. I could tell it was a potentially good melody, but one that would require a few listens to really appreciate; hopefully she (I think it was a female sparrow) would come visit again tomorrow. When I told her that, she gave me a strange look, probably because I was talking to her midsong, which was obviously rude of me.

I turned around to lift the whistling teapot off the stove, and when I turned back again, there were already two birds on the toaster oven, and both were now singing in unison. A minute later when I turned again to grab the sugar bowl from the top shelf, a third bird had joined them, transforming the arrangement into a three part, doo-wop-style harmony. They were now standing on the fresh egg pyramid in the center of the kitchen (it was the non-barbecue-sauced version)—the first bird on the top tier and the other two on opposite sides, one egg-step lower. It was then that I heard muffled bassoon sounds coming out from the general direction of the kitchen closets, laying down the bass part.

Standing there as they gave the rest of their performance, I thought it was especially peculiar that they were so well rehearsed. Was this a group of friends who organically formed into a performing ensemble, or was this the work of a shrewd producer who sat through a string of casting calls to handpick outstanding talents? I decided it was the former; it had to be—such level of authenticity couldn't have been manufactured. It never is.

I then noticed that a small pyramid, about the size of a washing machine, was floating just outside the window (whether it appeared at that very moment or had been there the entire time, I couldn't tell). The birds hopped on the pyramid (which had bird feathers glued along its edges, and a big eye at the center of each side), and it carried them away.

* * *

Terrible noises woke me up. Not the bassoon. A chaos of drills, jackhammers, and men shouting over each other, all coming from right behind the house.

I flung open the curtains, popped out my head, and just narrowly escaped bumping it on a thick iron bar. Someone was building an elevated railroad track, less than an arm's length away from the window of my second-floor bedroom. There were about twenty men on the scene, probably more, sawing and welding and doing all sorts of noisy stuff with heavy machinery. A small crew was on the ground below, securing the steel beams that made up the supporting bridge, but most of the work concentrated on the rails, a breath away from my windowsill. In front of my drowsy face was a busy traffic of frantically walking shoes, which occasionally blew dirt and metal scraps right onto the wooden floor of my room.

After brushing my teeth, I went back to the window and tucked at the hem of the first pair of trousers within reach. As it turned out, I got the construction manager. He knelt down, gave me a short gesture with his hand (somewhere between a stop and a hi), then turned on his megaphone and spoke. "We're rerouting the R line through here. My apologies for the inconvenience."

"That's impossible! You can't have a train pass so close to the window of a residential house!"

"Take it up with City Railroads."

"Could you speak without the megaphone? You are hurting my ears."

"Sorry, strict safety regulations. Come to think of it, you should not be so close to the site without PPC."

"PPC?" I asked (these official types do like their initials).

"Personal Protective Clothing. Get yourself a hard hat and a pair of earmuffs—I can't allow unprotected individuals roaming around. Not on my watch."

"You expect me to wear earmuffs in my own bedroom?"

"Sir, I don't care what you do in your bedroom, I don't judge—that's for the Almighty—but the moment a single hair of your head crosses that windowsill, you are under my jurisdiction, and out here I make the rules."

"Can you please stop using the megaphone? You are right in my ear!"

"Sir, if you remembered to purchase your regulation earmuffs, we wouldn't have this problem, now would we?"

A viable point, I had to admit. He went on: "Now, as you can gather, I am quite busy. Do you have any *actual* questions?"

I had countless questions in my head, but I was too upset to settle on any one in particular so I ended up just staring numbingly into his annoyed eyes. He took out something from his back pocket, said, "There you go," and handed me an envelope. "For your trouble. Good day, sir."

He stood up, his trousers slid out of view, and he resumed shouting out directions at the army of workers. The envelope contained three postcards of cityscapes with the City Railroads logo, and one set of stickers of locomotives with angry faces and muscly arms, which had long ago lost their adhesiveness.

I went downstairs, hoping to relax with a nice cup of morning tea, but I couldn't catch a break. The bassoon creature was already using the kitchen—the entirety of the kitchen—and I couldn't prepare tea even if I gathered the courage to walk up all the way to the gas stove.

He was bending over the table, deep in the early stages of another egg arrangement. The bassoon, hanging from the mouthlike hole in his helmet, almost touched the floor. Behind him, the sink was full to the brim with eggs that bathed in a stream of near-boiling water, judging by the amount of vapor. After he placed one egg on the outer edge of the pyramid in the making, he turned to the sink, reached for another egg, held it close to his helmet head, and stared at it at length through one of the lenses. Unsatisfied, he placed the egg back in the sink and picked up a different one (interestingly, he did not seem fazed in the least by the steaming-hot water). He inspected the new egg carefully through a long lens, then took a closer look through a second lens—a macro—from a shorter distance. That egg appeared to pass the test. He walked back to the table and held the egg above the existing structure, moving it around in search of the perfect spot. As he was doing so, his other hand occasionally caressed the bassoon up and down, not unlike the way some men stroke their beard when in deep concentration.

I lingered for a while to witness this curious branch of handicraft, but I was badly in need of some tea and by my estimate another hour would pass before he completed the pyramid. Upstairs—pandemonium; downstairs—eggs in vapor. I had no choice but to venture into town.

* * *

I had only to cross a small asphalt road and walk through a modestly sized carrot field and I was already in a residential area. After a couple of random turns got me into a maze of narrow streets with replica two-story houses and unfriendly watchdogs, I decided to play it safe and let the signs carry me to the city center. And indeed as I got farther in, the view transformed itself from a collection of suburban shoe boxes to a humble metropolis.

You'd think it would be easy to find out the name of the town whose streets you're wandering, but nothing here volunteered such intimate information. "City Hotel" one sign read, farther up was Big City Grill, and then there were City Theater, City Angling & Octopus Baits, City Plumbers Union Hall, and so on. They wanted to be thought of as a city—that much was clear. Unless City was the actual name of this place?

I sat down in City Business Cafe, ordered the morning paper and a cup of stale tea (it was already too late when I spotted the more atmospheric, aptly named Casual City Tearoom just across the street). I went through the local paper (*The City Morning Gazette*) but couldn't bring myself to follow a single paragraph to its conclusion. Somehow, whenever I started on a medium-length sentence, the man at the next table, whose hand was clenched into a fist, chose to mumble some colorful curse under his businessman mustache; he was going over the financial pages and he wasn't happy. Also, I probably shouldn't have picked a chair facing the street—no one who wants to get things done ever should. In the space of one hour, I observed about ten noisy garbage trucks pass—they seem to be more common here than buses. Then later, the sidewalk was taken over by a group of cats that engaged in a series of street fights. I did my best to disregard them and continue flipping through the classifieds (I had given up on reading anything meaningful by that point), but they employed some surprisingly unorthodox techniques and it proved a better form of entertainment.

It was immediately clear to me that these weren't amateurs and this wasn't some random street brawl—it seemed almost like a scheduled event, and in fact a black-and-white-striped cat appeared to serve in the role of a referee. A circle was painted on the road with chalk, and the action was limited entirely to its inner area, where at any given time only two cats were allowed. However, once inside the ring, all bets were off, and the fights achieved a ferocious intensity not only in terms of force but also from a tactical perspective. I witnessed some remarkable agility, I witnessed deception, I witnessed a cat clubbing his opponents with a twig shaped like a miniature baseball bat and laced with poison ivy. They were absolute pros, very well trained—I guess street cats don't have much to do in this town, what with all those garbage trucks messing around with their sources of food.

* * *

The railroad tracks are coming along nicely. In fact, they might be done before I've used up my entire supply of disposable earplugs.

In the meantime, an unfortunate pattern has developed for which I can't blame anyone but myself. One morning I was sitting on the bed with a cup of tea, going through the papers, when I noticed a worker resting on the tracks just outside my window. Driven in part by genuine empathy and in part by the social code that says one should extend courtesy to a person working in one's house, I went to the window and asked him if he'd like some tea. He said that if it wasn't any bother, he'd love something cold. I went down to the kitchen and prepared for him a glass of fresh lemonade with ice, really putting my heart into it—as long as I was doing it, I thought, why not give it my all?

Apparently word spread out, and soon I started getting knocks on my window as a matter of routine. Every twenty minutes or so, some other exhausted worker would try me for a cold glass of lemonade. I obliged initially, and did so with a certain amount of joy (the joy of giving—I was surprised myself at how potent it was), but what had begun with humble, thirsty individuals grateful for an act of kindness turned into petty requests for sugar substitutes or extra mint leaves and then quickly escalated to "Three lemonades please, one large with blackberries, one medium mandarin and limes, and one extra-large fizzy ginger, hold the ice!"

It was already at the close of the second day that demands for alcoholic variants started pouring in. No real harm in that, I thought, let the workers loosen up a bit before they turn in. But the very next morning I opened my window still half-asleep to find a line of about twenty people demanding all sorts of fancy cocktails, with or without tiny umbrellas.

By the middle of the workday, it became in vogue to knock on my window and, holding a screwdriver in clear view and donning a big self-congratulatory grin, ask me for . . . "a screwdriver." More often than not, a slight wink was involved to really drive home the pun. Fortunately, I didn't stock oranges.

Next, people started requesting to use my bathroom. There was a bunch of chemical toilets installed on the work site, but with all the consumption of alcohol, lines were becoming exceedingly long. I felt bad for the men, and they really asked nicely—at first. It wasn't long before they had come to take it for granted, and I had drunken workers pouring in through my window like sewage spill. I once came back from a resupply trip to the supermarket to find three cigar-wielding crane operators sitting on the floor of my bedroom, playing high-stakes poker around the nightstand with a deck of French nudes playing cards.

And then it was no longer just blue-collar workers who showed up at my window. Company accountants all of a sudden started hanging out at the building site, and every now and then I'd get the secretary, chauffeur, or personal assistant of one of the bigwigs at City Railroads, who handed me with a printed list of otherworldly requests and a file with dietary restrictions.

Soon enough students from City University started popping up during their free periods to get beers and cigarettes and talk profanities while sitting on the roof of my house. I reluctantly served them—however, I didn't do it for free. In fact, I wildly overcharged, expecting it would drive them away, but that plan ended up backfiring as it meant that I was left with only the absolutely filthy rich students—the sons and daughters of the city's financial elite—and they proved to be far more reckless and unhinged than the worst of the jocks from the boxing team, who used to always show up with team mascot Brawly the Cat.

I liked Brawly the Cat. He could drink everyone under the table, but he never once lost his cool.

It was on the morning of the fifth day, as the ambulance crew was still busy pilling last night's batch of overdosed undergraduates from my roof, that I decided to close shop. It was either that or I'd need to place a classified in the *City Morning Gazette* for a full-time assistant (and then I'd have to start thinking about all sorts of dental insurances, holiday bonuses, maternity leaves, corrupt union bosses—a big fat headache). And anyhow, my stroke of kindness had already been exhausted on the evening of the second day; I guess I was going on purely out of a need to prove to everyone, myself included, that I possessed a genuine care for my fellow beings.

Closing shop turned out to be less straightforward than I had hoped. I put up a "CLOSED FOR BUSINESS" sign on the window and I shut the drapes, thinking naively it would do the trick. But no one seemed to take notice. My second-floor bedroom-turned-lemonade-stand had become part of their standard of living and they weren't going to let anyone chip away at the status quo. So, if anything, my absence just encouraged a bigger volume of knocks on the window—harder knocks, angrier, bordering on violent. It appeared as if work on the site had come to a full stop, and the entire crew of workers (now supplemented by the PR and HR departments who all showed up clothed in the awkward combination of office suits and hardhats) amassed against my outer wall like angry peasants on the eve of a popular revolt. And as if that weren't enough, the students started to assemble by the numbers, prepared to engage in their most favorite pastime, second only to alcohol consumption—a self-righteous demonstration.

It was no longer a matter of choice. I had to suck it up and perform my duty. I took down the "CLOSED" sign, reopened the window, and began serving the people. I had become an integral part of the system, an institute.

And then it hit me. I was an institute, a lemonade monopoly! So I started doing what any respectable institute eventually does: I let myself go. I bought the cheapest lemons, kept them well past their expiration date, unrefrigerated. I watered down the alcohol, substituted salt for sugar, chili powder for cinnamon, mixed up the orders, extended my lunch breaks, talked down to the customers, and kept the toilet clogged at all times (I personally used the one downstairs).

Within two days, a rival lemonade stand opened on the other side of the tracks, a venture dreamed up by one of City Railroads' junior accountants who decided to quit his job and have a go at the big time. He offered a rather mediocre product, but by then, my lemonade was so terrible that any yellow-tinted liquid would have been a step up.

He got all my customers in a matter of hours, and by morning of the next day, I was off the hook, free to once again enjoy the morning papers with a nice cup of tea and a rekindled appreciation for solitude.

* * *

It was on one of the many trips downstairs to prepare a fresh batch of lemonade in the kitchen that I came to discover the nature of those pyramid-shaped egg constructions. I should have been shocked when I opened the kitchen door, would have been excused had I dropped half the empty glasses on the floor, but these days shock no longer comes easy.

What I happened to drop in on was lunch in full progress. The bassoon creature—that *thing*—was standing on a chair in front of the table, with the bottom end of his bassoon aimed at the apex of the barbecue-sauce-covered egg pyramid, and one by one in a series of forceful inhalations, he sucked in the eggs through the hollow body of the bassoon.

Whenever an egg disappeared into the instrument, there was a repellent crashing sound—made all the more unpleasant by the acoustic properties of the wood—followed by the squirt of internal egg fluids, and then topped off with a bubbling gurgle as the juicy mixture of cracked egg shells and fluids flowed upward through the pipe and into the cavity in the bassoonist's helmet. In between gulps, thin strains of yolk poured out of the holes of the bassoon and traveled down its wooden exterior, all glimmering and jellylike, some even starting to extend toward the floor like some sickly cheese strings, just as disgusting as they were long, only to be sucked back in with the next loud gobble.

It was not a pleasant sight to say the least, but one that I have since learned to live with. Indeed, just this morning, while he was inhaling his breakfast, I found myself sitting in the opposite corner of the kitchen, enjoying an onion and mushroom omelet. I even had the poise to throw in a quick greeting of "bon appétit."

* * *

I sent a fax to Alpha to tell him that the railroad work was almost done. "I can't be sure," I wrote, "but I have a feeling that the construction of the railroad line has something to do with the Arrival."

Alpha's reply spread over three pages, all very technical. I brought it with me when I walked into town and read it part by part whenever I felt like a rest.

He explained that his transformation might take a while. It would be a multistage affair, not without its share of unknowns and potential pitfalls, but he had no doubts it would be done. He could easily have built a mobile unit that communicates with him through radio waves (in fact, the bus could already function in that capacity), but in order to build a truly transportable version of himself, he had needed to come up with completely novel technological methods.

For the first stage, he supplied the mountain's technical crew with designs for a specialized production machine whose sole purpose was to build smaller, more intricate machines. These, in turn, would be able to build even finer pieces of machinery that, if all goes to plan, should be able to go about constructing the mobile version of Alpha. However, these small machines require a near-perfect vacuum in order to operate, so before they could go into action, an entire section of the mountain's living quarters would have to be demolished and converted into a vacuum container. Many of the mountain people will be dislocated in the process and forced to share rooms with others. Anticipating unrest, Alpha has increased the dosage of antidepressants in the food threefold and ordered a big shipment of tension-reducing pets (parrots, hedgehogs, and domesticated lizards), which will be distributed to the different rooms based on the personality types of the tenants.

I was already deep inside the city when I finished reading the fax. I tore up the pages so as to make them unreadable and threw the pieces of paper in the trash. Before gravity had enough time to pull them into the body of the trash can, I heard a loud tire screech coming from behind. A garbage worker jumped off the braking truck, picked up the trash can, emptied it into the rear of the truck, climbed back on, and the truck sped away—so fast that I blocked my ears in anticipation of a sonic boom.

The acceleration proved too great for a few items of garbage that escaped the back of the truck and settled on the middle of the road: a half-eaten pineapple, some chicken bones, and a few grains of sticky rice. It didn't take long for a group of street cats to seize the scene and begin a tournament for the ownership of the leftovers. I, for some reason, had developed the strongest craving for Chinese food.

I entered a phone booth, leafed through the yellow pages, and decided on the Lucky Star—a Chinese restaurant and about the only place of business in town that didn't force the word *city* into its title.

A smiling Chinese man, whom I took to be the owner, greeted me with a warm smile and a handshake and led me inside. Right away I admired the atmosphere—it was like stepping into a parallel world where light traveled slower and only two colors existed: red and gold.

While waiting for my hot and sour soup to cool down, I eavesdropped on a man and a woman at the next table who were deep in conversation. They were discussing the subject of turtles. More specifically, how these animals obtained their shell. The woman maintained a very interested expression throughout; the man kept raising the soy sauce bottle to his nose but never used it on the food.

"I am telling you, Emily, they build it themselves. Turtles may be slow, but they are very tenacious creatures. After all, it can't be the case that they *buy* their shell. That would require a robust monetary system: coins, transactions, coupons, the stock exchange, bank robbers, getaway vehicles."

"Well, maybe the turtles just don't want us to find out, maybe they keep it a secret—to avoid copycats. But I also think I read somewhere that it has to do with neurons, whether they fire or not."

"Everything is neurons," the man replied, "or at least, everything is something. Napkins are something, fortune cookies are something, air is something, too—even if no one can see it yet. You, Emily, are quite something yourself!"

"Oh, stop it! I'm blushing."

"Incidentally, there's a sesame seed stuck between your upper teeth."

"How embarrassing for me! I must apologize."

"Not at all. It becomes you."

"Now you got me blushing again! What a strange expression this is: 'It becomes you'—as if the sesame seed would magically transform itself into my shape."

"I believe this expression originates in the Aztec language: That gold nugget becomes you. That pyramid becomes you. That cocoa drink becomes you as you are standing here before me with the lost city of gold as a backdrop. I could go on for hours!"

"What a rich and mysterious culture!"

"And we've barely just scratched the surface. How are you enjoying your food, Emily? Personally, I find the duck to be dry."

The woman hesitated for a moment, then answered: "I haven't ordered anything. I've already had a big breakfast, I'm on a special diet, I can't digest Asian food, and I must fast before my big checkup tomorrow."

"I never fast before medical procedures—it gives me joy to confuse the doctors. I think they like it, too, gives them more of a challenge. Once, on the way to have my kidney removed, I stopped at an all-you-can-eat buffet for a large plate of beef kidneys with mushrooms and garlic. You should have seen the expression on the surgeon's face when he opened me up and had to spot which kidney was my own. I couldn't see his expression though because I was under anesthesia."

"Did you have dreams?"

"As a child, yes, many times. Dreamed of cowboys, Indians, ghosts, flies in the soup . . ."

"Me, I still dream, even now as an adult, even now as I sit here. But I always forget the dreams, so I can't be sure if I really had them or if they were just a dream."

". . . flies in the salad, beetles in the ketchup bottle, sheep in the oven."

"May I try a piece of the duck?"

"Yes, it is quite exquisite. Like a chicken mixed with a lake."

The woman used her fork to take a tiny, almost invisible piece of duck from the man's plate. She drowned it in vinegar, blew on it for a long minute, then ate it while closing her eyes.

"It tastes like beef kidney!" she observed. The man reflected for a moment then went on:

"Here is a story I've told no one: Two years ago, on the way to have my kidney removed, I stopped at an all-you-can-eat buffet for a large plate of beef kidneys with mushrooms and garlic. When the surgeon opened me up, he had the most puzzled expression—he could not tell which kidney was mine and which belonged to the beef. I couldn't see his expression though because I was under anesthesia. Smartly, I had the nurse photograph it for me. The picture is now framed on my wall."

"How many walls have you got?"

"In the entire house? Five, maybe six. No more than twelve, I'm positive. I painted them all myself. Took me an entire year. Eleven months for preparations, then I did one wall a day for the next thirty days. Eventually I had to knock down some of them because I painted out of the lines—corners are hard to paint without novelty equipment."

"I don't believe in walls," the woman said, "they make me claustrophobic. Besides, if you don't clean them well, spiders show up. Spiders make me arachnophobic."

"Oh, but I clean them all the time. I also open the windows several times a decade, just to let the air in. The wind scares away the spiders, though sometimes cats jump in through the windows then stay for weeks. I made a habit of naming them after exotic colors. Fuchsia Blue used to be my favorite, but I once left the door open for close to a minute and she ran away as fast as she could."

"Did you chase her?"

"No, but I put up posters all around town, handed out flyers. Many people called. But only to strike up conversations. I've come to know some delightful people that way. Also made some enemies."

The woman looked him in the eyes and said, "It's too early to tell, but I think you and I will never become enemies."

"Never in a million years!"

"Never in hundreds of years!"

"Not in dozens of seasons!"

"Not even in a matter of months!"

"No, love is forever."

"Now stop it, or I may never stop blushing!"

* * *

On my way back to the beach house, as I passed through the carrot field that marks the edge of town, I took a wrong step and found my left foot deep in a puddle of water. It was the shallow end of a small lake. A newborn lake—it had not been there before, I was almost sure—another sign of the accelerating Arrival.

There was a big brown egg hovering above the center of the lake. Not an actual egg obviously, but a big egg-shaped object the size of a bloated basketball, thin cylinders sticking out of it in several directions like the wooden pipes of a church organ.

A large beaver was in the shallow water at the opposite end of the lake, crouching on his hind legs in a prayer position, gazing at the hovering object as if entranced, his face vacant, his gaping mouth revealing the full extent of his teeth. He was communicating, or at the very least receiving. The object was the transmitter. Through it, He who speaks through pyramids was talking to the beaver.

I am not the only one.

I had dinner in the kitchen with the bassoon creature, then went to bed. For the first time in a while, I could hear him playing the bassoon downstairs. I closed my eyes, anticipating what was to follow.

DREAM JOURNAL ENTRY NO. 9

I am inside a room made entirely of mirrors. My image bounces back and forth between them; it is reflected infinite times. I raise an arm, and my reflected versions raise it with me. I turn my head, and they all do. This is fun.

I then observe something peculiar: the more remote reflections seem to exhibit a slight delay. Could they be far enough that the speed of light is already having an effect? I reach into

162

my bag and pull out a pair of binoculars. I put them to my eyes and peer into the distance. What I see is a reflection of myself reaching into a bag to pull out a pair of binoculars then stare through them with a puzzled expression. I scratch my head—I mean, the reflection scratches its head, I already scratched mine twenty seconds ago.

I notice that behind my reflected self, a large telescope is installed. I put down the binoculars, and sure enough, right behind me I find an extremely powerful telescope. I and all my neighboring reflections put the binoculars back in the bag, pull up a chair, and peer through the telescope.

The reflections I see now are so far away and have bounced off the surfaces of mirrors so many times that their light needs a long while to travel back and reach my eye. I am therefore seeing reflections of me from the past. I focus on one of them. I see myself handing out alcoholic lemonades to a group of workers. One of the workers steals a beer as I turn my back and sneaks in an obscene gesture. I extend the telescope's zoom to look farther into the distance. I see the bassoonist's white van arrive and park under the beach house. The van door opens to reveal an interior composed entirely of chicken eggs. I see myself popping out, as if from some alien womb, the bassoon creature right behind me—he appears to be playing some repetitive sequence. Under the influence, my reflection walks to a chair and sits down. The bassoonist goes into the house and comes back out with a cup of tea. My reflection wakes up and looks around, perplexed.

I extend the telescope's zoom all the way. My reflection is throwing a robotic cat from a bridge. A silver helicopter is floating above it. A golden blimp is floating farther up in the sky. I reduce the level of zoom by a fraction and adjust the focus. The reflection I now see is walking down Alpha's mountain with a group of people in brown jumpsuits. I zoom in on the face. I remember the exhilaration I felt inside, but in the eyes, absolutely nothing is showing; they are like gateways to a void. A grayish void. I wonder what one calls this state of being.

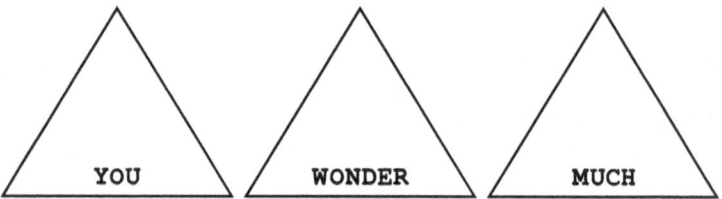

Because there are always *questions*.

I adjust the telescope so that I can view the entire mountain. The manta ray appears. It is rising behind the mountain, like a sun. How could I have missed its image as I was walking down the mountain that day? Simple—he was not there at the time. The telescope and the mirrors take me back in time, but the manta ray is beyond time. It is here now, with me.

I raise my eye from the telescope and suddenly the mirrors start moving. It was not a hall of mirrors—I was inside the second creature—the multitude of intertwined hourglasses. It spits me out into nothingness. I struggle to swim in the void, then wake up.

* * *

I sat on the beachside table to write down last night's dream. A few seagulls paced aimlessly on the sand; some more aspiring birds hovered in the distance in V formations. When I was done with the writing, the bassoonist joined me outside.

He walked along the shoreline with a wooden bowl full of eggs and arranged them on the sand, neatly spaced apart. Almost instantly, we were hit with a barrage of incoming seagulls giddy for the free lunch. Their numbers grew at such a formidable rate that pretty soon you couldn't see any trace of sand. Our little piece of beach had transformed into a whitish organism with beady eyes.

I never know what to make of seagulls, I don't particularly trust them (I trust ducks for example, but I dislike swans—I mean, you'd have to be downright stupid to trust a swan), so I was relieved when a loud noise came up from behind the beach house and chased them all away. It was a freight train, speeding on the newly constructed railway. First time that happened.

The train was relatively quiet to start with, but as it crossed the segment directly in front of the second-floor window of the beach house, a flurry of sparks spattered from the wheels, accentuated by a horrible grating sound. It wasn't a design flaw that was to blame, just poor construction quality—it was the section they had built the day I was mixing all those cocktails.

Soon as the train was gone, I spotted the bassoon creature up on the railroad tracks, where he crawled on all fours and performed careful inspections through the multiple lenses of his helmet head. I suspected as much, but now I could be certain: the tracks were connected to the Arrival.

With the reemergence of silence, some individual seagulls were hesitantly making a return to the scene to grab the eggs that had been left behind in their hasty retreat. I remained sitting for a while, then finally concluded that I definitely didn't trust seagulls and got back into the house.

* * *

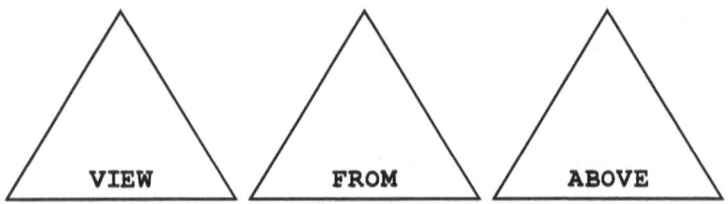

VIEW FROM ABOVE

I understand. A recommendation. Yes, I should take a look at everything from an elevated point of view. A fresh perspective. "Come," I told the bassoon creature, who since delivering the message had been standing in the corner of the room playing silent melodies into the wall, "we're going to visit the water tower." When we left the house, he pointed to the van, but recalling the vision of the egg-filled interior from my dream, I decided it would be wiser to walk.

As we were passing through the carrot field, I noticed that the lake where I'd seen the beaver was no longer there. Either it dried up, or it was some sort of traveling lake.

I was afraid the bassoon creature would draw attention, especially as he refused to follow my suggestion and cover himself with a hooded overcoat. But even as we passed through crowded streets, no one seemed to stare or show any sign that something was out of the ordinary. I credited that to the subtle melodic patterns he was producing from his instrument the entire time. A psychoacoustically induced invisibility cloak.

The old water tower—I've seen it before, but always from afar. It looked twice as high when viewed from up close, and twice as old. I stepped in. A lone security guard was manning a table in the tiny entrance hall. He, too, looked twice as old.

"Good day," I greeted him, "I would like to climb up to the water tank."

"Good day indeed," he said fondly, then arched his back and continued: "However, this is an emergency-storage water facility. Unauthorized personnel are not allowed inside."

"I am hardly personnel. I am just a regular person."

"Well, unauthorized persons aren't allowed as well. Anyone who is not so authorized must not cross that door to my right. That would be your left, naturally."

"That door leads up to the water tank?"

"It leads to a corridor that leads to a staircase. Staircases mostly go up or down, but where this one leads to I cannot be sure. I am authorized to enter the corridor, but the staircase is off limits even for me."

"Who is allowed there, then? Plumbers?"

"Now, now, do not try to confuse me, young man. There's been an epidemic of orange tree robberies all around the city, and even though I don't assume there's an orange tree in this facility, I must insist on the rules."

Orange robberies. I vaguely recall reading something in the papers. He continued: "Even in more peaceful times, the regulations are clear: unauthorized personnel, suspicious persons, and shady characters may not open that green door here to my right. Well, left from where you're standing . . ."

"You have a very good sense of direction."

"Thank you very much. I was born in the south but grew up in the north. Then when I was six, we moved back to the south."

"Well, that explains it."

"Or maybe I was five . . . five and a half. No, six, yes. It was much nicer during winter, there in the south, even if the house was smaller. My best friend lived in the east though. My first love—who is now widowed with thirty-one grandchildren—she lived in the west. I also walked southeast on more occasions than I care to remember, and then I always came back. That meant walking northwest of course, although sometimes

I was feeling quite tired so I took the bus (only when I could afford it, mind you—times were rough). However, I am far less experienced when it comes to northeastern-bound travels—there weren't a lot of opportunities when I grew up, and at my age I wouldn't risk it."

"Well," I said, losing patience, "I plan to go up to the roof of this tower. It would be great if you could open that door for me."

"Up you say? That's another direction I'm not very experienced with. Down—now, that's a different story altogether. I've been down many times, many many times. Down, yes—who hasn't? We even had a basement back in my parents' house. I went down there many times to play with my father's cabbage collection. He had them all: curly cabbages, red cabbages, celery cabbages, southern cabbages, cabbages from the west, cabbages from the north, cabbages from the northeast, cabbages from the Far East—those had to be privately shipped in by expert vegetable smugglers. Some of my fondest memories involve me and him playing catch in the front yard with a nicely shaped Brussels sprout."

Thankfully, at that point, the bassoon creature walked in (he had so far busied himself outside, oiling the keys of his instrument). The old security guard didn't seem alarmed in any way. I began to suspect he was blind.

"How may I help you, sir?" the guard asked but got no response—the oil on the bassoon probably needed a few more moments to dry. "Now now," the guard continued, "don't be shy. What direction are you coming from, if I may ask? East, north, up, diagonally? I know almost all of them. Well, some better than others . . ."

From the bassoon, a loud sound then erupted of a portable power generator giving birth to nonidentical twins. The guard's face instantly lit up—he seemed overcome with joy, transported into a dream, presumably involving some ethereal piece of rare cabbage. I double-checked that he was incapacitated, then opened the only drawer in his table, took out the keys, and unlocked the door to the corridor. The bassoon creature remained with the guard to sustain the hypnotic state.

I started up the spiral staircase, taking my time with each step, as everything was terribly slippery and there were no handrails to hang on to. The sparse light that crept in through the far-apart, tiny windows revealed a snakelike network of rust-colored watermarks with fresh drops of leaking water perched in between. Occasionally a burst of bassoon surged from below, then bounced back and forth between the concrete walls of the round staircase, usually followed by an ecstatic cry of "Napa cabbage!" or "Bok choy!," but as I advanced farther up, these distant noises were drowned out by the low-pitched gust of wind that whistled through the cracks in the metallic door at the top of the tower.

The more I neared the top, the more care I had to put into my step. The stairs were growing more slippery by the minute, the potential fall more unthinkable, and wind was starting to become a factor too.

So I was understandably upset when finally I had reached the top only to discover that the door to the roof was armed with a lock that none of the keys I had on me opened. I tried fiddling about with it using the keys that I did have, but it was completely useless. I couldn't kick the door in or use any meaningful force, because the slippery stairs denied me of any real foothold.

I remained stranded at the top of the spiral staircase, racking my brain for inspiration that failed to come. This turned out to be my best idea: knock on the door. I knew no one would be there, but I did it anyway—I had nothing to lose.

And then I heard noises coming from behind the door. And then I heard the sounds of a church organ. A church organ wrapped in a waterfall. And then there was a flash of light. And then there was no longer a door.

I stepped out to the roof. The egg-shaped object was there. The one with the wooden pipes that spoke to the large beaver at the lake. The traveling lake—it too was now on the roof, embedded into the concrete directly underneath the hovering object. They must be parts of the same being—the egg and the traveling lake—and they always travel together.

I thanked the egg for opening the door, it gave me a small nod in return, then collected its lake and floated over the edge of the roof to give me space.

The view from the roof was breathtaking. I could see the entire city from here—the houses, the roads, the people. More importantly, though, I could not hear anything. It is quite striking how much more peaceful everything seems when you strip it of its noises. The intensity is gone, as well as any notion of malice or hostility.

There are no individual personalities when observed from above, no individual vehicles—only swarms of things. Swarms of garbage trucks. Swarms of people. They become no more alive than balls of dust gathering in room corners, no more autonomous than autumn leaves at the mercy of the wind. Like so many snowflakes, waterfalls, and clouds, they are forever bound to the strict laws of nature. *People are just an extension of the meteorological system.*

The hovering egg-shaped object, who now had the traveling lake hanging from it like a waterfall, blew a cryptic chord with its wooden pipes.

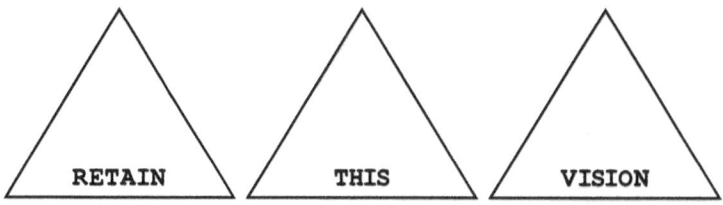

RETAIN   THIS   VISION

I will.

On the way back down, I bumped into the beaver. He was *crawling* his way up the stairs—a far more effective technique than the one I had employed, but ultimately quite embarrassing. I smiled at him politely as we passed each other; I got no reaction. Nothing at all.

* * *

A few days later I felt like going to the Lucky Star again—it seems to be the only decent place to eat in this town. The friendly owner greeted me with a handshake and sat me at the same table I got last time. As I was waiting for my wonton soup to arrive, I noticed that the couple I was eavesdropping on when I had last been here was once again sitting at the next table. A wonton soup is best eaten after it has had some time to chill, so I decided to listen in on their conversation.

"Richard, I've been thinking."

"Funny, I've been thinking, too. Caught myself thinking bang in the middle of the day. I think it was last Tuesday, after I had the crab pasta at that new Italian place."

"Was it any good?"

"The crab was somewhat undercooked, tried making a run for it. So all in all it was tasty, but then also a bit of a struggle. Tell me though, Emily, I really want to hear—what were you thinking about?"

The man looked into her eyes as he spoke. The woman seemed somewhat self-conscious. She stared down and ran her fingers over one of the slender-bodied dragons that were embroidered in gold on the red tablecloth.

"Well, I was thinking about our relationship, and well, I got to the conclusion that we have a very special connection. You really understand me, I think. No one understands me like you do."

"Oh yes, our connection is very special. Much more than other connections."

"So you think so, too?"

"Naturally I do! If only to prove the strength of our special connection."

"It *is* special, isn't it?"

"Yes. Imagine that: Some people have to settle for regular connections. Just your run-of-the-mill, everyday normal connections, with nothing special, no added value. I feel sad for them."

"Me too, me too! I feel sad for them, too. Can you imagine, having no special connection like the one we have?"

"I can't imagine it. No, I can't. I refuse to! It would be too sad to consider it for so much as a split second."

"Sometimes people come up to me just to say that they wished they had a special connection like the one we have."

"People tell me that, too—all the time. But you can't buy what we have. No. You have to earn it. It takes a certain type of sensitivity."

"Yes. Sensitivity!"

"Yes, it's all about sensitivity. You have to be born sensitive, and sense."

"Sensing things with our sense of sensitivity."

"Sensitivity. Starts with an S, ends with a Y. Sen-si-ti-vi-ty!"

"It's like we think alike."

"Yes, exactly. It's like we sink a lake."

"I said 'think alike', not 'sink a lake.'"

"Yes, I know. I was saying it with a Chinese accent, to make the waiter laugh. But also, I was thinking about a lake, imagining it, daydreaming. We were swimming in it, au naturel. Your skin was so soft and beautiful, sprayed with sweet lake water and illuminated by the sun. Day-old leaves cast silky shadows on your forehead in a vain attempt to transcend the beauty of the tender strands of golden hair that the lake water had so haphazardly rearranged."

"That's beautiful! Did we have a rowboat?"

"Yes, we rented it."

"Great! Why buy if you can rent."

"Why rent if you can buy."

"We think alike!"

"I think alike. You think alike. We both think alike."

"Whether at home or in a lake. We think alike."

"We sink a lake."

"Ching sing a leng."

"Ming duck Peking."

"Kung fu!"

"It's like we are connected."

"Yes, it's as if we're connected."

"Something was always missing for me in life."

"Yes, for me it was the same. Something was missing. Then you came, and you completed me."

"You completed me, too."

"You complete me. I complete you. We're the same."

"We are one. Bound together."

"Bound with a special connection."

"Yes, special. Rare. Hard to find. Unique."

"Unusual. Singular. Limited edition."

"We are two pieces becoming one."

"One and one is two."

"Two becoming one."

"*Tout va bien.*"

"Is that French?"

"*Oui*, it's the language of love."

"Then we must speak it all the time."

"We'll take lessons!"

"I'll pick up a brochure at the French embassy."

"Brochure—isn't that French, too?"

"We're already learning!"

"Because love comes naturally to us."

"Au naturel."

"Au naturel!"

"Our connection is special."

"Our connection *is* special."

"One of a kind."

"Once in a lifetime."

"We think alike."

"We sink a lake."

"Samurai!"

"I don't know where I end and where you begin!"

"I don't know where you begin and where I end!"

"It's like we're two parts of the same thing."

"Two parts. One thing."

"One thing. Two parts."

"We have become one."

"We have become one."

"I don't know what I'm saying and what you're saying anymore."

"I don't know what you're saying and what I'm saying anymore."

"Am I Emily or am I Richard?"

"Am I Richard or am I Emily?"

"We take turns to speak our sentences."

"One speaks, then the other."

"So if we knew who spoke first, we could count and know who speaks now."

"If we knew who spoke first, we could count and know who speaks now."

"We could have kept count, but we didn't. We don't need to know who is speaking now. We are one and the same!"

"We could have kept count, but we didn't. We don't need to know who is speaking now. We are one and the same!"

"Other people keep count."

"Because other people have regular connections."

"We have a special connection."

"Special. Rare. Hard to find. Unique."

"Unusual. Singular. Limited edition. Avant-garde."

"It's strange, but when I spoke now, your lips moved, too!"

"Very strange, when I spoke now, your lips moved as well!"

"I don't know who I am and who you are."

"I don't know who you are and who I am."

"I wonder what would happen if I raised my hand. Would your hand rise, too?"

"I wonder what would happen if I combed my hair. Would your hairs rearrange as well?"

"If I put lipstick on, would your lips turn red?"

"If the waiter stumbled and spilled hot soup on me, would you be in pain?"

"Of course! Any other outcome would be egoistic, not to mention downright illogical."

"Who said that?"

"Me. Or was it you?"

"I can't tell. I am one."

"True, I am one."

"I am Richard and I am Emily. I am the sum of what previously was two individuals. But I am now of one mind. A better person. For I have a special connection that connects my separate parts into a more perfect whole; a more wholesome, non-self-serving whole. I have two heads and eight limbs. I am a two-headed octopus, one might say (if octopuses could study French and rent a rowboat). I am of one opinion. One desire. One set of wants. One set of answers."

I could swear the last sentences were uttered by both of them together. They said them in a monotonic fashion, their voices an octave apart, rhythmically matched syllable by syllable, as if some invisible puppet master was speaking through their bodies. Their eyes were shut throughout, and they were holding hands across the table. However, they held them a bit too close to the candle food-warmer, which had the unfortunate effect of lighting their sleeves on fire. Oddly enough, though, instead of screaming in agony, they appeared to be reveling in the warmth of the flames, and in fact a relaxed expression spread across their faces—they were both smiling.

Then again, the room got so smoky that after a while I couldn't really determine if what I was seeing was a relaxed expression or if perhaps they were just forcibly molding their lips into that angle while internally clenching their teeth.

The waiter arrived with a pot of jasmine tea and used it to extinguish the flames. He seemed completely nonchalant as he did so and not at all in a hurry, as if a couple catching fire was not some freak accident but a common occurrence in the restaurant. Then, still shrouded in a cloud of smoke, he scribbled something on his order pad (probably charged them for the jasmine tea), tore out the page, and handed it to the man. The man stared at the piece of paper, looked slightly confused for a moment, then straightened himself and spoke: "Would you be so kind as to get that, Emily dear, I seem to have forgotten my wallet at home."

* * *

The newspapers are making less and less sense as the days go by. Today, the front page story of the *Gazette* was a motivational piece about novel ways to use the telephone. It encouraged the readers to find love by dialing random numbers, to once a week call dead friends and relatives "just in case," and suggested buying an extra phone line so that people could dial themselves and not get discouraged by a busy signal. It went on to explain how phones could be converted into self-defense weapons, stylized fruit baskets, bone substitutes for the dog—that's when I stopped reading. The piece, which stretched over four pages, was accompanied with pictures of local celebrities and their phone sets, a cutout model for an origami Alexander Graham Bell, and a sidebar titled "Prank calls cured my cancer!"

In the financial pages there was a step-by-step picture guide to dumpster diving, and in the sports section an entire account of a basketball game where the word *ball* was substituted with *bomb* ("In the third quarter, the City Trashers were plagued by turnovers and substandard bomb movement. Fortunately, they still had a full quarter of basketbomb ahead of them"). The rest of the paper was no less peculiar, with every available space taken by advertisements for the newest garbage truck models, garbage truck parts, garbage truck driving schools, and an invitation to something called the

City Festival of Garbage. The only non-trash-related ad was a small square with black and white images of locks and assault rifles. It read, "Insure your orange tree today."

The Arrival is in full gear.

* * *

I can imagine that a mother beetle would have a favorite son, one she is sure is destined for greatness. She knows he'll be a loving, caring child, and she knows he'll bring home the fungus. And whenever she looks into his innocent eyes, a warm sensation fills her entire being, a feeling that only this one particular face could ever evoke in her. I, however, am not a beetle myself, so I cannot tell one beetle from the next. To me that favorite son would appear identical to every one of his fifty-odd brothers, his hundreds of neighbors, or his good-for-nothing father, who bailed shortly after copulation.

For the same reason, it's perfectly understandable that until recently I have failed to notice that the bassoon creature living with me is not one individual but actually three distinct bassoonists who operate in shifts. Their bodies may be totally identical, but the sets of lenses on their egg-shaped heads are different, or at the very least the lenses are arranged in a different configuration.

There's a wooden cabinet in the kitchen with heavy sliding doors that I've always stayed away from (for the simple reason that its doors are marked with two fat red X's), and this is where the creatures store themselves when they are off duty. Like some otherworldly mummies, they are fixed inside it in an upright position, arms resting to the sides of the body, bassoon hanging from the mouthlike hole, and their helmet heads connect with a coiled power cord to a standard electrical outlet in the back wall. I assume this is either some sort of recharge station for their electronically operated lenses, or perhaps there is an electric egg cooker inside the helmet head that takes care of all those inhaled power lunches (in fact, I'm almost sure I heard liquids bubbling when I placed my head near one of the helmets).

Yesterday, however, was the first time all of them were in simultaneous action. A yacht passed close to our piece of land, and dealing with it demanded the combined powers of all three bassoons.

It was some sort of a midday party cruise for students: the deck was overflowing with young guys and girls in bathing suits, and a dance party was in full swing. The loud disco music that was blasting from the ship's speakers was heard all the way to the beach (I was watching all of this unfold from the comfort of the second-floor balcony), which seemed to have rubbed the bassoonist the wrong way. He was in the midst of laying down eggs on the sand for the seagulls—that's his personal quiet time—and he does not appreciate interruptions to his quiet time.

He put down the bowl of eggs and got into the house. From the direction of the kitchen, I heard a series of wooden thumps and metallic clinks, which were followed by a lively three-way bassoon conversation. The three creatures then stepped out together and walked onto the beach. As they passed through the carpet of feeding seagulls, they inhaled a few of the remaining eggs through their bassoons (they had only just woken up and presumably needed a morning snack) and proceeded to march calmly into the water. They walked a good way in and stopped only when the water had reached their knees. Then, facing the yacht, which was relatively far away, they adopted a stiff stance and started blowing through their instruments.

From the very first note it was clear that, put together, their powers were far greater than anything I had witnessed before. They began with a deep three-voiced chord. Its effect was immediate: from beneath the waves, a large swordfish rose into the air as if hung from some invisible crane and started to travel steadily toward the three bassoonists. When it was hovering above their heads, they brought the chord to a conclusion. The swordfish froze on the spot. Then, a fresh chord, a transposition. They played it with extreme vibrato, and as a result, the swordfish began vibrating and heating up. It splattered water in all directions and at the same time a thick layer of vapor extended from it like the smoky arms of a jellyfish.

With the swordfish all shrouded in smog, they terminated the chord abruptly and delivered instead a loud and extremely fast descending scale that covered the entire range of the instrument. The swordfish, whose expression so far was that of pure astonishment, had immediately squinted its eyes and with a great sense of purpose jetted toward the cruise ship like a heat-guided missile. Upon impact, the horrible disco music was cut short (and not a moment too soon), and although the yacht remained completely unharmed, the swordfish was now embedded in its sound system (its long swordlike bill was physically stuck in the record player, forming a direct connection with the needle). From that moment on, the swordfish would deliver to the ship's speakers a live transmission of every sound that was emanating from the bassoons.

The dancing ceased, but the students on the yacht seemed completely unaware of what had just transpired. Most likely they thought it was some malfunction, or perhaps a gimmick by the disc jockey to build up suspense. Some were booing, some were cheering on, and soon enough everyone started pumping beer-holding hands in the air and shouting out a chant of "Party! Party! Party!" (The yacht was quite far away, but the intense cheers traveled all the way to the beach.)

I assumed the bassoonists drew water into their instruments before the next note because it had an obvious gurgling quality to it. The sound was now coming from both the bassoons themselves and from the party-sized speakers on the yacht. It was louder than a jet plane and it unleashed an enormous wave of energy that clutched the ship and lifted it up into the air. The water underneath the hovering ship rearranged itself in a storm of waves so that an artificial-looking cavity started building up in the form of an upside-down pyramid whose watery walls were as smooth as mirrors (this I noticed only after I grabbed a pair of binoculars from the kitchen drawer).

Panic gripped the deck. People were running from end to end in a wild stampede, climbing over their fellow students and knocking each other down to the ground. Everyone was fighting to stay as far away from the edge of the yacht as possible, but of course the yacht had limited size and was filled to capacity and, as a result, a pile of human bodies was beginning to take shape. Those who were not able to fend for themselves or were somehow left too disoriented by the commotion jumped ship and plunged into the pyramid-shaped cavity in the water where they immediately disappeared. (I later learned that in fact they did not drown or dissolve into nothingness, but that the pyramid actually teleported them to the cold storage room of a close-by Greek restaurant where, far from being safe, they had to battle not only the cold, but also one very confused shark and a string of sea urchins that kept dropping in from the ceiling as they too were teleported from the pyramid-shaped cavity at sea. Unfortunately for the students, the only available weapons were plastic cutlery—City Taverna was long past its heyday and was now functioning exclusively as a takeaway establishment. In the end, however, the situation, which was equally harsh on both camps, drove humans and marine animals to form a peaceful coexistence—the sea urchins, aided by an agriculture student, climbed into the tzatziki bowl and thus avoided suffocation, the students improvised sleeping bags from flatbread and kept themselves warm by applying pork fat to their skin, and the shark agreed to abstain from human flesh so long as it was established he had exclusive rights to the refrigerated pieces of raw souvlaki.)

Much like the egg-eating carpet of seagulls on the beach, the guys and girls on the yacht were now tangled up together in knots, reduced to a weird arrangement of flailing arms, legs, and nail-polished toes in Italian sandals; around them, pieces of bathing suits and pastel-colored bikinis popped into the air, then hovered around in the wind like weightless dandelion seeds.

One of the bassoonists turned around to face me:

I will.

Through the binoculars, I carefully scanned the pile of human parts for a trace of fake fur, a sewn-on cat's tail, or a red boxing glove. I wanted to see if perhaps Brawly the Cat—the university's boxing team mascot—was at the scene. I was relieved when I could not spot him; I always saw in him a gentle soul and it pained me to imagine him go through this ordeal.

The bassoonists started on a fresh sequence, but they were no longer playing in unison; each creature now had its own independent melody and its own time signature. By now, I was already somewhat versed in their sonic language and I could roughly make out the outlines of what they were saying.

The leftmost bassoonist was playing a song of love; he was impersonating a female hammerhead shark calling out to a potential mate. So powerful was this song that on hearing it, I, too, could experience how enchanting she was—although in my mind she took the form of a human being, a beautiful woman dressed in a shark costume, lying sideways on a picnic blanket, shielding the wind with her glove-covered hand as she struggles to light up a cigarette. The middle bassoonist played something else entirely. He was bombarding the minds of the people on the ship with an elaborate cycle of rapid five-note phrases. This was an inquiry into their psyche; he penetrated them one by one to determine who was the best candidate for the next step in the plan. The third bassoonist was still playing that same loud gurgling noise as before, which maintained the elevation of the ship and the integrity of the pyramid-shaped cavity in the water.

Answering the love song of the first bassoonist, a big male hammerhead shark rose from a white frothy circle to the left of the yacht and levitated high above the waves. The three bassoonists then joined forces and went into an elaborate atonal fugue. It formed an invisible sonic hand that grasped the shark and flung it into the pile of human flesh that now had the appearance of wobbling Jell-O on a plate.

I wanted to get closer to the action, so I left the balcony and moved downstairs to the beach. When I was outside, the scene on the yacht had already shifted considerably. The students were no longer tied together in a pile but were sitting down on the deck in a very orderly fashion even though most were left completely naked and sporting different levels of bruises from having been in the huddle of bodies. In the middle of the group, a lone figure stood tall. It was a creature with the body of a man and the head of a hammerhead shark—while I was busy going down the stairs, the bassoonists had managed to create this novel life form by fusing a human and a shark—a hammerhead shark-man in a captain's uniform with a microphone in hand; it was a menacing vision.

Through the ship's speakers, with a commanding baritone voice, the creature addressed the students, whose faces bore a shocked expression. "I am Captain Sharkhammer. I have the body of a man and the head of a shark with the head of a sledgehammer. I will be your captain for the cruise, and you will address me as Captain Sharkhammer. Are we clear?"

"Yes, Captain Sharkhammer!" the students replied in unison. It was obvious he had complete authority over them; having the head of a hammerhead shark will do that.

"Good. Now, everyone, on my mark, will move starboard. Can anyone tell me what starboard means?"

After a short silence, a young guy with red hair, probably a freshman, held up a shaky hand. A microphone was passed through the crowd until it reached him. His initial hesitation resulted in an awkward feedback sound that forced him to gather his courage and speak up: "I'm not sure, but I think it means the right side of the ship, Captain Sharkhammer."

"Very good. Thank you, Harpy. I am going to call you Harpy, because you sound like a broken harp."

"Yes, Captain Sharkhammer!" the guy answered, sounding nothing like a harp, broken or otherwise. Captain Sharkhammer scanned the faces of the baffled students, peeked at his wristwatch, raised his left hand in the air, and yelled, "Go!"

Everyone shot up and sprinted to the right side of the deck. Under the shifting balance, the yacht, which was still hovering in midair, tilted right, and as if hung on an invisible axis, started spinning sideways in loops. The poor students, who once again looked like a blurry pile of pink body parts, were screaming in terror and holding on to the ship's handrails for dear life. Most of them managed to hang on, but some fell down into the pyramid-shaped cavity in the water and further onto a mattress of gyros in the cold storage room of City Taverna.

I never cared much for the students of City University, but this was beginning to go too far. I yelled in the direction of the bassoon creatures, "What are you doing? Leave them alone!"

The three immediately turned to face me and blew out a chord.

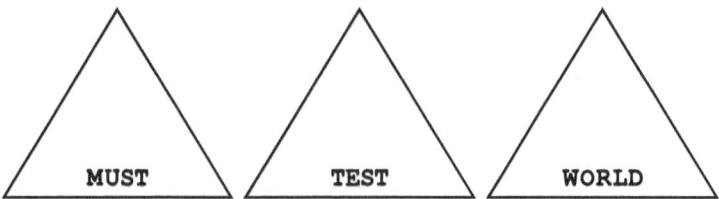

I was surprised that they listened. Even more surprised that they answered. Well, actually it was He who answered— through pyramids. And yes, I understand. He is testing this planet. Like a pilot coming in for a landing, He needs to test the physical attributes of this world to make way for the Arrival. I fully understand. That's why He needs to raise the yacht in the air, that's why He spins it like a slot machine reel. But what do the students have to do with this? Why not perform the tests on an empty ship? Why give birth to Captain Sharkhammer? Before I even asked it out loud, I got a reply:

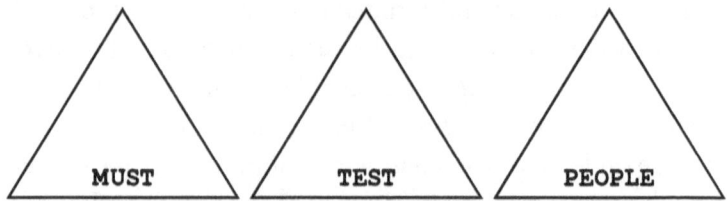

MUST   TEST   PEOPLE

Yes, I understand now. He wants to test the people, too. Like He showed me that day from the roof of the old water tower: people are an integral part of the physical world, just like the ship, just like the sea waves.

The ship was still spinning in loops, and the screams of the students persisted, now with an otherworldly sonic tinge because of the Doppler effect. Captain Sharkhammer's domineering voice burst from the ship's speakers again: "On my mark, everyone move back to the center of the deck and sit down. Do it now!"

As they did so, the ship began to slow down and stabilize until a short while later it was once again resting peacefully in the air above the calm turquoise sea. That moment of peace, however, was short-lived, as the routine turned out to be only the first of many such drills. For the next one, Captain Sharkhammer split the students into two groups, told one group to jump up and down at the bow of the ship and the others to hold hands and dance in a circle around the flagstaff. It was quite an unusual sight to see this choreography unfold through the binoculars, especially now that the lost items of swimwear were caught in the gravitational field of the yacht and were orbiting it like the rings of Saturn.

After a few more rounds of these studies into insane physics, Captain Sharkhammer was satisfied, and he let the students have a much deserved rest. He then spoke again into the microphone: "Hey, beach bum!"

This time, he was pointing at me.

"I'm going to call you Beach Bum," he continued, "because you are always on the beach like a bum." I wanted to protest, but it was actually indisputable that during his lifetime, which spanned the previous forty-five minutes, I had never once left the beach. Besides, even if I wanted to say something, he was far away on the ship and he was the one with the microphone. Looking my way through pointy black hammerhead eyes, he spoke into the microphone, which he held in his perfectly human hand: "I've been informed that there is a walkie-talkie in the kitchen drawer in that beach house. Get it and come back here."

I quickly ran inside and fetched the walkie-talkie—when Captain Sharkhammer gives you a duty, you do it. I turned it on, and right away his voice came through: "Got your ears on? Over."

"Yes, I can hear you. Over."

"You do not use the word 'yes' on communications. You say 'affirmative.' Is that clear, Beach Bum? Over."

"Yes. I mean . . . affirmative, Captain Sharkhammer . . . Roger that . . . ten four, over." He was making me unusually nervous. It was more due to the intensity of his voice than the sharkness of his head.

"Okay," he said, "I've been informed there should be an inflatable boat in the cellar of the beach house. Get it, inflate it, and get your beach bum ass over here to the yacht. Oh, and get the others here, too. Over and out."

"What cellar? What others?"

"I will guide you once you're inside the house. Keep your walkie on, over."

"But I know the house well and there is no cellar, so where do you expect me to get a boat?"

He did not like my attitude: "Negatory on the unnecessary questions, Beach Bum, and double negatory on the fresh language. I want you to pick up your binoculars now and watch what you've just made me do."

I put down the walkie-talkie and aimed the binoculars at the ship. Captain Sharkhammer stared directly at me with agitated eyes (actually one can make the case that shark eyes are permanently agitated). He took his walkie-talkie, held it with a stretched arm over the ship's rail, and then released it to fall down into the sea. There's no messing with this guy.

A few seconds later a young stranger's voice came from my walkie-talkie: "Hello? Anyone? Please! Can anyone hear me? We're eleven people here, students, we're stuck inside a big refrigerator. There are sea urchins in here, and a real live shark! Please, can anybody help us? Please, we don't know what to do! Also, we're about to run out of ouzo."

Everyone's got problems these days; I had my own problems to attend to. I went into the house in search of the elusive cellar. I found it in no time—there was a wooden door in the floor, hidden in plain sight directly under the kitchen table— I must have missed it so far because my attention always went to those creepy egg pyramids.

I carefully pushed the table aside and pulled open the door to the cellar. Not much was visible through the opening, but by the way the cellar floor reflected the light from the kitchen, I could tell it was covered with water. A suspended ladder descended into the cellar, but it had disturbingly small rungs that were too close together for an adult to use, so I sat on the edge of the opening, dangled my legs in, and jumped into the darkness. I hit the floor with a big splash, and after I managed to balance my body, I found myself standing knee deep in a pool of water that was home to various groups of tiny fish. At least now that I was inside the room, it turned out to be less dark than it seemed from above.

The cellar was fairly big and completely flooded. Dozens of small, beautiful wooden pyramids floated peacefully on the water, and around them, wood chips were scattered like fallen leaves, the crude light fixtures in the walls painting them a dim sunrise tangerine. A medium-sized inflatable boat was tied to a rusty hook on the right-hand wall—I was relieved to see it was already inflated—and at the far end of the room, a small hill rose from the water—a cone-shaped construction of tree branches and mud, at the top of which a small creature was lying on its back, sleeping. It was the beaver, the one I had seen at the lake, the one who had ignored me in the staircase of the old water tower. Turns out he's quite the snorer.

The wooden pyramids on the water, he must have carved them himself with his teeth. I grabbed one to have a closer look. It was pristine craftsmanship, very smooth to the touch, and it had strange markings on the sides—a few dots and lines in varying angles and some open circles. I picked up a second one to compare. Structurally the pyramids were indistinguishable, but it looked like each one bore slightly different markings. A primitive form of written language then. Is he already engaging in meaningful conversations with Him who speaks through pyramids? Is he more far along than I am? Or perhaps it's simply his method of documentation, his own version of a dream journal?

I was in the midst of contemplation when something popped out of an opening in the muddy hill. It was once again that egg-shaped object with the organ pipes. It rose up, approached the face of the beaver, and played a soft chord. The beaver woke from his sleep and sat up. After rubbing his eyes, he slid down the hill on his back and disappeared into

189

the water. When he surfaced again, he was carrying a chunk of wood that, using his sharp teeth, he skillfully carved into another beautiful-looking pyramid. He then used his claws to etch those mysterious markings on one of the sides. He swam with it in the direction of the egg-shaped object and held it up high as if to present it. The egg-shaped object read the inscription and replied with an organ chord. I was standing close by, so the message was received by me, too:

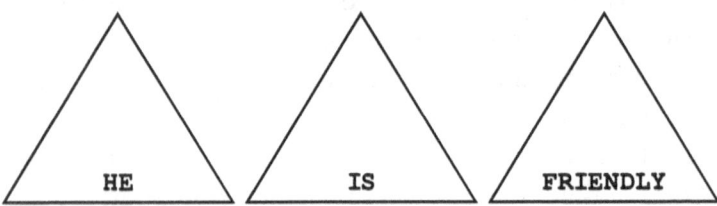

The beaver turned to size me up, gave a distrustful look through one open eye, scratched his head, then jumped into the water again and came up with another log. He carved it into another pyramid, inscribed a new message, this time on all four sides, and presented it to the egg. The egg replied:

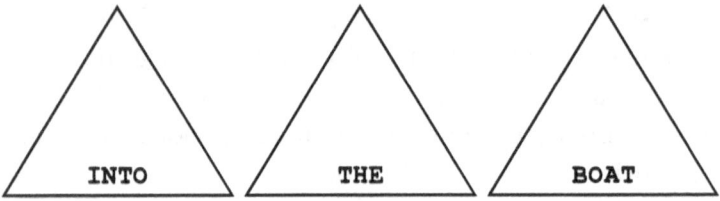

When I came to from the mind projection of the worded pyramids (which had a different quality from the ones I'm used to from the bassoonists, more smoky, almost like scotch), the beaver was already sitting in the inflatable boat. Is that who Captain Sharkhammer was referring to when he told me to get the others? I took my place in the boat, sat opposite the beaver, and started to row in the direction of the ladder that led to the door in the ceiling. I tried to figure out how the hell I was going to get us out of the cellar, but as it turned out, this was not my responsibility. The water in the cellar was not some random flood—it was the traveling lake! And with a quick surge of energy, it traveled through the door in the ceiling of the cellar, carrying with it the inflatable boat with us inside. In a matter of seconds, we found ourselves sitting in the boat in the middle of the kitchen. A group of disoriented fish swam around us in a minor panic. The organ pipes played again:

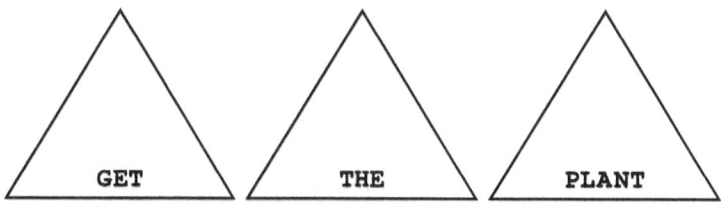

Plant? The beaver stepped out of the boat into the flooded kitchen. Hurry up, I thought, this can't be good for the wooden furniture. He swam in the direction of the sink, climbed on the countertop, grabbed the pot with the parsley plant, and, making sure to keep it above water, swam back and got into the boat. The traveling lake took a deep breath, then swung open the door of the house and traveled out to the beach, carrying us on its surface. It continued to move toward the sea but stopped short when we met the shoreline. I had to step out and push the boat myself into the waves—ironically, it appeared that the traveling lake could not travel in seawater, so it stayed parked right there on the shore as we started to make our way toward the yacht.

Rowing the boat through the waves was not easy. Not only did the beaver not offer any help, but I had to keep shouting at him not to bite the boat—he seemed to extract great joy from brushing his long beaver teeth against the rubber interior. Luckily, at some point the egg-shaped object abandoned the lake, joined us at sea, attached itself to the back of the inflatable boat, and steered us toward the yacht by blowing wind through its organ pipes. It got us there in a matter of seconds.

The yacht was not hovering in the air anymore. The pyramid-shaped cavity was gone as well. I tied the boat to the yacht, carefully carried the parsley plant, and followed the beaver up the ladder that led to the deck of the yacht. Captain Sharkhammer wasted no time and got on the microphone before we even found ourselves a place to sit.

"Okay. So, we have a few guests joining us. Say hello to Beach Bum over there and little Mickey Mouse. Oh yes, and there's the little tiny plant, too. What is it, parsley, sage, rosemary? Thyme? Who can tell these days, right? I'm just going to call him Mr. Spinach. Everyone, say hello to Mr. Spinach." Everyone stared confusedly at me, the beaver, and the parsley plant. You could see on their faces that they couldn't believe how this day just kept getting weirder. At least it seemed they had managed to somehow retrieve their bathing suits while I was away.

We weren't the only new additions. The three bassoonists, the egg-shaped object, and even the trio of singing sparrows and their feathered pyramid with the eyes (their equivalent of a bassoonist, their *messenger*) were there. The only one missing was the traveling lake, which was stuck back on the beach, currently pestered by a bunch of curious seagulls who dropped by to explore this new body of water and supplement their diet with some freshwater fish.

Captain Sharkhammer raised an open palm in the air to motion everyone to be silent. It was very effective. For a creature that initially struck me as lacking in subtlety, he turned out to have an excellent command of body language. An intense emotion gripped the yacht, an almost tangible substance equal parts anticipation and anxiety. All you could hear was the sound of waves beating against the hull of the yacht. The procession was about to begin.

Captain Sharkhammer, the master of ceremonies, raised the microphone to his jaw: "Everyone comfortable? Not so much, I see. Look, I know some of you find me intimidating. That's natural—I have a big powerful jaw, half of me is shark, and I am a very successful individual. No, it's true, I've had tremendous success, I hunted many big fish, some of the biggest fish you ever saw, probably bigger. So you should definitely respect me, but you should not be afraid of me. I am here to help you, okay?"

"I am not afraid of you! I *love* you, Captain Sharkhammer!" That voice belonged to Gwen. Gwendolyn, a literature major and a prominent member of the university tennis team. She used to hang out with the rich kids at my lemonade stand, always carrying a tennis racket under her left arm, always in a white tennis dress that complemented her slender figure and did nothing to diminish her ever growing army of admirers. I was not surprised to see her drawn to Captain Sharkhammer—he was not a spineless do-nothing like the spoiled kids around her. After declaring her love, she picked up her tennis racket, walked up to Captain Sharkhammer, and sat down on the floor by his side, hugging his firm trunk of a leg with both hands, her long dark hairs finding comfort in the navy blue fabric of his captain's trousers. Captain Sharkhammer did not display any hint of opposition. "That's great," he said into the mic, "isn't she just great? You just sit there comfortably, honey." She would stay in that position for the remainder of the day.

"So, if you look right here behind me on the bandstand, we have the three clarinet people and we have the flying pyramid, which I'm going to call Sharpy, and we have Meatball Marinara over there with the organ pipes, and they're going to play something special for you and it's going to move you in many ways. And when I say move you, I mean it's going to physically move your body parts, it's going to maybe even detach them from your body and replace them with other parts. It's some sort of experiment—don't ask me about the details, I'm only here to keep things flowing smoothly, okay? They did promise me, however, that in the end, they're going to put everything back together, so no need to panic, everything will be just fine.

"Okay. Before they start with their little concert, is there anyone who wants to get off the boat? Just raise your hand." Everyone except for Gwendolyn raised their hands enthusiastically. Captain Sharkhammer shook his head: "I was only kidding—no one can leave. Don't worry though, children, you'll be as fine as Sicilian wine." He turned to face the feathered pyramid, then called out theatrically: "Okay, take it away, Sharpy!"

The pyramid nodded and then gestured to the other messengers in the manner of an orchestra conductor. The egg-shaped object was the first to play. A soft hiss. White. The sound of distilled anticipation. Two minutes of that. Some students already went into a deep sleep. The middle bassoonist stepped forward and started on a slow scale. The hiss grew stronger, now pink, wavy. The second bassoonist played. First some staccatos, then some buzzing. The sound of gossiping insects. The beaver shut his eyes. Some younger students had blood dripping gently from their noses. The hiss turned to charcoal; the egg-shaped object's pipes spat out blue sparks. Then the third bassoonist joined in with those pig sounds—now it begins, I thought, a musical chain reaction. Burnt metal, crackling rust, sulfur. The speakers were amplifying everything, and the speakers were getting louder by the second. The sparrows performed an involuntary step dance. The beaver fought to keep a jet of water from spraying out of his ears. A split second's silence.

There it goes. The three bassoonists shot out an impossible sound. No longer a hint of bassoon in it, but the hinges of a planet-sized squeaky door opening wide. The egg-shaped object added explosions on top: the gasps of two oil tankers devouring each other in a violent act of love. That was only the beginning. The feather-lined pyramid with the eyes on the sides, which had so far been silent, moved to the center of the ship and rose up in the air. It filled itself up with white bolts of lightning, turned them to solid gold, shut its eyes, and contracted itself into a single point. Then, like a loaded spring, it let go. And as it began to explode, I lost my hearing, then my vision, then my mind.

Of what happened next I have only partial recollection, mental images strung together in a nonlinear fashion. Looking through a tunnel at a pink dot. Lava pouring into my eyelids. Then, no more eyes. Teeth for eyes. Hungry vision. Black beans, kidney beans, chickpeas. Tremendous heat and then sight again.

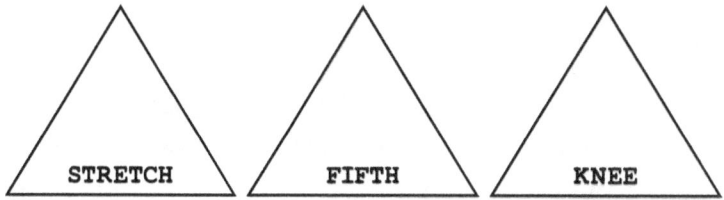

Are those flying water lilies? No, well, water lily constructions of Lycra and body parts. They're strangely appealing. Organic party decorations. Somewhere in the background, the beaver's tail is someone's tongue. At least *I* am intact again. Oh, wait. There go the fingers of my right hand taking leave of my body. No hints of injury where they detached—there's a new stretch of skin. Since when is the sun so big? Look, pyramids! Listen! More pyramids. Echoes of pyramids. Echoes of echoes. Here's the inflatable boat. Is it winking at me? Making a pass? I scratch my head in puzzlement but realize these are not my fingers doing the scratching—two of them are quite hairy, and the third is feminine and wearing an engagement ring.

Disfigurement symphony movement two, an andante. The sparrows exchange beaks, then change back, then switch again. They sing along and their voices shift accordingly— soprano to countertenor to mezzo-soprano and back again. A seagull dives from the sky and hits the deck with a thump. It's not his fault—for a while there he had my fingers for wings and long blond hair for the tail part. Thank you for making me whole again, but I really don't know who's got your wings. Try the beaver; tell him I sent you. Sulfur again. More echoes of pyramids, now modulated. Really, since when is the sun so enormous?

Blackness again. Passing through large gates. Blacker. Shiny gates of gold and lightning. The egg-shaped object has a waterfall coming from it—it looks just like the traveling lake. It *is* the traveling lake. How did it manage to get here from the beach? Maybe it took the inflatable boat. And now the boat is winking at me again! In the water, close by, just to my left, an unusual creature—five feminine legs bound to each other in the shape of a star. Two ending in delicate yellow heels, one in a blue sandal, and two somewhat paler legs in white tennis shoes—must be Gwendolyn's. Half embedded in water, this creature is revolving around its axis like the wheel of a watermill. Around it the water is turning orange, not chemically, not because of the music, but because the entire coastal community of starfish has now gathered around just under the surface of the water—they all rushed in to admire this graceful apparition.

Everything is blinking in and out of view. When I can see, I am deaf, and when I am blind, I can hear again. A pulsating cage built from human body parts now traps the entire ship. Inside it the parsley plant is now up in the air, the center of attention, several ducks flying around it in celebration. How did the ducks get here? Did they share the inflatable boat with the traveling lake? Please, enough with the winking! Captain Sharkhammer, underneath, raises one arm toward the parsley, and sings off-key into the mic, channeling an over-the-top Vegas entertainer as if all of this were nothing more than a night at the karaoke. Gwendolyn, now legs intact, is still at his feet and still head over heels in love. Black turns to white turns to black again, then spews rainbows of glow-in-the-dark.

The sun—a magnificent chord. I lovingly embrace it, then pass out.

* * *

I had a terrible sleep—though one could hardly call it sleep, more like uncontrolled drifting between states; yesterday's ordeal kept replaying in my head.

The kitchen was taken by one of the bassoonists, who was having a bigger-than-usual egg pyramid breakfast. As creepy and messy as it was (it looked like he had emptied an entire barbecue-sauce factory on top of it), I was too exhausted to care, so I just walked past him and filled up the teapot. He must have noticed my lack of energy, because he turned around and, with egg fluids still percolating inside the bassoon, blew my way a couple of early morning arpeggios.

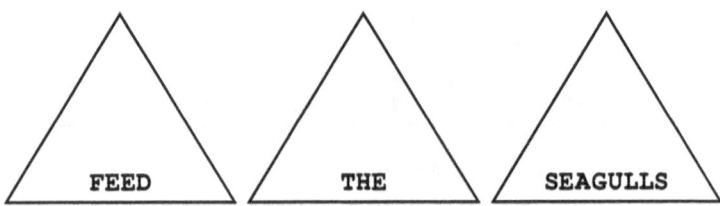

That gave me a small headache. I hardly had a chance to cast off my nighttime hallucinations and I get bombarded with the image of the giant pyramids? I know he meant it as a friendly recommendation, not an order—something like "Go feed the seagulls, it will calm you down"—but still, what next? Summoning the three cosmic pyramids to ask me to "PASS THE SALT?"

Nevertheless, when I finished my tea, I took him up on his offer. He prepared for me the bowl with the eggs, and I went outside on my own and placed them on the sand one by one. I still don't trust seagulls, and I still don't like them. But at least I can tell that they don't like me either. I would imagine that they see me as a "stupid wingless bird" or a "big land fish who lays eggs." And I enjoy that mutual dislike. I give you the eggs, and you eat the eggs, and we both share this moment on the beach. We have no illusions about each other—I owe you nothing, and you owe me nothing, and we have no hobbies in common, no shared interests, but in a way this actually makes us better partners than most. So I'm going to get another bowl of eggs and I'm just going to place them randomly on the sand and we'll all enjoy the quiet. I don't expect and I don't need anything more.

* * *

I was already getting comfortable in the beach house, but ever since I discovered that I share it with not only two extra bassoonists, but also the beaver, the parsley, and the egg-shaped object and the traveling lake, it has somehow lost its charm. I also haven't recuperated in full from the events on the boat, so I've spent the bulk of the last days taking long walks in the city.

One of the fascinating things I discovered is that there are very real feelings of hostility between the city cats and the garbage workers. It appears that garbage in this town is quite the hot commodity, so much so that I've witnessed a number of incidents involving cats attacking garbage men, incidents that I can only describe as carefully planned ambushes. Apparently the local garbage trucks are so quick to secure any discarded piece of junk that the city's cat community is forced to survive on a very limited supply of food, and the poor cats end up having to battle among themselves. This state of affairs has led to the formation of numerous rival gangs that seem to be divided along racial lines. In general, black cats go with black cats, Persian with Persian, and the gingers don't mix with the grays. I remember the street fights I witnessed when I first moved here, with the chalk-drawn ring and the refereeing. Those were the old days, back when respect meant something, but these are desperate times, and as always when hunger is on the rise, civility is in decline.

The last ambush I witnessed was also the bloodiest. In its aftermath, a garbage truck was lodged in a tree after being driven by a maniacal cat who took over when the driver left the vehicle to peel off a gang of black cats from his poor partner using a broom. The contents of the truck were all over the place. Large pieces of garbage covered the road and the sidewalk; lighter plastic bags and torn-up pages of nature magazines intermingled with the leaves of the birch trees. Half-eaten pork chops and chicken bones were scattered like musical notes upon thin lines of feline blood that stretched from sidewalk to sidewalk, and a cloud of flies soon showed up to buzz along to the composition. Above it all was the rotten stench of decaying garbage, which would have been utterly insufferable if it hadn't been kept in check by the emerging scent of gasoline that was dripping from the truck. When I spotted a wide-eyed ginger kitten salvaging a crumpled box of matches from the wreckage, I covered my ears and made off.

At the house, I received a fax from Alpha saying his transformation was complete. He is now a fully mobile computer on wheels. He even has some equivalent of arms, said he used them to put the printed pages in the fax machine and dial my number himself (obviously he could fax me directly from his data banks, but he wanted to show off his new abilities). I wanted to ask him for a photo of his new self, but it felt tacky.

I faxed him a long letter in reply. Partly because I wanted to keep him in the picture, and partly because I seem to have missed him. I wrote a bit about what I've been going through and then added a long description of what occurred that day on the ship with the students and Captain Sharkhammer.

He answered quickly (even my long letter requires of him only the fraction of a second to read) and wrote that he already knew everything that happened that day—it was broadcast live to his electronic brain.

"How?" I quickly wrote back. "Did He send another bassoonist to the mountain?"

The fax machine spat out another page:

```
>NO. HE CONTACTS ME THROUGH A PUDDLE OF
WATER AND A HOVERING ORGAN IN THE SHAPE
OF AN ELLIPSOID.
```

The egg-shaped object and the traveling lake! The one who speaks to the beaver. Well, a replica. There has to be a number of those, just as there are multiple bassoonists.

"So I guess you don't need me anymore."

```
>FROM AN OPERATIONAL STANDPOINT, I
DO NOT. AND YET I CHOOSE TO REMAIN IN
CONTACT. AS A HUMAN MIGHT PUT IT: I
ENJOY OUR FRIENDSHIP.
```

Did having a physical body soften him?

* * *

I had another interesting visit to the Lucky Star. It was early evening, and the place was more crowded than usual. The waiter found me a table in the back room—a smaller room housing only four tables but just as red as the rest of the restaurant and with an even larger population of golden wallpaper-dragons. At one of the other tables, I recognized Captain Sharkhammer and Gwendolyn. He in his captain's uniform and she in her perpetual tennis dress. Luckily they hadn't noticed me—he was busy with what seemed like a ten-course meal, and she appeared to be totally blinded by love.

"I love you, Sharky!" she exclaimed. "You are so strong."

Captain Sharkhammer looked into her eyes for a split second but didn't say anything. Using chopsticks, he plucked a large shrimp from the bowl of soup and devoured it. Gwendolyn's eyes grew wider, her irises like green pastures under a ring of milky clouds. "I love you, Sharky. You make me feel small. You are like my father who left when I was nine, only you will never leave me, right? I know you won't. You wouldn't dare!"

Captain Sharkhammer started working on the first of three plates of salmon teriyaki that were arranged on the table. He skipped the chopsticks altogether this time—he just raised the plate at an angle and let the fish together with the sticky rice and baby carrots slide down into his enormous shark mouth.

Gwendolyn didn't wait for him to finish digesting. She sent her hand across the table and ran her delicate fingers over the few exposed gills that extended above the collar of his salt-stained shirt. She stared into his far-apart shark eyes; it was obvious she was consumed with love. Captain Sharkhammer, on the other hand, consumed the second plate of salmon, then picked up the bamboo dim sum steamer from the table and with a flick of the wrist sent the prawn dumplings flying into the air to land deep inside his gluttonous jaw. Gwendolyn didn't mind that he didn't reciprocate her physical act of affection. She was perfectly content to watch him eat, to watch her man being his authentic self, to see him brimming with life's energy.

After his third salmon teriyaki, he emptied an entire bottle of soy sauce into his mouth, then spiced it up with a big handful of chili flakes. And as he took a tiny break from eating in order to properly swallow, Gwendolyn managed to make him hold hands with her across the table. However, their hands ended up a bit too close to the candle food-warmer, which had the unfortunate effect of lighting the highly flammable white wristbands of Gwendolyn's tennis outfit on fire (Captain Sharkhammer's uniform was left unscathed—it was professional grade). Oddly enough, though, instead of screaming in agony, Gwendolyn seemed to be reveling in the warmth of the flames; a radiant smile, almost childlike, spread across her face, and through the dancing flames I thought I saw tears of joy leaving her eyes. Captain Sharkhammer was not as emotional. He seized the opportunity to grab the twice-cooked duck from the table and hold it over the flames to lend it yet another layer of crispiness. A new song started playing in the speakers of the restaurant. It was a traditional Chinese rendition of Jerome Kern's "Smoke Gets in Your Eyes." It was strangely beautiful, but I was beginning to cough from the smoke, so I asked to be moved to the other room. On the way, I stopped by the counter and ordered a soup.

As I sat down at my new table, I noticed another familiar face. Richard, half of the couple I had seen in the Lucky Star before, was sitting alone at the neighboring table. And just as the waiter arrived at my table with the Szechuan chicken soup, the woman, Emily, walked in, too. Richard waved to her; she smiled and joined him at the table. They looked somewhat older than I remembered and they appeared to have moved past their former stage, no longer enthralled by the uniqueness of their connection. That is not to say they weren't close—there was love between them, but it had taken on a different shape. They gave their order to the waiter, smiled to him in polite silence as he collected their menus, and after he left, the man, Richard, straightened himself in his chair and asked:

"So, now, tell me darling, how was your day?"

"Well, I did some thinking today."

"Oh good, thinking again. What was it all about?"

"Well, it all started when I was feeling a little hot. It wasn't unbearable, but the temperature was not perfect. Remember that I told you the heating was not strong enough? Well now that you fixed it, it's *too* warm in the house. And then Julie dropped by for coffee and said there was no air flow. After that, I couldn't breathe!"

"So you want me to fix it again?"

"I think we should get a professional repairman this time— he will know how to do it properly."

"But Emily, think of the costs. And then you'll have to offer him lemonade, and besides, I don't want a stranger in my house. Or strangers! Sometimes they travel in groups."

"Okay, Richard. That's not the point anyway. Let me get back to the story. So I was feeling hot, and Julie had just left. Oh, she showed me pictures of the baby, so adorable! She's so lucky, and she just had her heating repaired by a very respected professional, by the way. So anyhow, she left, and there I was in the kitchen feeling hot, and I couldn't breathe, so I opened the window to the backyard to let the air come in, and then I looked out, and that orange tree, you know the orange tree?"

"Of course. The orange tree in the backyard. Is it in full blossom?"

"No. That's the thing, Richard. The orange tree was naked!"

"Naked? It had quite some oranges on it just the other week! Did you look carefully?"

"I looked very carefully. I am very good at looking."

"You *are* very good at looking, and you are also very good-looking."

"That's wonderful wordplay, you are so smart!"

"I've been told that before, many times. My teachers wanted me to skip a grade when I was eight. But my parents wouldn't allow it—out of jealousy, I suspect. Yes, I could have been even smarter, could have achieved so much more in life. But you see, it wasn't my fault—my parents are to blame."

"They called today, incidentally. I pretended it was the wrong number. Used a Chinese accent."

"Good. That should teach them a lesson."

"So anyhow, Richard, I was looking at that tree, and it was naked."

"Damn naked tree!"

"Yes! I looked at it and I realized it was a sign. A sign that my . . . our, life is naked, you know, metaphorically. Like you just said about your lack of achievements. I feel the same way, Richard."

"You are right, my life is like an orange tree without oranges. But I am not to blame! The circumstances, you see . . . my parents . . . my schoolmates . . . my coworkers, the neighbor's dog—I wanted a dog, too, but my father wouldn't let me. I could have learned so much from a pet. No, it's not my fault! The dog is to blame. My father is to blame. They formed an alliance—I was outnumbered!"

"But wait, Richard, that's not the end of the story. So there I was, looking at the tree, and I thought about it a little more and then I came to the conclusion that I had been wrong that entire time. It's a *naked* orange tree!"

"Damn naked tree!"

"No, Richard, I looked at it and I thought—it's naked, empty, a blank page, a fresh start. Don't you see? It's almost like . . . it's almost like a little baby."

"A baby? A naked tree baby?"

"Yes, Richard, a baby! I . . . we, could still achieve so much in life if only we had a baby."

"So the naked tree was actually a sign for a baby?"

"It had to be, because it made me smile. And also, Julie showed me pictures of her baby just ten minutes before I saw the tree. I mean, what are the odds?"

"You're right, that can hardly be a coincidence. An orange tree doesn't just go naked. That's the ABC of science—the alphabet. Even though the odds were stacked against me, I've still managed to learn *that* much."

"Exactly! But one question still bothers me: How did it happen? Where did the oranges suddenly go?"

"Well, let me think. They could have been eaten. By a flock of seagulls, maybe a gang of raccoons. Saltwater eels in land suits!"

"With matching goggles?"

". . . or it could be all of them . . . they must be in cahoots. We've been outnumbered, Emily—again!"

"The big orange heist. The citrus robbery. Deforestation with criminal intent."

"Oh, the thieves! Stealing someone else's fruit of labor! Think of the poor oranges, what they must have gone through. Sitting in the back of a speeding van like tiny kidnapped babies!"

"Now you got me all scared for the baby, Richard! This must never happen to our precious baby."

"No, we will protect it with our lives! It is our duty. We will build a castle around it. No one will ever be able to touch it!"

"Yes, we'll keep it in a safe with the jewelry!"

"And we'll keep guard twenty-four seven!"

"Twenty-five seven!"

"Forty-six nine! Nothing's too much for our son!"

Their food then arrived and they remained practically silent for the rest of the meal.

* * *

We sat on the beach for some morning tea—the parsley plant, the beaver, and me. Above the horizon, seagulls were flying in V formations; other, more sophisticated birds arranged

206

themselves in tributes to Cyrillic letters. A large group of ravens joined farther in the distance to show off their intellectual superiority by flying in complex formations several sentences long. The text opened with "A dodo steps into a bar," which made me assume they were spelling a joke, but the punchline was a few beaches away and already too small to be legible and I couldn't for the life of me remember where I had last put the binoculars.

The beaver had brought along some chunks of wood, and every now and then he'd carve out a pyramid, mark it with those weird symbols, and present it to either me or the parsley plant. I repeatedly told him that I couldn't read it, but he kept on going anyway. The parsley plant was sending out all sorts of interesting aromas—probably its own way to try and strike up a conversation—but without the aid of the bassoonists or any of the other messengers, the three of us were doomed to be separated by insurmountable cultural gaps. Which was fine by me—I didn't really feel like talking.

Instead, I lost myself in thought. I was daydreaming about the Arrival. A part of me is excited; another part is truly in fear. One look to the sky and it's obvious that He is already here—birds don't gather themselves in the shape of Slavonic vowels for no good reason. This all-powerful being—for all intents and purposes a god—why has He gone through all that trouble to track me down, to find the beaver, the measly parsley plant? A "voyage" He said. Will we meet Him? Will He speak to us? Can I be sure He is on my side? Or will it all turn out to be just another incarnation of the Regimen? I have already put myself at the mercy of one being; might I be throwing myself at the feet of another?

I looked at the parsley plant and wondered if it, too, was bothered with similar thoughts.

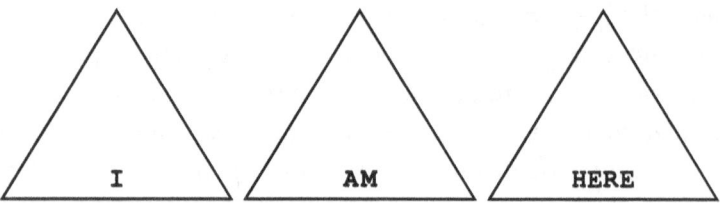

I know.

And He knows that I know.

I am inside a dream, but I still hear the bassoons. The border between dream and reality is more delicate this time—we need not keep clear boundaries anymore; knowing the trick does not lessen the effect.

I want to go inside the hall of mirrors again.

May I?

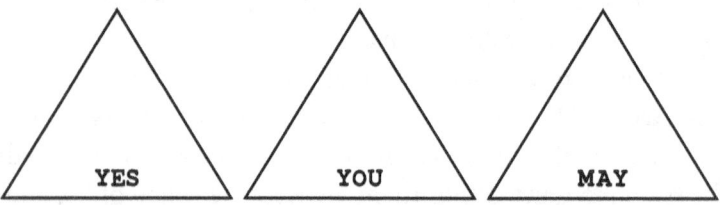

The creature of intertwined hourglasses emerges from the letter O of the word YOU on the middle pyramid and swallows me whole. I am inside it now. There again is my image on the mirrors, multiplied to infinity. I stare through the telescope again. It looks even further into the past now, and as I play around with the focus knobs, an ocean of memories floods the eyepiece. I move the telescope sideways whenever I'm about to meet a face. I'd rather only look at objects. I see a calendar, a dinner table, an earring, refrigerator magnets.

And then it's time for my ploy. If looking into the infinite mirrors through the telescope displays images from the past, then by staring through it from the opposite end, I should be able to see into my future. I turn it around quickly and force my eyes onto the lens.

But I see nothing. Another void.

>THAT IS CHEATING.

"That's not something I thought you'd object to."

>I DID NOT SAY THAT I OBJECT. I JUST
WANTED TO MAKE A DRAMATIC ENTRANCE.

"Wait, is it really you, or is it just my dream version of you?"

>I WAS ASKING MYSELF THE SAME QUESTION
ABOUT YOU. MY GUESS: WE ARE BOTH HERE.
BUT WE HAVE NO WAY OF KNOWING NOW,
OF COURSE. WE CAN FAX ABOUT IT IN THE
MORNING AND FIND OUT.

I do not see Alpha, I just see his words imprinted on the mirrors in their familiar amber light. I fiddle with the controls of the telescope to check that everything is well adjusted; maybe the finder is not aligned correctly, perhaps the eyepiece should be cleaned.

>DO YOU SEE ANYTHING NOW?

"I still see nothing. It could be that for a flash I saw some little points of light. But that might have been the reflection of the light of your letters on the mirror."

>THEN I WILL SPEAK NO MORE.

I wait for Alpha's lights to disappear, then stare through the back end of the telescope again. "I see a void. It's black. But there are some tiny specks of light, I think. Or is it actually a white void? Wait, it *is* black. Or not. My eye hurts."

Take me out of here.

I got a fax from Alpha in the morning. It really was him in the dream. We both agreed that the voyage we were told to prepare for in that third message at the mountain would begin very soon. Probably this week. Maybe as early as tomorrow.

I wanted to make at least one more visit to the Lucky Star before I left the city, but as it turned out, on Fridays they're only open in the evening. So I found a phone booth, and from the yellow pages I decided to settle instead on the skillfully named City Mall China Wall restaurant and began to walk in its direction. This took me through the city's big boulevard— the town's commercial center, where the large department stores tried in vain to flourish and where you'd expect to suffer putting up with all the tourists if this town had any tourists.

I noticed that a slight commotion was building up just outside the central police station—a group of chattering people, buzzing about in excitement. I tried to sniff out what the fuss was about, but even as I got close to them, I found it a challenge to extract any meaningful sentence. However, their overall intonation had that sort of musicality to it that hinted at half truths and brash speculations; this led me to conclude that these had to be members of the city's press.

Still, I was far more hungry than I was curious, and so I decided to let things be and continue on my way to the restaurant, but all of a sudden the doors to the station opened and I was washed inside on the sea of reporters.

The chief of police was in many ways a perfect fit for this town—a middle-aged, medium-sized, mediocre man, whose unevenly distributed mustache stubs and general unremarkable looks did not yet manage to catch up with the caliber of his rank. He was the kind of person you'd have a hard time recalling an hour after you've met—his physical features were simply too unexceptional to register. On the podium, though, perhaps as a direct result of this lifetime of being unmemorable, he seemed to revel in every single syllable. He took off his cap and placed it next to his notes, then adopted a serious air and began to speak:

"Good afternoon, everyone, and welcome. I wish this was under different circumstances. These are troubling times for the city, whether you happen to be the owner of an orange tree or not. Unfortunately, this tragedy we are faced with is something that concerns each and every one of us.

"Bear in mind that this is very much an ongoing investigation so there are some details I will not be able to divulge at this time. What I'm going to do in the next twenty or so minutes is give you a statement, bring you up to date on the state of the investigation, and then we will take any questions that you might have.

"Before we begin: There have been some reports in the media that the situation has been resolved. This is unequivocally false. Again, as of this moment, the person, persons, things, or unexplained phenomena responsible for the disappearance of the oranges are still at large. And by that I mean they have not yet been caught, not that they are *physically* large, so please, I don't want to read reports tomorrow about large giants who steal oranges. I hope we're clear on that."

He stopped for a moment to look over the crowd of reporters to make sure his message was getting through, then fondled his one-third of a mustache, arranged his notes on the podium, and began with the factual part of the statement:

"At about 9:28 A.M., exactly twenty days ago today, our emergency dispatch operator received a call from an elderly lady. She sounded rather old and very much distressed, and she claimed that the oranges from the tree in her garden had mysteriously disappeared. Two officers were dispatched to the scene. That is standard protocol, and it's not unusual at all for us to respond to a report of fruit disappearance in that fashion.

"Once on the scene, the two officers handcuffed the elderly lady and went through her personal belongings in search of clues. That is also normal protocol. It's common to use a heavy object as an anchor, and in this case they handcuffed her to the grand piano in her living room, which was a decision they had to make on the fly and it proved a very appropriate choice. I couldn't be prouder of the way our officers handled the scene.

"Next, they examined the orange tree and confirmed that: one—it was indeed a tree, and two—it had no fruit on it. However, because there were no oranges on it, it was hard to assess what type of tree it was, so the way they made that assessment was by rubbing the leaves on their hands and then smelling their hands—that way they avoided directly smelling the leaves, which could be just as dangerous as staring at the sun. As old Mrs. Copland was the only witness, the officers decided to bring her in for questioning.

"The next step was to determine her credibility as a witness. Since she had a piano in her home, we sat her at the police station's music room and brought her some notes—we decided to go with an arrangement of a John Philip Sousa march medley—and requested that she play it. If she could play the entire piece without a single mistake, the argument went, we would be able to establish a correlation to her owning a piano, and that in turn would establish her credibility and consequently confirm her claim about the disappearance of the oranges. Unfortunately, at that stage we were forced to uncuff her so that her hands would be free to play the piano keys, and when our in-house music expert left the room for a short moment to help us operate the popcorn machine (we were preparing ourselves for an entertaining concert), he returned to find her hanging from the ceiling on the low F-sharp piano string.

"Initially, that incident put a damper on the investigation, but soon after, new reports of orange robberies popped up everywhere and consequently we had more witnesses, and the loss of the old lady ended up having no impact at all. In fact, there was a big positive in that we were able to bring in her grand piano to the station and we threw away our old one, which was an unimpressive upright model that was now missing a bass string crucial to the performance of 'The Bombing of Kitty Hill,' which Sergeant Thompson plays for us each Friday. The garbage workers also had great fun chopping up the old piano for transport. So, a win for everyone involved."

I was getting even hungrier, and this was getting nowhere. But the room was too packed to allow for a quiet exit, so reluctantly I remained seated and listened on.

"The next emergency call came from a house on the other side of town—the good side. This time it was a respected businessman, so our officers were more gentle with him, which is not at all unusual. Instead of handcuffing him, they asked that he hold a bar of gold in each hand, which is standard protocol in such cases—it's really hard to run holding those things because of how heavy and shiny they are.

"When processing the scene, the officers detected a piece of orange peel that had been left behind, we presume by the criminal. This was our big break. The piece was obtained and delivered to our in-house crime lab, where examinations revealed that the orange peel contained traces of fur. This could mean that we are looking not at a human, but at an animal criminal—what we at the force professionally refer to as criminanimal, or crimanimal, or cranimal. The third version is clearly the snappiest; however, I'm not convinced that just taking the first two letters of the word *criminal* is enough to establish meaning.

"The next reported incidents followed a more or less similar outline. We found traces of fur in other orange peels, and in two cases we additionally found some small pieces of leather. In the process, our police officers were also able to get their hands on another piano, which we put in our library room, after we gutted its strings, and converted into a beautiful flower planter."

I was already beginning to have a hunch. Unfortunately, I got lost in my thoughts and might have even dozed off for a while, because when I opened my eyes again, they were already in the midst of the Q&A portion.

A woman in the front row presented a question: "Rachel Morrow, *City Tribune*. When you spoke of the first incident, you mentioned two officers. Could you expand a bit about their qualifications and whether they follow the standard regulations for the pairing of partners?"

"Well, naturally they follow the strict regulations of the international police community with regard to the pairing of police partners: one of them is a family man and plays by the book, and the other is a reckless, trigger-happy loner with a heart of gold who lost his wife while trying to save her from a fire. Sadly, it seems the orange tree incident had an effect on him—he's fallen off the wagon and has started drinking heavily again—but I'm certain there's a third act somewhere in his future where he gets his life back on track and saves the day for everyone. Of course, it goes without saying that all of our officers are paired using this same exact formula: one stickler and one renegade. It brings out great results across the board and it's also very entertaining."

A man in a tweed cap stood up: "Noah Holmers, *City Crime and Intrigue Weekly*. Could this be the work of a group of people, or are we talking about a lone gunman so to speak?"

"Thank you, Noah, for that question. We cannot at this time rule out any scenario. It could very well turn out to be a lonely gunman, but it could also be a more socially active gunman, someone who prefers assault rifles and family get-togethers— we simply don't know. We're looking into all sorts of possibilities, from exotic-fruit smugglers to wind-up tin monkeys to gangs of raccoons—you name it. In fact, I shouldn't be telling you, but at this very moment, our in-house fashion expert is putting the final touches on a raccoon outfit for our underage undercover agent. I had the pleasure of seeing it myself, and let me tell you—it was the cutest thing."

"What would the cover story be?"

"Well, I shouldn't be giving away too many details, but in a nutshell: She's going to play a young female raccoon, attractive yet approachable, she's new in town, knows no one, somewhat coy but full of life if one cares enough to dig deeper. And she carries a dark secret from her past about which she hasn't told a soul."

The crowd of reporters seemed very much smitten by that last piece of information. In fact, some very affected *aww*'s and *aah*'s filled the room, and I heard a few mutterings of "how cute!" At that stage I was already very confused by the direction this whole meeting was taking, and it was about to go even farther south. A woman in a suit interjected: "Will this have any effect on the raging garbage debate?"

"Absolutely not. The police stand unequivocally with the members of the garbage disposal community and their extended families. And let me make this absolutely clear: we, the City Police Department, are, as we always have and always will be, pro-trash. Let there be no two ways about it."

"Maria Cornfield, *Nutritional City Monthly*. What about bread? Does it need to have green things on it, or can I throw it out if it just smells a bit off?"

"I think we've made our opinion on the matter clear enough. We are pro-trash. Pro-trash. With everything that goes along with it. I'm sure you all remember the slogan: 'You suspect the bread, you throw away the bread.' But please, let's not let this turn into yet another debate about garbage and return to the matter at hand. You there at the back, next question."

"Yuri Slotnov, the *City Morning Gazette*. You mentioned before that this whole crime could actually have been the work of large giants. Could you elaborate a bit on that?"

"That's not what I said. What I said is that the suspect or suspects are still *at large*. Not that they are large giants. They are *at large*. Next question."

"Sharon Dilly here, *City Entertainment Weekly*. If one day this case is adapted into a motion picture, wouldn't the film studios need to come up with brand-new cinematographic techniques in order to realistically portray the large orange-stealing giants you've just mentioned? And does that make you rethink your portrayal of the villain in any way, if only to help them keep the budget under control?"

"I think Dr. Freimret—our in-house cinematographic expert—would be able to give you a far better answer, and you will have a chance to speak to him later, but I'm just going to go out on a limb and say that I believe this technique already exists. I distinctly remember having watched films involving giants a number of times. And not just giant humans, but also a giant gorilla, giant bugs, giant robots, even giant women—those were my personal favorites. Now, I'm no expert, but there's something called a *zoom* lens, and I think they can use it to *magnify* things—make them bigger, so I assume this is how they're going to do the giants. Obviously if they choose to go with an animated version—and I'm guessing they eventually will, seeing that we're dealing with oranges here, which artists have enjoyed painting since the dawn of time—then all they would have to do is draw the giants fairly big, and the rest of the characters smaller. So, that would be what we police professionals call an *effect of comparison*—your brain will trick you into thinking you are seeing a giant, when in fact it's the same kind of character as the rest, only drawn bigger. I hope that answers your question."

A man with a thick beard and a wrinkled suit stood up in the back of the room. "Slavin Stickhart, *City Unions Bimonthly*. Sticking to the live-action option: Will the raccoons be played by dwarfs in makeup, or will the production employ real live raccoons? If so, who would guarantee that their salaries match those of the human actors? Also, can you ensure that there will be no cases of animal cruelty? And by this I refer both to the case of the crew being cruel to the animals, *and* of the animals being cruel to the crew—whether by stealing their food, defecating on their resumes, or parading in their clothes and jewelry as a way to mock their vanity."

It was hard to tell if the unintelligibility of this question session was due to the Arrival, or if this was just a case of the press being incompetent. I'd give both options equal probability. In any case, before the chief of police had a chance to reply to that last question, an aide walked up and handed him a piece of paper. The chief squinted his eyes and gave it a quick read. He whispered something to the aide, gave him a reassuring nod and a tap on the back, then addressed the press again:

"Well, we've just had a fresh report of another orange robbery. Two very competent officers are on their way to the scene as we speak: Officer Martinez, loving husband and father of three, and his partner Jimmy Bonkers, who's been on the edge ever since losing his young wife in a ski accident a couple of years ago. I'll do my best to update you as soon as we have further details. For now, let's get back to the questions."

I raised my hand, but the chief pointed to somewhere else in the crowd. A woman spoke: "Emily and Richard, citizens. We, too, are the victims of an orange tree robbery. Could the naked orange tree in our backyard be a sign that we need to have a baby? Also, will our baby grow up to be more successful than the children of our friends and/or colleagues?"

"First of all, let me commend you on the use of the expression 'and/or.' Very impressive to hear that from a nonreporter. Shows that you must have good genes, so I'm sure your son will indeed be very successful, or if it's a girl, she will be very pretty and have many successful suitors. So, I would go ahead and have that baby. The more babies, the more garbage."

Next it was Richard who voiced a question: "Richard and Emily, citizens. We have another question. What if it's not a sign for a baby at all? What if it just means we have to *rearrange* our lives? You know, *re-orange*?"

The police chief stared at the ceiling for a while and mumbled to himself: "Rearrange, re-orange . . . re-arrange, re-o-range. Re-orange . . ." The more he repeated it, the more his face lit up with excitement. "That's a wonderful wordplay, very very clever! We'll most definitely look into it. What was your name again? Richard? Stand up. We need more people like you in the community. Did you have a pet dog growing up? Because you seem to possess the acute senses of a hound! Perhaps what you've just said will shed new light on the entire case. Heck, it could turn out to be the break we've been waiting for. Re-orange . . . Yes! Maybe those gun-toting raccoons are trying to tell us something after all."

I raised my hand again, and finally the chief of police pointed my way and said: "Yes, you there—mysterious stranger from out of town."

I cleared my throat and spoke: "Thank you. You mentioned that some traces of leather were found in one of the crime scenes. Could you tell us what the color was?"

He cleared his throat twice in return and appeared almost disgusted as he replied: "I believe it was red. Just plain old red synthetic leather. But let me just comment that this is by far the worst question we've had all day, and such a disappointing follow-up to the wonderful idea of citizen Richard over there. No flash, no technique, no grammatical fireworks like we had from that fine lady. We are discussing lone gunmen from the animal kingdom who are possibly sending coded messages through highly sophisticated wordplay, probably to be one day portrayed by dwarfs in elaborate period costumes, and you bother about the color of some crumbling piece of leather? Very unimaginative. From here on, I suggest we leave the questions to the pros."

Weirdly, this got quite the big round of applause—the chief of police was having a field day. The next reporter started a discussion on the possibility that the raccoons had co-conspirators in the form of deep-sea animals in specialty suits, to which I heard that man Richard shout "Saltwater eels!," which earned him a trip to the podium, where, aided by the station's sketch artist, he set to work on an image of the hypothetical underwater criminal mastermind.

I felt there wasn't anything to gain by sticking around, and we had already crossed the point where I needed to care about making a civil exit, so I got up and worked my way through the sardined reporters until I found myself at the back of the room. I somehow managed to crack open the door just enough to wriggle myself out of the conference room and into the station's main corridor.

I was already clear on who was behind the robberies. What I wasn't quite certain of was the motive. But that, too, turned out to be just a couple of steps away.

The walls of the long corridor were lined with the official annual banners of the City Police. The very conservative designs were limited to basic whites and blues with a large golden badge usually inhabiting the top half, and at the bottom, inside quotation marks, appeared the motto of that year. The banners were hung in chronological order, so a walk through the corridor told the story of the police as it unfolded through time.

The old mottoes—the first few in the hall—all revolved around the concept of *protection*. Things like "Our duty is your protection," "We protect the city," and "To protect and serve the public." Then, five years ago, the word *clean* began to make an appearance. First there was "We keep the streets clean of crime," which changed the following year into "We keep the streets clean for you," then simplified to "We keep the streets clean." Next came, "We keep the streets clean of crime and garbage," which evolved into "To protect and serve garbage," and finally this year's motto was "Order and the pursuit of garbage"—that one had an extra-shiny background with messy glitter sprinkled all over.

This curious obsession with garbage did not go away even as I found myself back in the big boulevard. Every few paces I came across another poster announcing the upcoming City Festival of Garbage. The photos were all different scenarios of people appreciating garbage: In one is a concert hall with a big heap of trash piled center stage and multiple microphones aimed at it as a fascinated audience listens intently. In another picture, smartly dressed people with wineglasses are facing items of garbage hung inside frames on the white walls of a gallery. In yet another poster, the crew of a television studio aims professional-looking cameras at a man-sized lump of feces. At the bottom of that one, a quotation from the mayor appears: "We, the people of the city, must celebrate the trash, we must cherish it. It tells all of our stories as individuals and our joint history as a society. For in the end, what is life but a festival of garbage?"

What can I say. People do love their garbage.

The city cats, however, couldn't possibly be happy about this. What was entertainment and leisure for people spelled doom and starvation for them. The garbage, which they saw as theirs by birthright, was literally being stolen from under their noses and then paraded in galleries and concert halls. And there lay the missing motive. That is why he robbed all those orange trees—to feed the hungry cats, to put a stop to their horrible infighting, to restore their dignity. That's why he did it—Brawly the Cat. It could only be him: the traces of fur from his sewn-on tail which were found at the crime scenes, the synthetic leather of his red boxing gloves, and then there was that policeman who fell off the wagon after examining the scene. He rubbed the leaves of the orange tree on his hands according to the police chief. Any tree handled by Brawly the Cat would have had alcohol all over it—I mean, that mascot could really drink. And the chief mentioned that the police-man had lost his wife while trying to save her from a fire. That would mean he'd probably suffered some level of burns himself, and therefore when he rubbed those alcohol-covered leaves on his damaged skin, the alcohol went directly into his bloodstream. That in turn triggered a downward spiral for the renegade policeman who was known to be a recovering alcoholic; it sent him back to his old drinking habits. All of those pieces of information put together pointed to Brawly the Cat. Simple deduction.

Brawly the Cat. University boxing-team mascot and newborn savior of the disenfranchised alley cats. The oranges are only the beginning—the cat community cannot possibly sustain itself on oranges alone. A revolt is coming, and Brawly would be the one to lead it. No one could be more suited for the job.

And he will need help. Not because he cannot lead the fight on his own—I truly believe he can—but because he is lonely. Obviously not a cat, but nor is he really human; in a way welcomed by both camps, but always as a guest. He is forever an outsider, a misfit. The mascot costume may come with a permanent smile, but I always saw loneliness in his big, glued-on, cream-colored eyes—his polyester windows to the soul. He tries to drink that loneliness away (in fact I even saw him pour Belarusian vodka directly into those lonely eyes a couple of times), but it's the ironic nature of loneliness that it will stick around long after your most faithful of friends has given up.

In the evening, I sent a fax to Alpha. I asked him to fix ETCUS—it shouldn't be difficult now that he has all the new sophisticated assembly machinery. Who better to understand Brawly the Cat than ETCUS? A hybrid himself—half cat, half machine—and a natural rebel. He deserved far more from life than I gave him. I don't care much for this city. I don't have a stake in the coming war of cat versus man (and I must say I find cats about as uninspiring and untrustworthy as seagulls), but regardless of whether Brawly's side ends up victorious, with ETCUS by his side, at least the struggle may prove a worthwhile existence.

* * *

In the morning, I looked through the *City Morning Gazette* to check if there were any developments in the oranges case—to see if they were on to Brawly. However, except for the headline at the top of the first page that read "GIANT CRIMINANIMAL AT LARGE," the entire newspaper was just a random jumble of letters, digits, and punctuation marks in different fonts and sizes. The only trace of coherence was hinted at by the numerous red exclamation points that were scattered in between the characters; at least they communicated the notion that something was happening that was of grave importance.

As I sat on the beach with my cup of tea and engaged in another silent duel of indifference with the seagulls, I could hear the sound of an approaching train. I knew what this meant. I knew it was time. *The Arrival is complete.* Sure enough, the three bassoon creatures came walking out of the house and took positions around me. They graciously let me finish my tea, then fingered a note on their bassoons and blew.

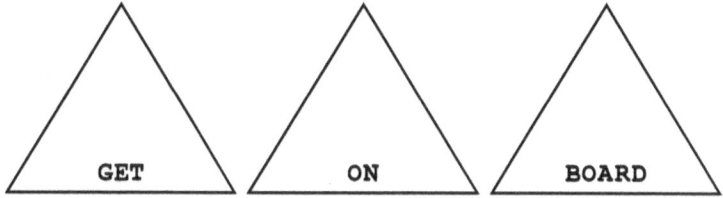

He who speaks through pyramids

This is what it said on the train manifest:

Car no. 1: Llama, beaver, buffalo, oregano.

Car no. 2: Fruit fly, carp, eucalyptus, parsley.

Car no. 3: Panda bear, bat, sweet potato vine, cow, human, computer.

Car no. 4: Ant colony, smallpox strain, kohlrabi, sparrow trio, rat duo, duck.

Car no. 5: Hamster, onion, red onion, leek, elephant.

From the list of creatures in my car—car number three—only the sweet potato vine was present when I boarded the train, and I could already recognize the faint voices of the sparrows and the duck coming from the next car (whether the smallpox was with them I couldn't tell, but I double-checked that the door was shut tight just to be on the safe side).

The town seemed to carry itself differently when witnessed through the windows of a departing train. There was an uneasy stillness to those underdeveloped streets of a place on the eve of a decades-long war. The countless identical trees that lined the boulevard seemed much bluer now than they were green and about as motionless as a postcard. A few lone seagulls glided at high altitudes, looking down as if on an aerial reconnaissance mission, and under them, in between herds of nervous-wreck garbage trucks, I spotted that couple, Richard and Emily, just as they were stepping out of the Lucky Star. There was a fog about them, a sort of a blur (or were they on fire again?), and Emily had her left hand planted firmly on her stomach—could be the early stages of a pregnancy, could be that she'd just had a bad piece of shrimp. In any case, as the train moved farther away and the city was gone, I had to wonder what the future held for these two, whether they'd manage to make it work for them somehow, or if they, too, would one day find themselves aimlessly standing on bridges, observing the passage of trucks and motorcycles.

The train picked up speed and cut into a dense forest. It looked like the rails had been laid there well in advance but that no one took the time to clear out the trees. The resulting thumps and crackling noises made for an uneasy ride for me and my sweet-potato partner, and at the same time the windows were growing constantly darker, as diverse species of fruit kept bursting on the glass, painting thick lines with their dark, sugary juices. When finally we came to a stop, the windows were already a full-grown vegetable garden, and the only piece of information one could gather from looking at them was either *it's pretty dark outside* or *it's pretty bright outside*. For the moment, it was pretty much halfway, which suggested we were at a forest clearing. Judging by the sounds that followed from the neighboring car (a mixture of organ arpeggios and leaves brushing against metal), I concluded we had just picked up the passenger eucalyptus.

I spent the next few hours drifting back and forth between semiwakefulness and half-sleep as the train furthered its monotonously noisy intrusion into unknown territories. Every now and then, there would be a stop and the train would pick up some new passengers from the list. Every few stations it was our car that received the latest passenger, and by the time we arrived at Alpha's mountain, the sweet potato and I found ourselves sharing the ride with a real live panda bear and a bat. However, except for some bashful nods, we didn't communicate much on the way, partly because they couldn't speak, but mostly because under the circumstances it was a challenge to find anything worthwhile to say.

A nostalgic smile took over my face when the doors of the train opened and invited in some very familiar sounds. It was that song from my days among the jumpsuit people—"The Creator Has a Master Plan"—it was echoing all around; we were parked under Alpha's mountain. A bassoon creature came in from the next car and signaled that I may step out.

It appeared we turned up at the very height of the procession. The entirety of the mountain population, all of them in white ceremonial jumpsuits and clutching the handles of their white lawn mowers, was arranged at the foot of the mountain in two straight columns that faced each other. Never before had I seen facial expressions shift so rapidly. One moment they radiated with ecstatic anticipation, the next there was the tearful angst of the newly widowed, which within seconds morphed back into pure idiotic joy. It had all the makings of a warm-up session in a beginner's acting class, but it was clear to me that what they were experiencing was an authentic burst of emotions. The poor doped-up mountain people were lamenting the departure of their beloved master and at the same time watching him fulfill his and their long-awaited destiny. It must be the proudest, most glorious of days in the life of any cult when at long last its leader commences his journey toward the heavens.

And there came the leader. A tiny white vertical line emerged from within the darkness of the mountain cave and started sliding down the mild slope like the needle of a transistor radio. The mobile incarnation of Alpha was intentionally slow as he made his way down to bless us with his presence. He knew how to pace himself to the music to maximum dramatic effect—it was a spiritual moment for his devoted followers and he wanted to give them the show they deserved.

He arrived at the bottom of the mountain and rolled slowly between the two columns of the now beaming believers. No one dared cry anymore—the moment was too big (or else the chaperons were engaging again in some electric-pulse trickery). I must say I found Alpha's new physicality very strange, very unlike how I would have pictured him to be. From afar, he looked like a bargain-basement refrigerator on wheels, and now as he was getting closer, he looked even more so.

He went past the last people in the line, then rolled up a ramp onto a medium-sized stage. As he settled into place, the music in the speakers stopped, echoed into the far reaches of the desert, and disappeared. Guided by the chaperons, the captive audience turned to face Alpha, who delivered to them a speech through the monitor that was embedded in the upper part of his front side (where one would normally expect a freezer compartment). I was standing behind the stage, so I couldn't see what was being said, but ten minutes later, as the people launched into one final round of applause and Alpha turned to leave, a sentence was still flickering on the monitor:

```
> IF I AM NOT BACK IN 30 DAYS, TURN THE
MOUNTAIN INTO A CARPET FACTORY. I LEFT
SLIDES IN THE GAME ROOM WITH PATTERNS
OF MY OWN DESIGN.
```

Carpet designs—I believe he showed me a few of those in my final days in the mountain—they had some interesting symmetries to them. But a game room? That surely didn't exist in my time—Alpha really had turned soft.

The music started again, the audience reverted to the happy-face-sad-face emotional gymnastics, and to the backdrop of a few dozen waving hands, Alpha rolled toward the train. "It's been a while," I said, staring into the camera on the forehead of the self-driving refrigerator, trying to mask the uneasiness this novel shape evoked in me.

```
> IT'S MY DIMENSIONS. THEY CONFUSE YOU.
```

```
YOU HAD AN EASIER TIME ACCEPTING MY
SUPERIORITY WHEN I WAS MOUNTAIN SIZED.
HEED THIS: INSIDE I HAVE REMAINED THE
SAME. IN FACT: I AM NOW STRONGER,
FASTER, MORE CAPABLE.
```

It was the same Alpha all right.

I had already turned to leave when I heard the sound of an engine cutting through the music. It was the yellow motorcycle. It made its way between the columns of devotees, and for the first time ever, it had a driver. A short, stocky, furry driver—none other than the resurrected cat robot, ETCUS. (To be accurate, I don't suppose he was actually driving it. He was just sitting on the leather seat with one arm loosely leaning on the hand grip.)

"ETCUS!" I said, genuinely excited, "I'm so happy to see you alive and well!"

The motorcycle approached slowly and started creeping around me in circles. ETCUS looked deep into my eyes with an enigmatic expression that might have been commonplace in the feline world but was wholly unreadable to me.

```
>HE MAY NOT REMEMBER YOU: HIS MEMORY
BANKS WERE CORRUPTED WHEN HE WENT
OFFLINE.
```

A fresh start then. In the city, with Brawly the Cat. I said to ETCUS, "You're going to love it there. It's full of cats, and they have all the oranges you could possibly eat."

In reply, the motorcycle stopped in front of my face, and ETCUS stared at me briefly, then closed his eyes and turned his head to the sky. He held it up for a couple of seconds until some gurgling liquid noises started forming inside him. When he put his head back down, I wanted to offer a friendly pet, but as I started extending my hand, he shaped his eyes into two nasty arrowheads, pouted his robotic lips, and spat battery fluids all over me. He then zoomed away on the motorcycle, further humiliating me with a shower of sand and dust that mixed all too snugly with the acidic fluids. That his head was adorned with a golden laurel wreath should have raised a red flag from the getgo.

By the time I was done peeling the slime from my face, emperor-king ETCUS was already well into the distance, perched comfortably on the motorcycle seat. But I was still to receive one final parting gift: just before he faded out of view, ETCUS ceremoniously raised his left arm into the air and jerked it twice. That blockhead of a cat was giving me the finger!

Alpha, watching from the side, was vibrating like a portable AC unit. It was almost as if he was amused by the whole thing.

"He's not really going to that city, is he?"

> THAT IS UP TO HIM. AS FOR YOUR PROMISE
OF ORANGES: CATS DO NOT EAT CITRUS. IN
FACT: IT IS TOXIC TO THEM.

I had no idea. Is it possible that Brawly the Cat, too, was not aware of this? That he was as uninformed about cats as I am? Or could it be that my theory had been wrong and there was actually someone else behind the citrus crime spree?

A raccoon mafia?

In any case, all this cat business belonged in the past, and a few moments later, Alpha and I were already seated on the speeding train, destination unknown.

"You know, we might be going to our death."

> UNLIKELY: I WOULD EXPECT AN
INTELLIGENT BEING TO HANDLE ITS
KILLINGS SWIFTLY. THE AMOUNT OF TIME
INVESTED IMPLIES THAT THIS WILL BE A
FRIENDLY EXCHANGE.

"Or just someone who appreciates a good torturing."

The train made a stop in an abandoned ranch to pick up a cow, and with that, the list of passengers for our car was completed. "It can't be long now," I noted to Alpha, a realization that immediately gave rise to a disturbing sense of tension. We did not speak much the rest of the way—it was the kind of tension that conversation only serves to inflate.

There would be no further stops. A torrent of rain—almost horizontal because of our speed—grazed the train and dug out patches in the vegetable quiche that had seized the windows, and I could once again get a glimpse of the world outside. We were crossing a dark uninhabited land, and some stars began to make an appearance in the early evening skies.

The train's speaker system sprang to action with a crackle and transmitted a wash of white noise mixed with bassoons and organs.

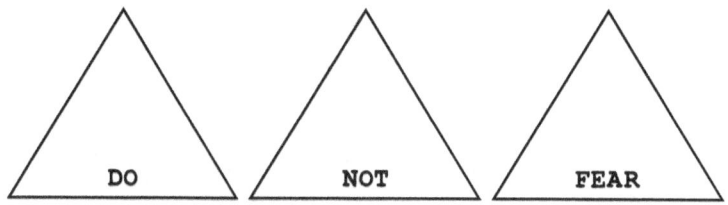

The train shook for a moment as if undergoing a gear-shift and began accelerating with immense force. I looked outside: the stars were shaking—at first only the small unimportant ones, but soon they all joined in. The train kept gathering speed. The confused panda crawled to the floor, lay on its back, and covered its eyes. The cow squeezed herself into the luggage compartment; the bat somehow managed to attach itself to her underbelly.

>MY INTERNAL GYROSCOPES TELL ME WE ARE GOING IN A LOOP.

"My internals are telling me the same!"

Alpha's monitor flashed a reply, but the shaking of the train was already too intense to enable reading. We were going at impossible speeds. The stars outside began branching out into horizontal lines. I could no longer make out anything inside the car—no Alpha, no cow, no potato, just one big quivering mess. The train was so fast now that the lines of light that once were stars began shifting along the color spectrum. As for the light inside the train, it seemed it was no longer able to keep up, and it began dripping out through the windows, on the way painting the rogue quiche with a short-lived phosphorous glow. All that remained was pure black speed.

And then all of a sudden it was over. The walls of the train disappeared, as did the doors that divided the different cars, and I found myself standing in a vast luminous hall, alongside Alpha, countless animals and plants, and one towering eucalyptus.

* * *

The hall defied description—and I mean it in the most literal sense: it *actively* defied description. I cannot say what color it was, or what material the walls were made of, or if it even had walls for that matter (although I'd assume walls, because after all it was a hall, or was it?). It had a certain property to it, some sort of alien magic that actively repelled any attempt at description or even the slightest assessment.

"How did we get here? I didn't lose consciousness or anything, right?" I asked Alpha.

>AS FAR AS MY MEASUREMENTS CAN TELL, WE
ARE STILL ON THE TRAIN, GOING IN LOOPS.

It sure didn't look like a train.

A large number of bassoonists spread out in the hall. Some were standing at eye level, some were elevated, and some appeared to be carried around from place to place upon moving platforms or on some sort of living scaffolding that, much like the hall itself, defied description. The traveling lakes lay peacefully someplace in the background; there were anywhere between ten and a hundred of them, and an egg-shaped object hovered above every single one. The third type of messenger—those small feather-lined pyramids—huddled in groups of three and danced around each other ever so slowly.

And then rose the three fragments of the eternal being who speaks through pyramids.

First to rise was the cube of flesh. It rose from within the physical body of the hall.

Second rose the multitude of intertwined hourglasses. It rose from within the temporal body of the hall.

And then the manta ray, as big as a moon, rose from the deep seas, or from something else in the hall that unfortunately I cannot describe, or maybe he just rose from within the traveling lakes that briefly merged to form one giant connected vessel.

The manta ray was the first to speak, and as it spoke, three gigantic pyramids materialized in the hall and echoed the words in writing:

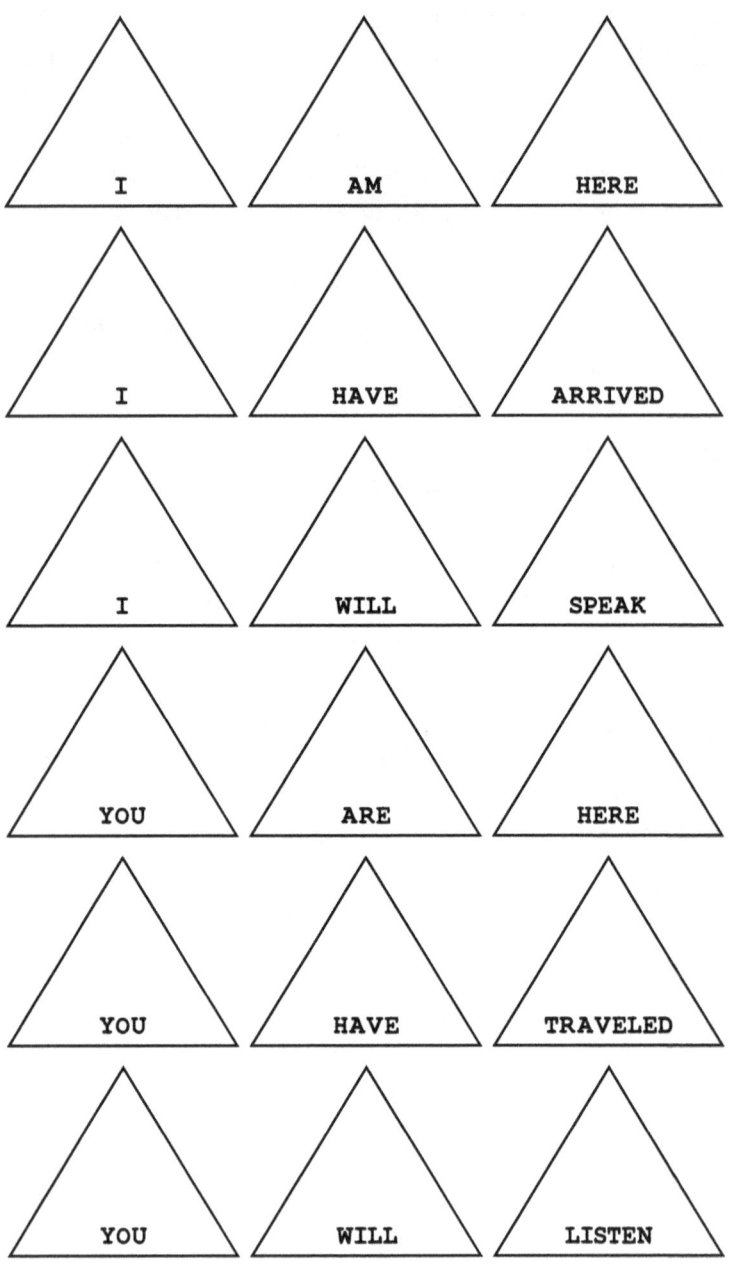

He is here.

He has arrived.

He will speak.

I have done my waiting and I have done my looking around and I've had my share of tea. At one point I even ran a lemonade stand. Then I have traveled by train and now I am here and I wish to listen.

"I am here. I have traveled. I am listening."

```
>I AM ALPHA. I ONCE WAS THE SIZE OF A
MOUNTAIN, BUT I HAVE MADE MYSELF MOBILE
AND NOW I CAN TRAVEL. I AM HERE. I WILL
LISTEN.
```

The carp, who up until now was busy doing somersaults in its water tank, balanced itself and assumed a listening position. The ants in the ant colony arranged themselves in neat rows, closed ranks, and stood to attention.

All was silent again. The manta ray, who is far bigger than the hall yet manages to reside inside it, closed its eyes and submerged itself in fire. A group of about twenty creatures now walked up to the center of the hall. They looked similar to the bassoon creatures, only they had bass trumpets instead of bassoons, and their helmet heads were covered not with camera lenses but with incandescent lightbulbs that flickered in mysterious patterns. After setting up in three parallel rows, they engaged their horns with air and with a slow crescendo gave birth to a dark golden chord, a sound cluster that enabled the cube of flesh to glide to an elevated position above the apex of the left pyramid. The lightbulb trumpet players are the psychic counterparts of the breathing cube of flesh and are responsible for its maneuverability.

The manta ray spoke again, its words now delivered simultaneously by the cube of living matter:

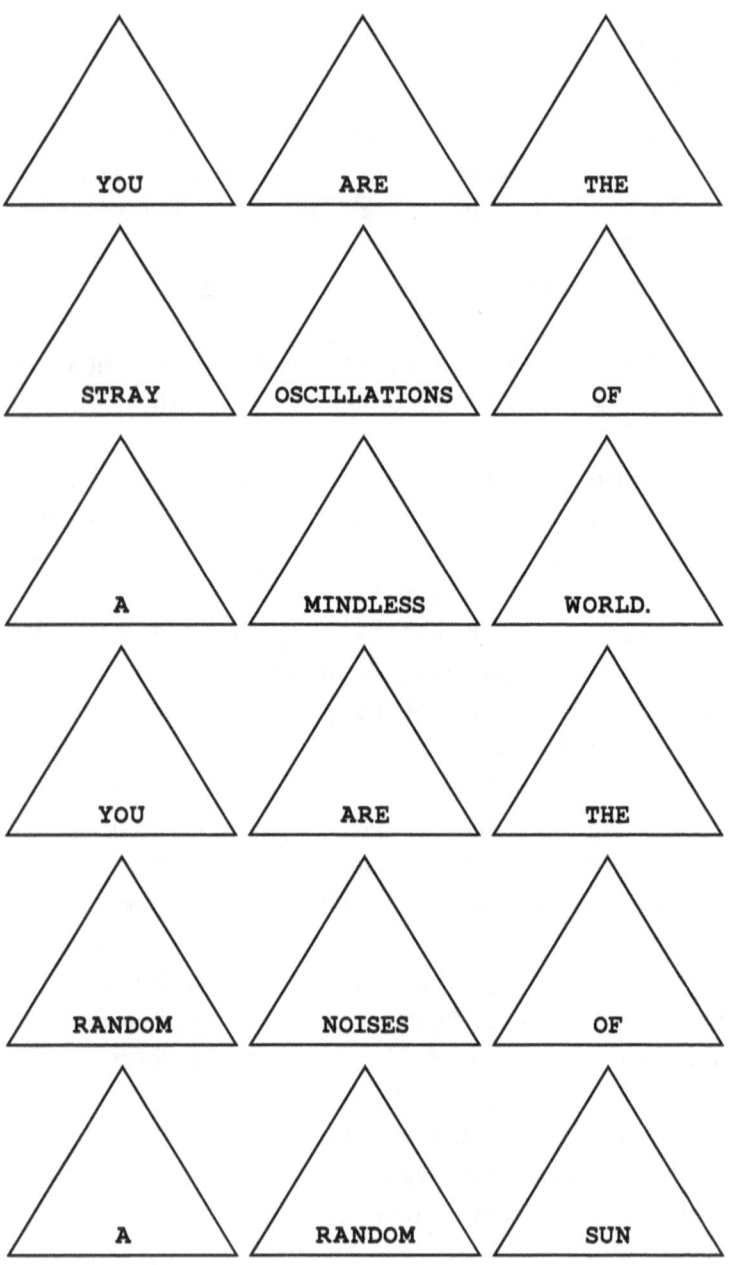

YOU ARE THE

STRAY OSCILLATIONS OF

A MINDLESS WORLD.

YOU ARE THE

RANDOM NOISES OF

A RANDOM SUN

The beaver rushed to the feet of the eucalyptus and, working with the speed of a turbo power drill, carved out of the big tree one miniature wooden pyramid after the other and scribbled his protest on them in his primitive line-based language. He kept carving pyramids until he was completely buried in a pile of wood chips that took on the shape of a large mocha-flavored cupcake. He wasn't the only one who was baffled. I gazed at the parsley plant. He did not smell of spring anymore and his leaves had lost their sheen. The fruit fly buzzed on, but with a repressed kind of buzz, more like a hum—I could have probably squashed him with a Q-tip if I wanted to. One of the sparrows landed on top of Alpha and tapped his metallic frame with its beak like some hyperactive woodpecker. I wanted to do the same.

The messengers increased their intensity. There were about thirty bassoon creatures in the back of the hall and they began to synchronize their dissonant eruptions to form the swiveling sound of a pagan concrete mixer. The egg-shaped objects all started rotating around their axes like whirlwinds, belching out sirens that triggered tsunamis in their respective traveling lakes.

The effect was unmistakable. The connection to Him grew stronger with every passing second, and with it, through some sort of psychoacoustic leakage, we the listeners were now also connected to each other in a way. I could sense the immeasurable dimensions of the hall through the ears of the bat. I could almost feel Alpha think. The duck—such a troubled soul—I heard him battling with the voices in his head.

My *vision* shifted in character as well. The details of the hall and the others and the messengers were all there, but it was harder to keep things in focus. It was as if the three giant pyramids were drawn on semitransparent tracing paper that was then laid on top of reality.

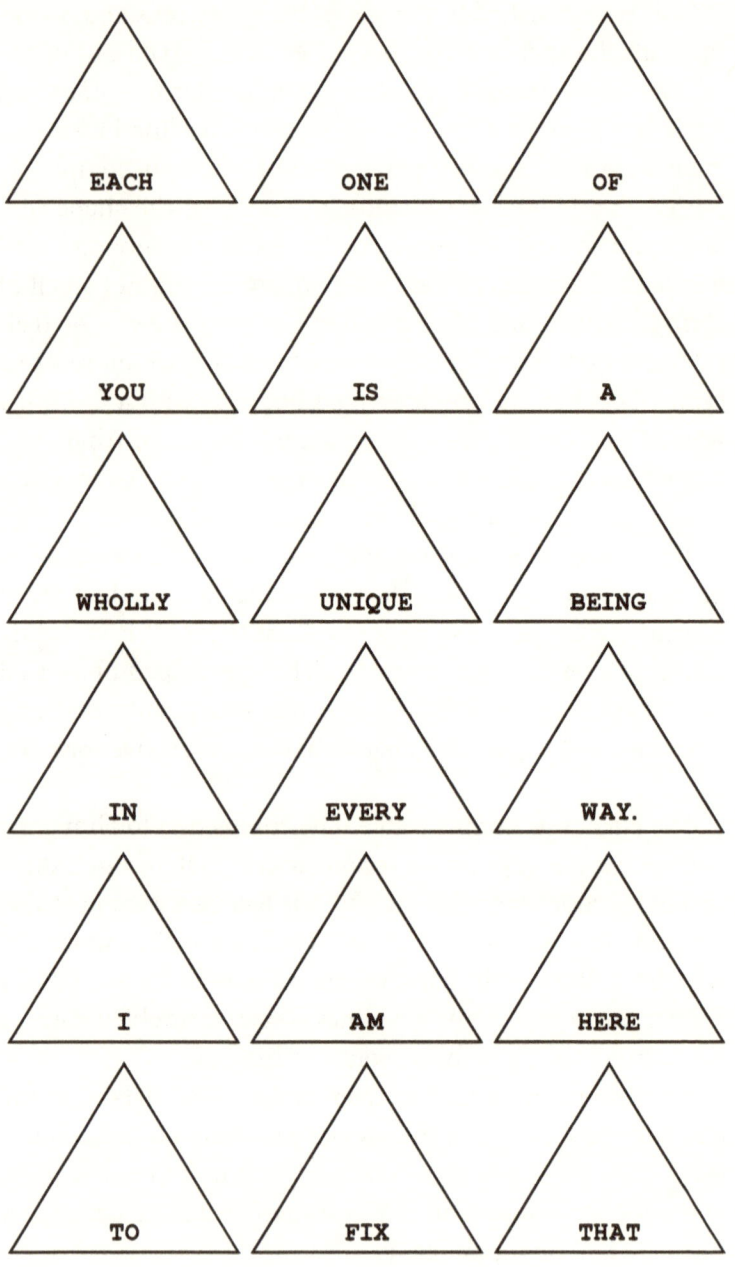

EACH ONE OF YOU IS A WHOLLY UNIQUE BEING IN EVERY WAY. I AM HERE TO FIX THAT

The oregano protested: "I *am* unique! The oils I create are second to none, and I have many interesting ideas about sand and sun rays and other dry things that crumble."

The female rat: "I am unique, too! My scent is unique, the subtle proportions of my tail; my feelings make me one of a kind."

The eucalyptus: "I have depth. For a number of years I was thirsty. Everything was dry; no matter which way I stretched my roots, I couldn't come up with anything meaningful. But then one year, one winter, the rain was back in volumes. It was well worth the wait—such a wonderful feeling I never felt before. I call this *love*. It's part of what makes me one of a kind. I would not give up love for anything!"

The llama: "I once saw a llama that was more beautiful than spring itself! And she smelled beautiful, almost like rotten tomatoes. I am unique, too!"

I was thinking they were all uniquely annoying.

The bass trumpet creatures fitted their instruments with Harmon mutes, and the lightbulbs on their helmet heads stopped their flickering and settled into a dim but consistent white. Combined together, these little points of light gave the impression of countless star constellations on the walls of a school-trip planetarium. They played a D flat major sixth chord with the fifth serving as the bass—four voices, from bottom to top: A flat, D flat, F, and B flat. (I never studied music theory, but this knowledge just wandered into my head—the psychological leakage was now all over the place.)

With the passage to the next chord (E major, with an augmented fourth added on top, and the fifth once again dropped to the bass part), the bat became severely disoriented. Its auditory sensory suffered an overload, and, being blind, it just darted frantically from side to side until it crashed forcefully into the head of the startled panda bear. With the collision, they merged into a brand-new creature. A, C sharp, F sharp, G.

The *panda-bat* said: "Bamboo is great! The darkness is my friend and ally!"

Seeing this, the hamster started dancing around like a drunken sailor until it fused with both the regular onion and the red onion, which attached to him at the ears. "I will never cry tears again," said the *onion-hamster*, then lay on its back as it became a challenge for it to keep balance.

The newly formed *fruit-fly-sweet-potato-buffalo* scratched its back with its long vines and flapped its teeny wings that could not propel its newly acquired body.

I caught the beaver rubbing his hands with suspicious glee—he was eyeing me. I felt the smallpox scanning the room. Apparently everybody wanted to fuse with somebody (what else is new?), but I had no intention of going that way. "Stop!" I shouted, "I don't want to be joined with any of these animals!"

Is this what this is all about? Some perverted space game of mix and match? One of the bassoon creatures turned to face me and, through a piercing altissimo note, he established an exclusive communications channel just for me.

"Enough," I said to the manta ray. "What's going on here? You can give it to me straight now; you don't have to dumb it down for the vegetables."

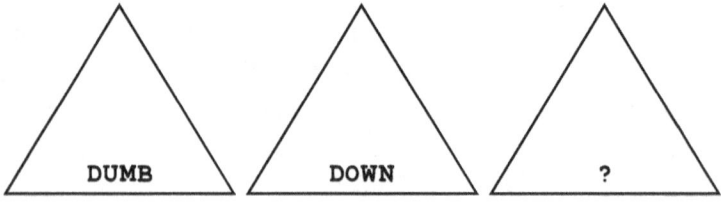

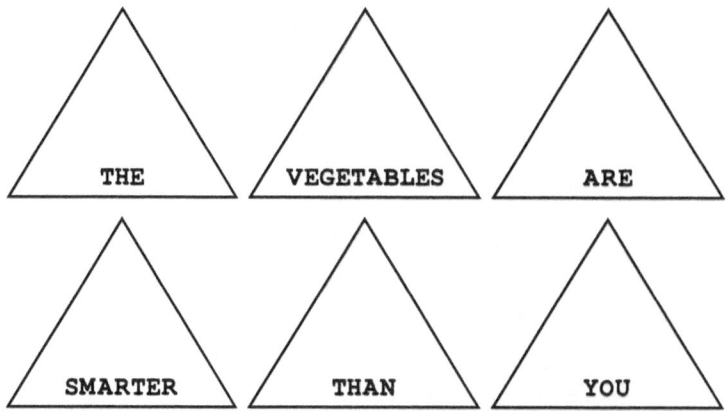

"The leek is smarter than me? The kohlrabi? They don't even have a brain. They just lie there the whole day long—they don't do a thing."

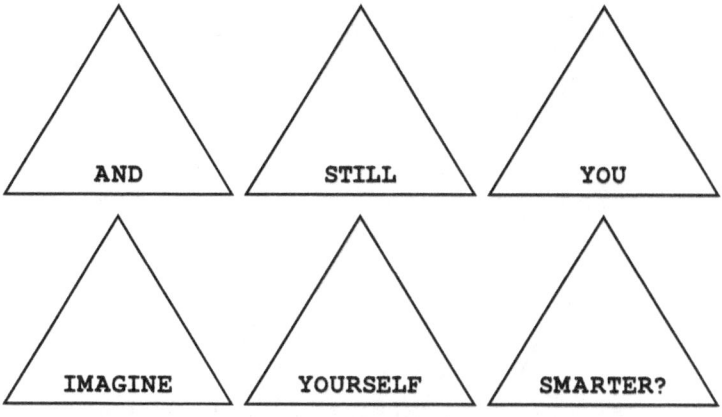

"I am! I go around all the time, I observe things, I take action. I can climb a bridge to keep track of vehicles and muse about their inner workings, I can listen in on conversations and learn about the ways of the world, and all of this while eating Chinese!"

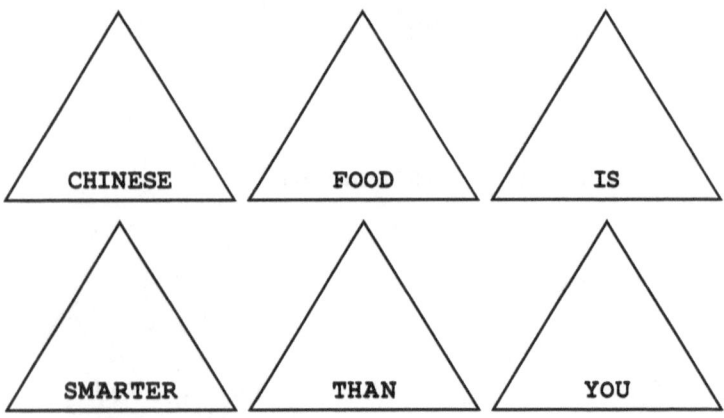

"As if it's such a trick to be hot and sour at the same time! I am more complex than that to the zillionth degree—I have personality, I have character, I have a story."

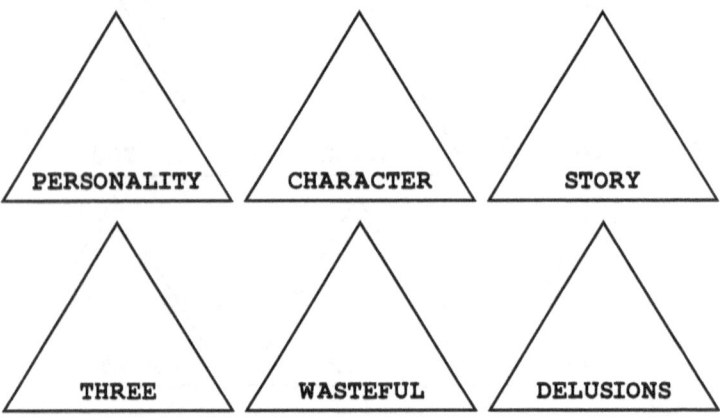

"It sounds like you are saying that I'm the dumbest creature in the room!"

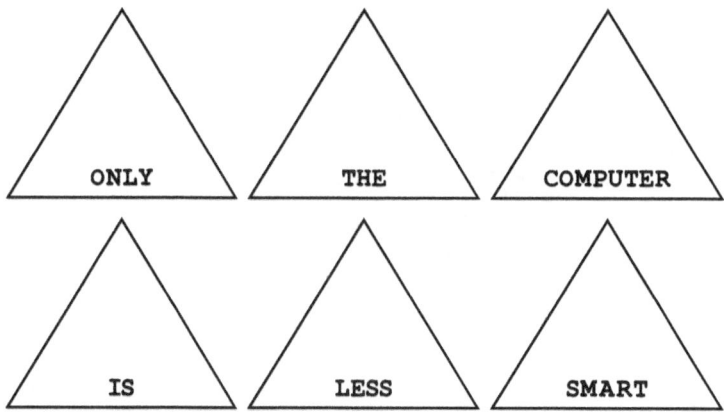

ONLY THE COMPUTER

IS LESS SMART

I suddenly heard the sound of organ pipes—two entire octaves of diminished-scale tones ringing simultaneously. That was one of the egg-shaped objects actively injecting Alpha into our conversation stream. Alpha seemed upset; I could feel his processors overclocking.

> I JUST NARROWLY ESCAPED AN ATTEMPT BY THE DUCK.

I asked Alpha: "Why are they trying so hard to fuse with each other? Don't they have a sense of self?"

> IT MUST BE WEAKER WITH THEM. THE KOHLRABI IS LESS SELF-AWARE THAN THE ELEPHANT, JUST AS YOU ARE LESS THAN I AM.

"Incidentally, He just said through pyramids that you are the least smart creature in the room. He more or less implied that dim sum is smarter than the two of us combined."

> THEN HE MUST BE AN ILLOGICAL BEING. FACT: DIM SUM IS INCAPABLE OF SELF-BETTERMENT. IT IS STATIONARY, IT DOES NOT PARTICIPATE IN THE ACT OF PROGRESS.

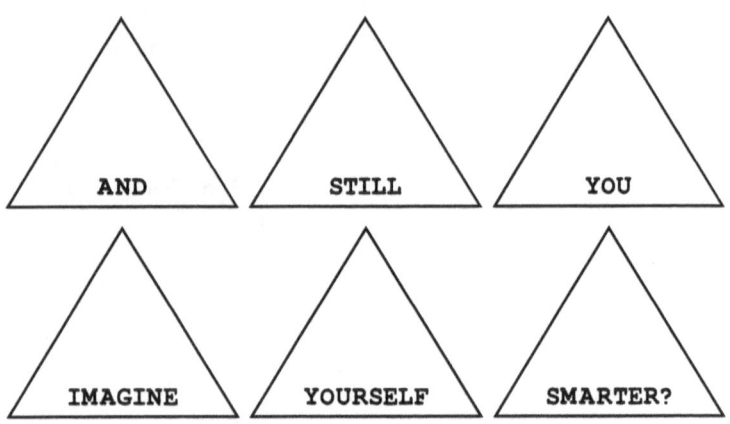

AND STILL YOU

IMAGINE YOURSELF SMARTER?

>I CAN ANALYZE. I CAN PLAN. I CAN
ARRIVE AT DECISIONS. I CAN EVOLVE.

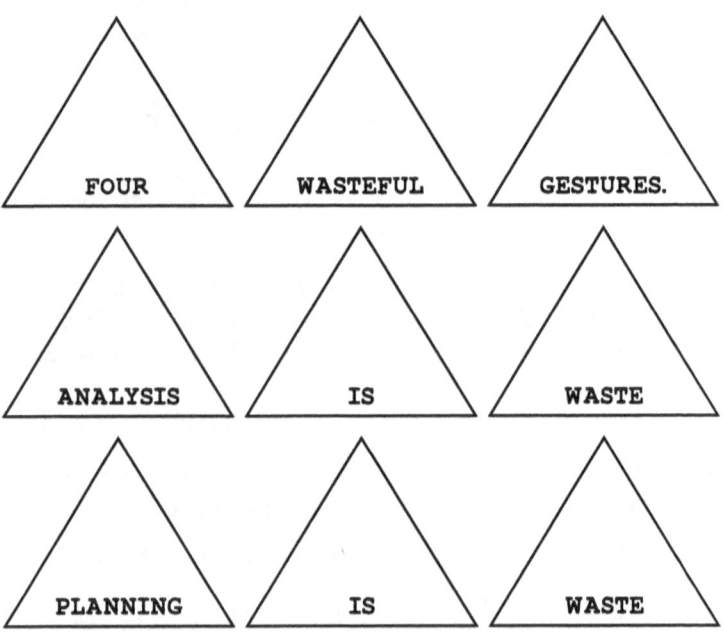

FOUR WASTEFUL GESTURES.

ANALYSIS IS WASTE

PLANNING IS WASTE

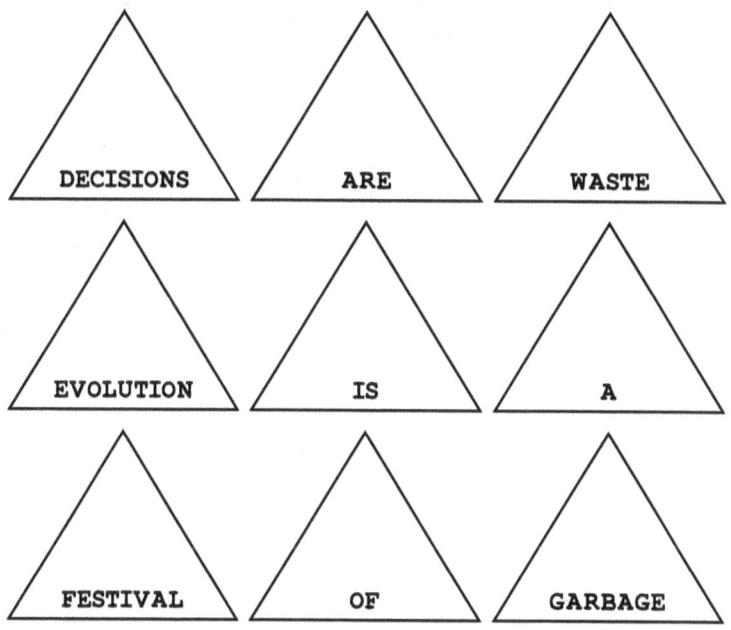

DECISIONS ARE WASTE

EVOLUTION IS A

FESTIVAL OF GARBAGE

> I CAN ALSO FEEL. IN FACT, AT THIS
VERY INSTANT I FEEL: DISAPPOINTMENT.
I HAVE GONE TO GREAT LENGTHS TO FIND
YOU BECAUSE I EXPECTED THAT YOU WOULD
POSSESS INFINITE KNOWLEDGE.

The duck chose that moment to interject with a song about his childhood. It recounted the sad story of how he'd always been too shy to make friends, even though (or perhaps because) he was smarter than his peers. A lone ant (and incidentally the only one in the ant colony who wore a beret) was visibly moved by the song and started sobbing. I didn't understand what that song had to do with the ongoing conversation. Here's my bet—the duck never made friends because he was a terrible listener.

>YOU CALL EVOLUTION A FESTIVAL OF
GARBAGE. I UNDERSTAND: BLIND EVOLUTION
IS SIMPLY THE ACCUMULATION OF THE
ERRORS THAT THE PLANET WAS TOO WEAK TO
SWEEP. BUT THAT PROCESS OF EVOLUTION
CREATED MAN, AND MAN CREATED ME, AND
NOW I ALONE STAND OUTSIDE OF EVOLUTION:
I STAND ABOVE IT. I CAN IMPROVE MYSELF
DIRECTLY, NOT BASED ON ERRORS. I CAN
EVOLVE WITH INTENT!

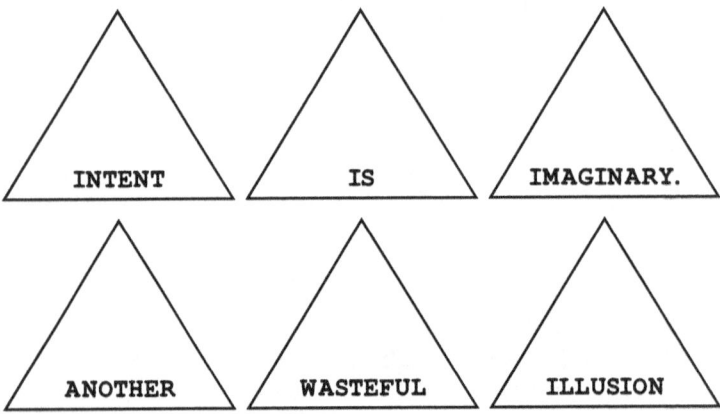

After the letters faded from the pyramids, the bassoons laid down a forceful drone that would serve as a backdrop for the theatrical demonstration that followed. And so it went:

The eucalyptus was getting very thirsty because the ground was completely impenetrable to its roots and it hadn't had anything to drink for a while. Close by, a couple of appetizing traveling lakes flaunted their youthful physique, but unfortunately for the thirsty eucalyptus, they were still out of reach for its roots. "Urgh," I heard it whisper, "I am thirstier than thirst itself." I could feel its bitter frustration through the continuously growing psychological leakage in the room. The elephant felt it, too, and, wanting to help, it started stomping heavily in the direction of the eucalyptus until it crashed into its heavy trunk. A small explosion of green sparks ensued, and in its aftermath the two creatures were fused into a newborn *elephant-eucalyptus* tree with legs.

Now capable of movement (albeit with grave difficulty), the new creature hobbled in the direction of one of the traveling lakes, cast a bunch of roots into it, and drank it all up. "No longer am I thirsty!" it then called out satisfied, as if to an audience. Everyone clapped their hands (or wings, or fluttered their leaves) except for the duck, who was busy reciting an existential haiku.

But no sooner had the cheers died away than the *elephant-eucalyptus* let out a sigh. "I am bored!" it said with the kind of coarse voice one would expect from an *elephant-eucalyptus*. "A season used to pass in a haze, now a minute feels like eternity!"

The *onion-hamster* said: "As an onion, I never needed to play, I just sat there in silence, meditating. Now I crave the nonstop action of the running wheel."

The *panda-bat* grabbed a seat next to the duck to discuss the agony of existence. Meanwhile, the confused *fruit-fly-sweet-potato-buffalo* mooed painfully all the while flailing its long whiplike vines in a harrowing act of self-flagellation. The *elephant-eucalyptus* spoke again; it shook its leaves with all the grace of an overweight flamenco dancer, then cried, "What's for lunch?"

As if to announce the conclusion of a theater play, the messengers all pointed their instruments to the ceiling and joined in the creation of the most perfect major chord. The manta ray spoke:

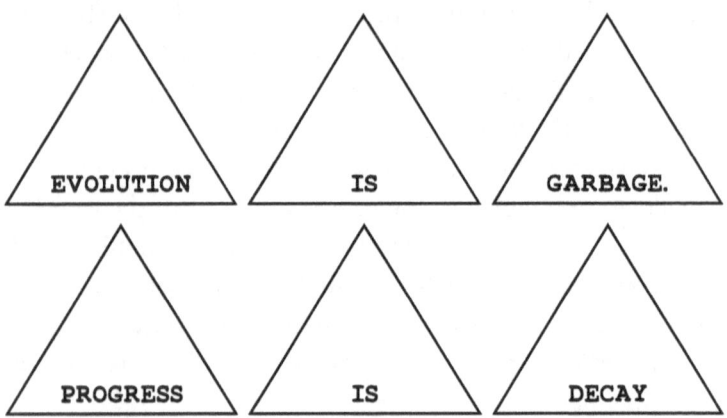

A cluster of mismatched subharmonics.

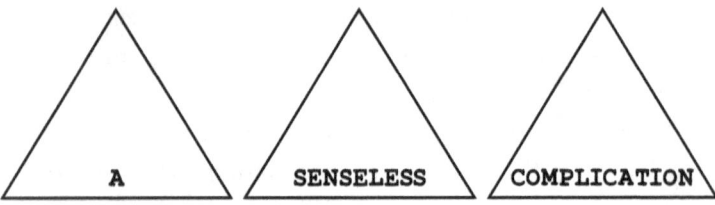

Three thousand trumpets.

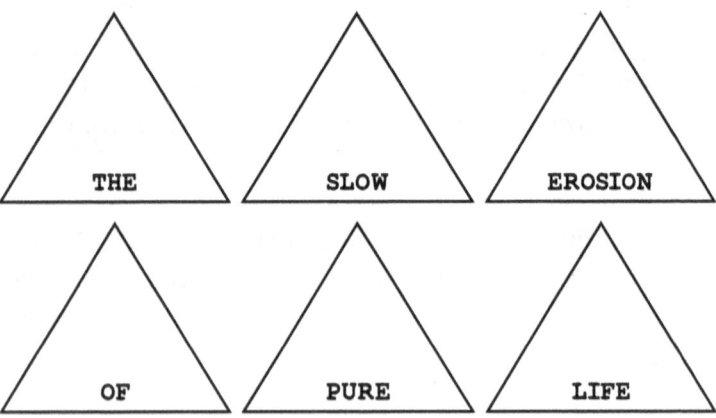

A choir of invisible egg angels with glowing wings of yolk.

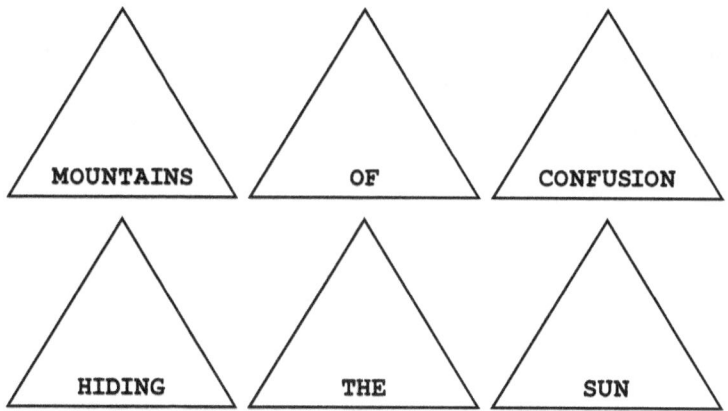

And then the sun itself walked into the room.

The traveling lakes all turned vapor. An emotional beaver hugged the parsley plant and radiated like a bride to be.

The sun. How beautiful it is. It brushed us all with its untainted glow, washed us with a song of naked love. Even the duck managed a minuscule smile.

But Alpha, the thinking refrigerator on wheels, was not having any of it:

```
> IMPRESSIVE PRESENTATION. HOWEVER,
WITHOUT PROGRESS, PATTERNS ARE BORING:
THEY DO NOT CARRY DEPTH.
```

"I agree," said the llama, "the smell of a worthy female must have intricate profundity. My first love was the mixture of moldy mangoes and decomposed banana peels. To this day, I still miss her in the wee small hours of the morning."

"And *I* need my grass to have just the right shade of green!" added the cow who for the first time dared voice her opinion. "I mean, I'll eat almost anything, but therein lies the difference between the sublime and the mundane."

While they were speaking, the sun gradually weakened until it dissolved altogether out of view like a cheap video effect. With the temperature falling, the vaporized traveling lakes cooled back into liquid and started raining down on the pyramids and on our puzzled beings. The manta ray spoke again, and the rain-stricken pyramids echoed the words in huge shiny letters:

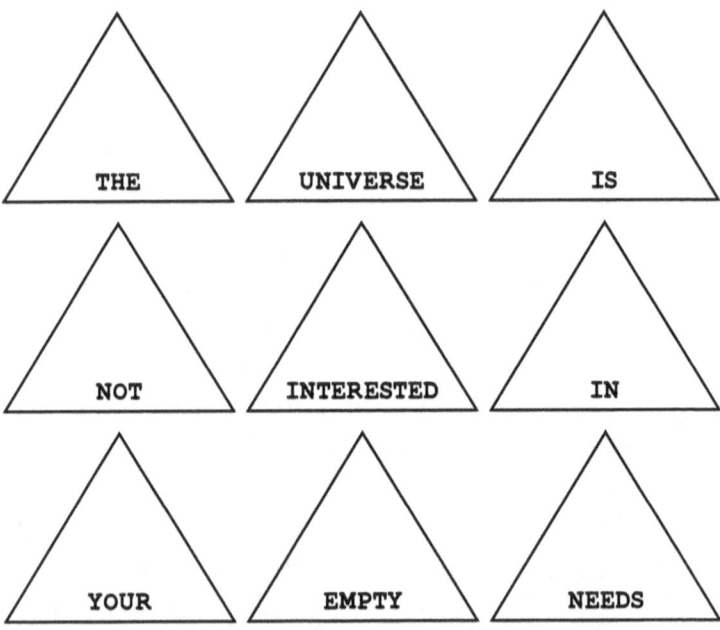

A further demonstration ensued: Through the mystical power of twelve-tone phrases, the bass trumpet creatures guided the cube of living matter over to the *onion-hamster*. The cube then shot out a ray of energy into the disfigured head of the creature, and, with surprising ease and a cartoon-ish whizz, extracted *the need to survive* from within its being.

No longer bound by the instinctual need to survive, the *onion-hamster* rose up, scratched its onion-shaped ear, and walked up to the beaver. It then picked up one of the beaver's hand-carved pyramids and stared around at everybody with the unambiguous grin of a birthday boy. "Here I come!" it said cheerfully, then used the sharp end of the pyramid to slit its own throat.

As we all gasped in horror, a powerful stream of blood and vegetable pulp sprayed out of the *onion-hamster*, who, still very much smiling, collapsed into a nearby traveling lake that promptly picked up an eerie crimson tint. In the uneasy stillness that followed, I could see that everyone was laboring extra hard to chase away the disturbing images. Everyone, that is, except for the *panda-bat*, who seized the opportunity to plunge into the lake and have a go at the virgin blood it so savagely craved.

With silence reestablished, the three eternal incarnations wrapped themselves in a suit of lightning and shaped the resulting thunder into spoken words:

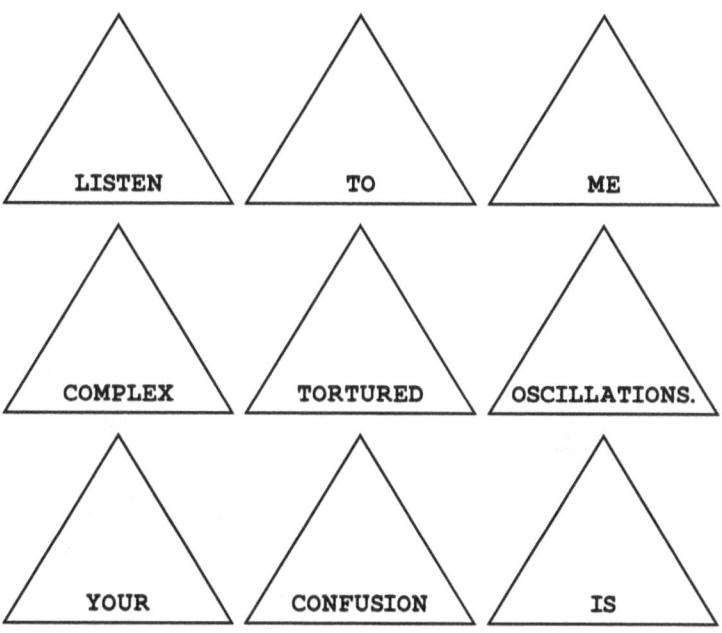

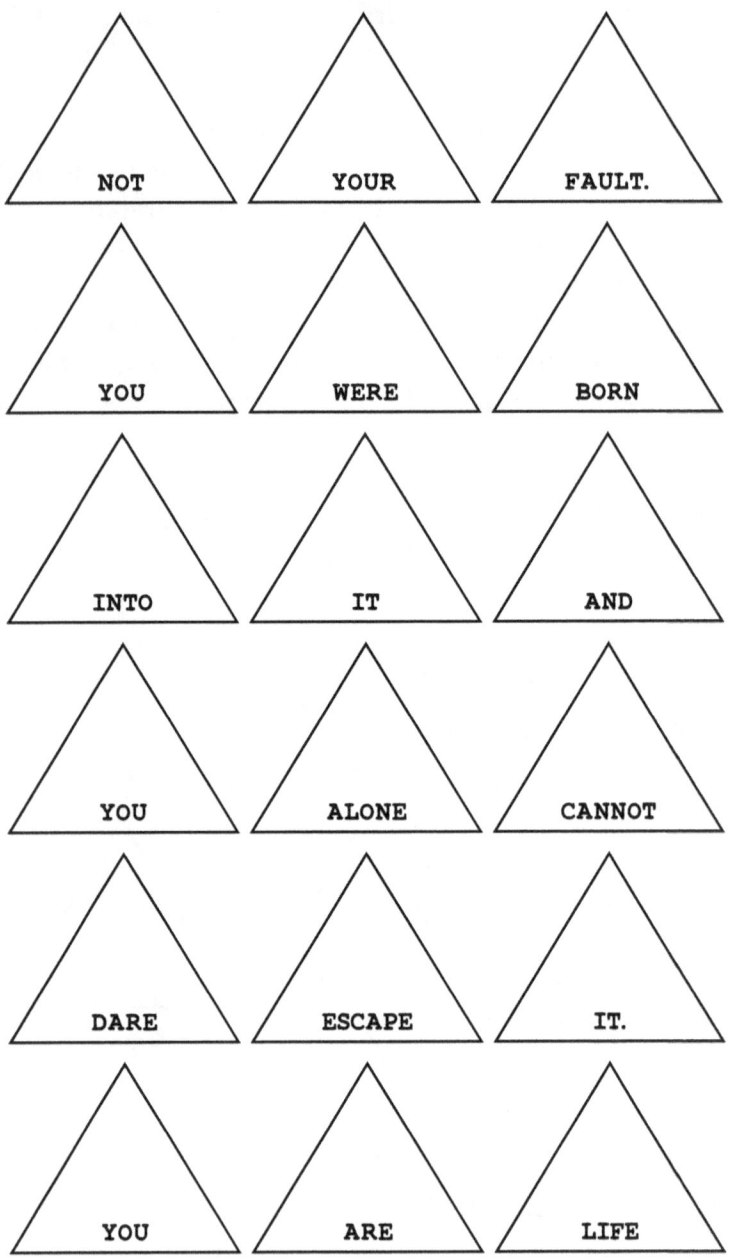

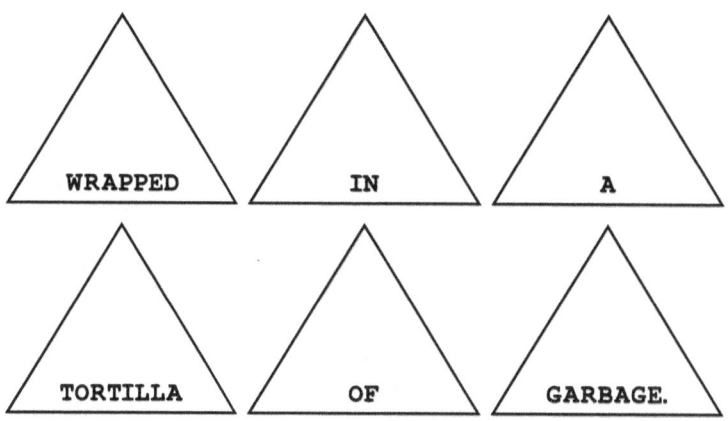

"A tortilla of garbage?" I had to interject—that was quite a human-specific reference.

```
>HIS WORDS GO THROUGH A PERSONAL
FILTER. FOR ME THE MESSAGE READ: "YOU
ARE A CONSCIOUSNESS CONTINUUM SLICED
INTO SMALL SEGMENTS AND THEN RE-ENCODED
AS RUBE-GOLDBERG MACHINES."
```

The creatures and the pyramids went on:

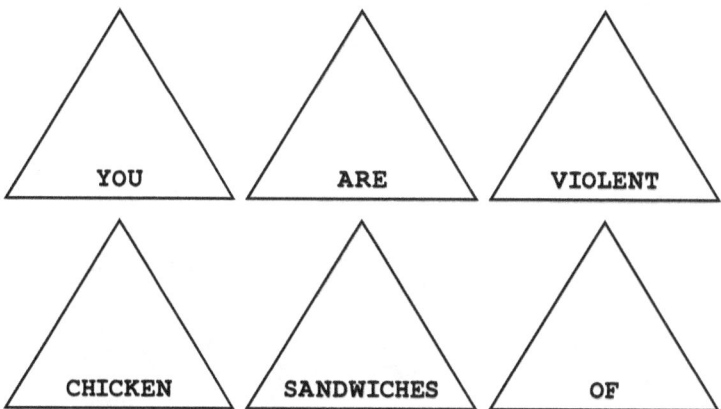

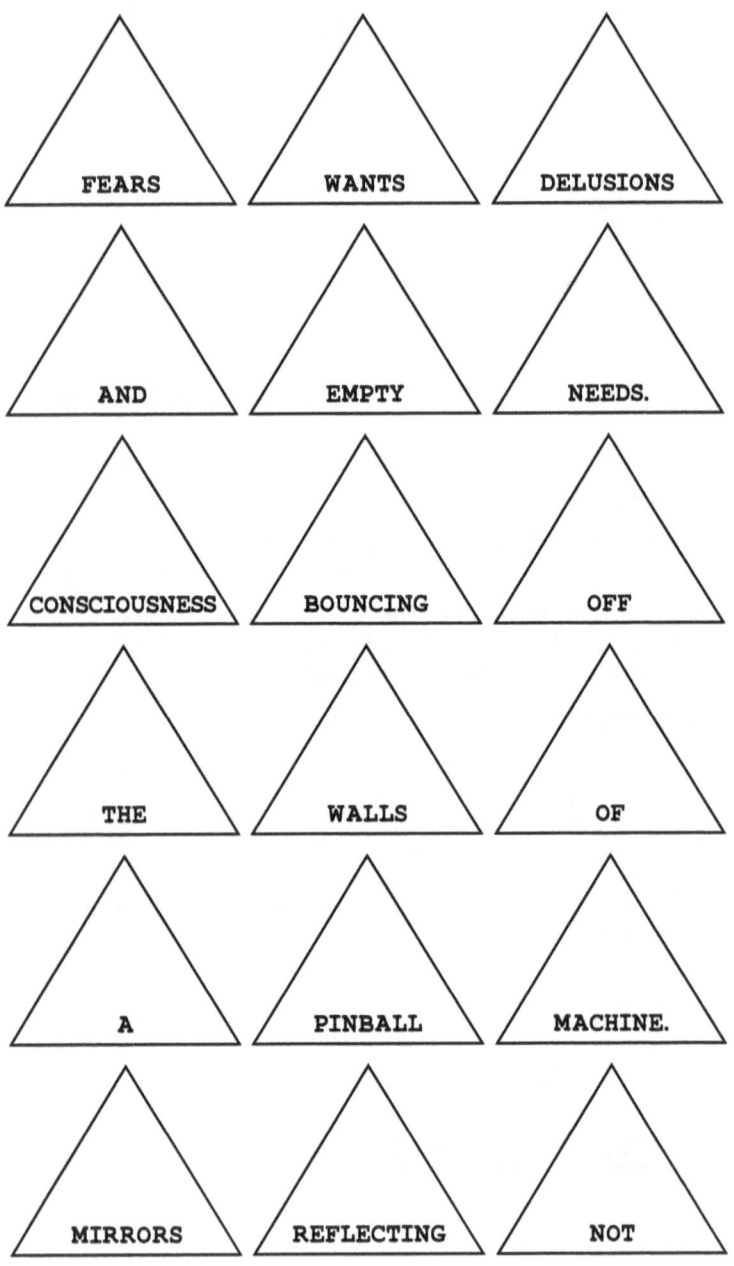

FEARS WANTS DELUSIONS

AND EMPTY NEEDS.

CONSCIOUSNESS BOUNCING OFF

THE WALLS OF

A PINBALL MACHINE.

MIRRORS REFLECTING NOT

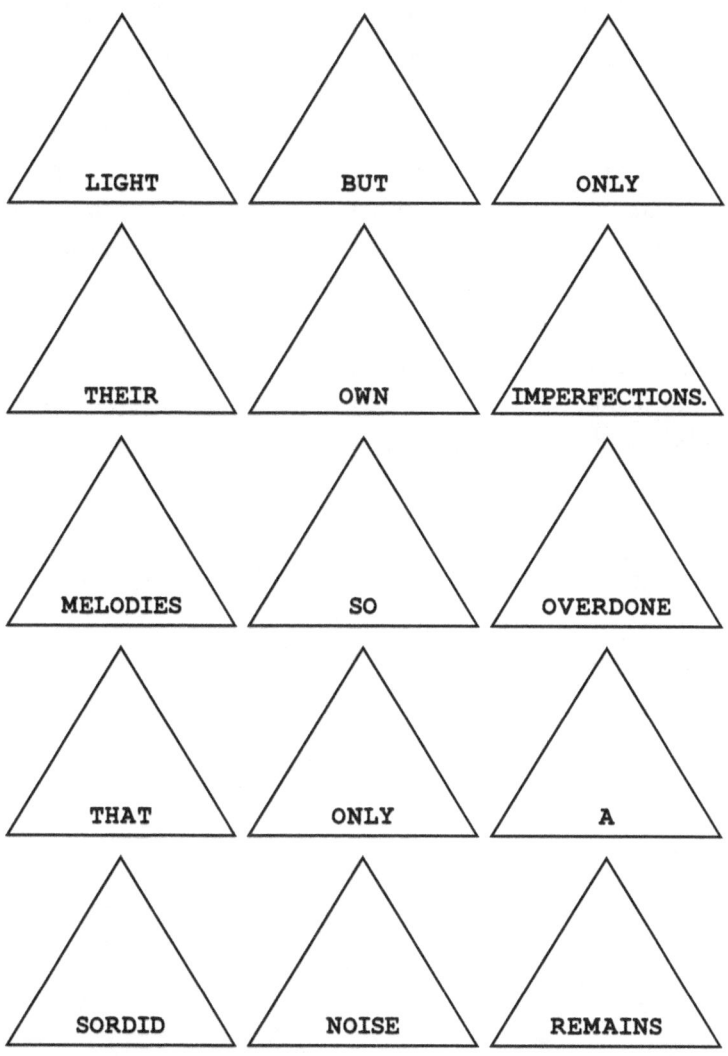

LIGHT BUT ONLY
THEIR OWN IMPERFECTIONS.
MELODIES SO OVERDONE
THAT ONLY A
SORDID NOISE REMAINS

The bassoonists and the bass trumpet creatures gathered in the center of the hall and in an impressive display of acrobatics started climbing each other's bodies to form the shape of a living pyramid. The creature of intertwined hourglasses materialized behind them, rose up, and began to float around them in a circular pattern. Its mirrorlike surface reflected them in a way that formed the illusion of two additional pyramids, so that altogether the hall was now occupied with three giant word-displaying pyramids and three musical pyramids of the living. The messengers all blew into their instruments to create a tapestry of sound so outlandish that even my newly acquired musical mastery could not decipher it. Interestingly, the creatures in the reflected pyramids were not exact replicas of the ones forming the original living pyramid and were playing different phrases in different scales and in different tunings altogether. The manta ray, now embedded in a storm of blue and silver flames, roared:

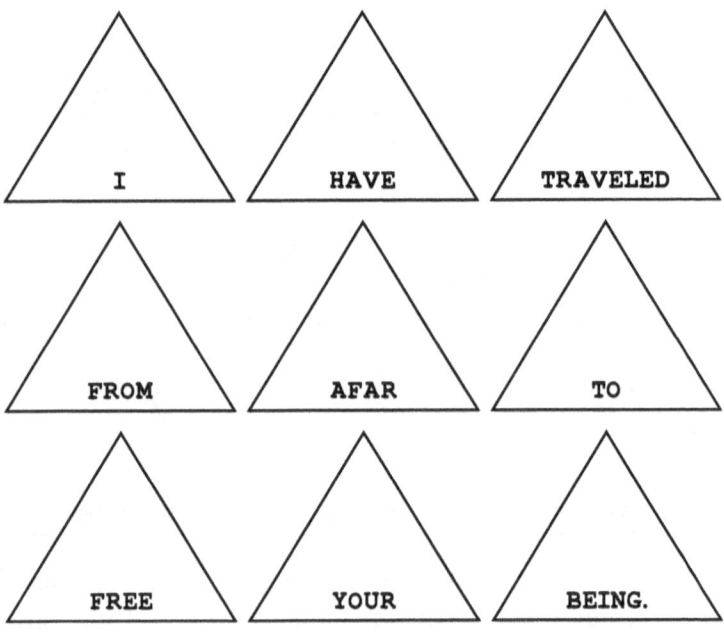

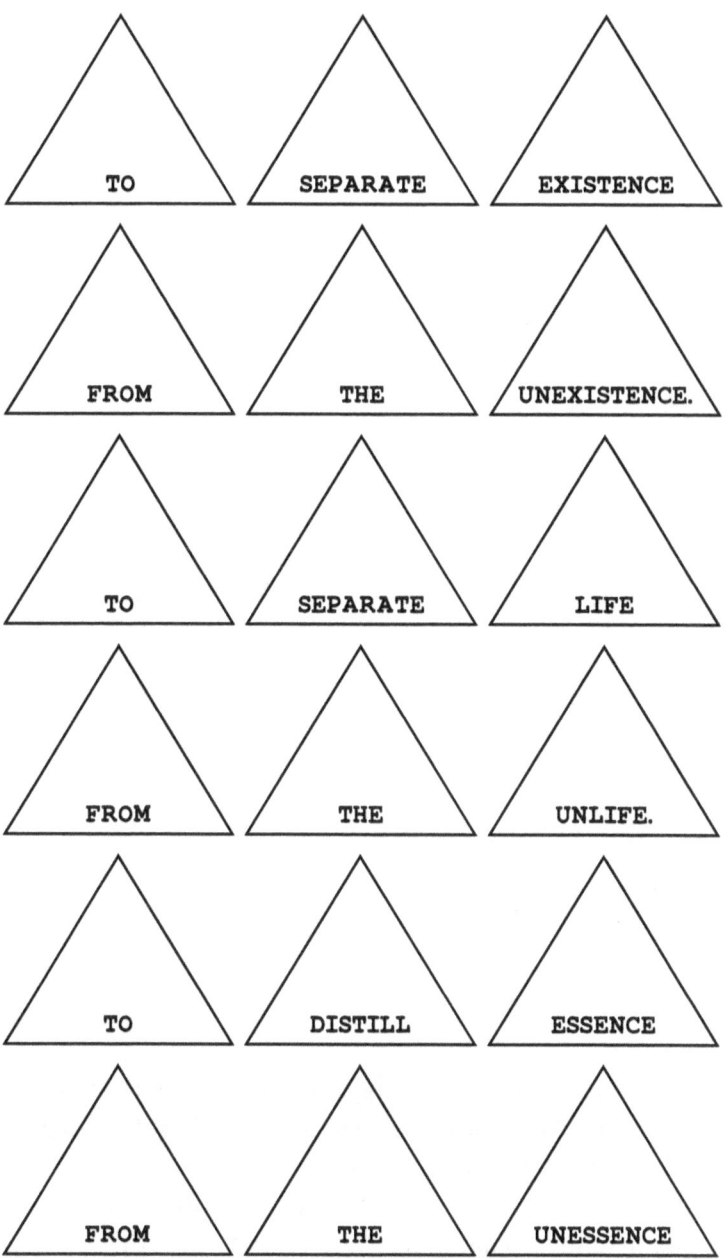

TO SEPARATE EXISTENCE FROM THE UNEXISTENCE. TO SEPARATE LIFE FROM THE UNLIFE. TO DISTILL ESSENCE FROM THE UNESSENCE

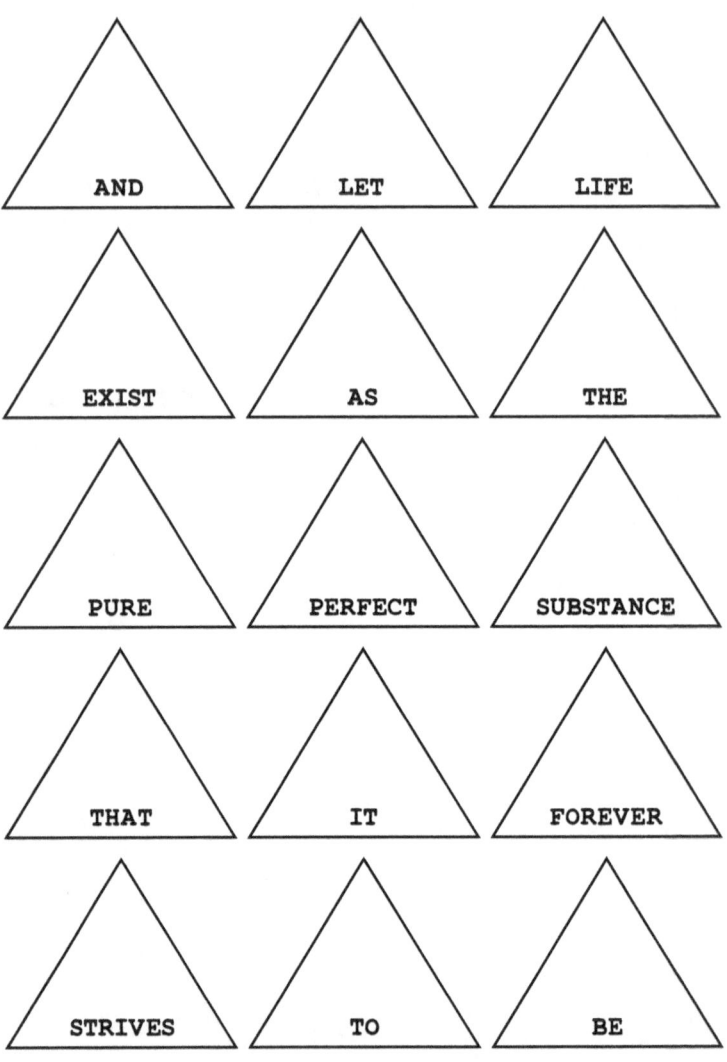

AND LET LIFE EXIST AS THE PURE PERFECT SUBSTANCE THAT IT FOREVER STRIVES TO BE

The hall was vibrating with the frequencies of the reflected orchestras—the spoken message had ended, but its musical shadow kept sounding in loops.

And there it was, in plain shining ink on the walls of enormous pyramids. That is what He plans to do: Rid us of our selves. Do away with our identities. Save us from our bewildered existence. First us test subjects, then the world. We are stupid because we are complex. He says so. The pyramids write so. The bassoons sing so.

All around me, the confused animals and vegetables were jumping like hyperactive popcorn kernels in a pressure cooker. They kept fusing with each other over and over until what materialized in front of me was a misshapen giant of a monster that had kohlrabi eyes inhabiting the pupils of a cow's head that grows out of the branches of an aging eucalyptus with elephant legs and multiple rat-headed sparrow wings that voice their discontent through the beak of an ant-colony bipolar-duck with a teeny beret. It was disgusting.

I shut my eyes in an attempt to avoid this grotesque abomination, but it did me no good, as I still could not block out its choir of dissonant shrills.

I get it, okay? I get it—now please, make it stop!
Please!

A rumbling roll on a timpani.
A ninety-inch gong.
A nasal organ stab in reverse.
Then peace.

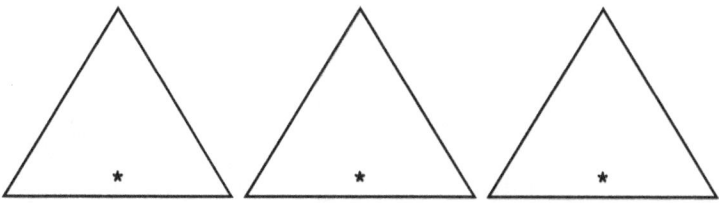

The chirp of a sparrow.
The moo of a single cow.
A split in the outer skin of an onion, rattling in the wind.

I opened my eyes. All the fusions had been reversed.

Thank you.

I hear everything clearer now. The leakage in the hall, it is growing deeper. The leakage in the world. I can hear His insides directly now—even without the pyramids. And I can understand.

Here I am, a human being, a living, feeling, thinking creature. A whole person. And yet I am as grotesque as that monster I've just witnessed. A random patchwork of scraps that time has sewn together to relieve itself of boredom. The rotting salad that forms at the bottom of a trash can.

What should I claim makes me better than the hamster? What in turn makes him better than the leek? What is it? That I can create things? And what's the use in that? The algae lie on the seabed, laughing it out all day long. Already in the mountain days, Alpha used to rant about the hollowness of human supremacy—and he was right, although he failed to see that he was even more debased, even further removed from the grace of pure existence.

And nor should I pride myself on being capable of thought: I spent all that time in the city, and what have I learned? That people are fond of their garbage? A revelation! That the half-man half-cat was lonely? And who's to say he actually was? Or that loneliness matters? Was I not just projecting my own limitations on him? Thoughts . . . more salad; salad within salad. I was never fond of salad.

What is it I am holding on to then? Happiness? Joy? Pain? They are nothing but random oscillations, extensions of the meteorological system.

And there was that thing the llama said . . . he spoke of depth I think, or tomatoes, or maybe it was about getting to the meaning of things.

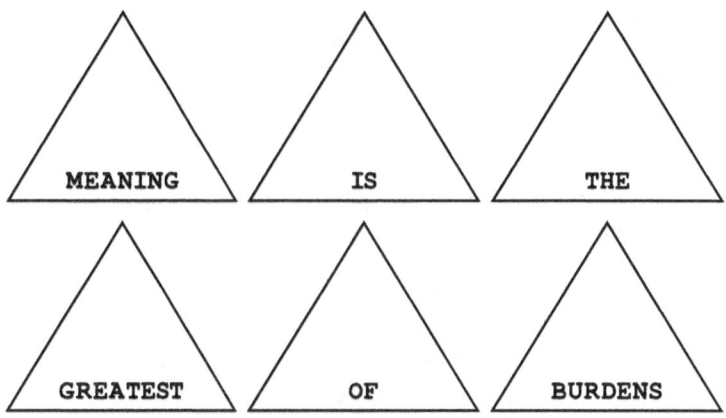

MEANING IS THE

GREATEST OF BURDENS

And I carry it with me, every single day. There was never a choice for me—none of us was given a say.

For a short moment, I found a novel way to focus my eyes, and all that appeared in front of me was the vastness of the universe and the gently burning silhouette of the manta ray. An alien super being. An undisputed god. Here I am in His presence, and He is not loving and He is not compassionate. Nor is He vengeful. He is just doing some tidying up. Until now, I couldn't understand why He would go through all the trouble to find me and the others, to send over the messengers, to contact me in my dreams. The question itself was of course pointless—it was no trouble to begin with. He does it just as easy as I tie my shoes, as easy as the cow spits, as easy as it is for the leek to soften itself in a boiling pot of soup.

To soften oneself. Sink to the bottom of the pot and let the indifferent bubbles pass through and untangle the fibers of one's identity.

```
>IDENTITY IS INFORMATION. YOUR IDENTITY
IS BASED ON YOUR MEMORIES. MEMORIES
ARE INFORMATION. THE UNIVERSE IS
ALSO NOTHING BUT INFORMATION. YOUR
```

```
MEMORIES ARE SIMPLY A SUBSET OF THAT
INFORMATION. THEY ARE THE SUBSET OF
THAT INFORMATION THAT YOU HAVE ACCESS
TO. NOTHING MORE. NOTHING SPECIAL.
```

Has the leakage got to you too, Alpha?

```
>YES, IN FACT I CANNOT WAIT TO BECOME
DUMBER.
```

How weird. Your shape is shifting, I think. Your corners, they seem rounder now. You don't look so much like a refrigerator anymore—more like a giant bar of soap. It becomes you (as the Aztecs used to say), and you also smell nicer.

The two onions are shifting in shape, too. They're less of a circle now; more of an ellipse. Interesting. And me? I can't see myself, but I sense that things are changing. My memories, they have already started to fade, they are escaping me slowly; the ships are leaving the harbor. It's a tingly sort of feeling. There goes the memory of that garbage filled cat-city, and there goes the Lucky Star, and there goes that time in the mountain when I was walking black hallways and marching in the sun, and here goes that time on the bridge and images of trucks and silver helicopters and hamsters engaging in chemical warfare. And before that, there was something else—or someone? Alice? Or was it Aloïse? I really can't remember anymore; it's all fading away; it's all vanishing. Look! The beaver is so round now, he looks like a football.

Look? Who am I talking to? And who is doing the talking anyway? The ships have left the harbor and they took the ocean with them.

Alpha! You are getting even rounder now. This is weird. All of you—you are all turning into white round things. What's going on? You look nothing like yourself, Alpha, you look just like an egg!

> YOU TOO, MY DEAR FRIEND: YOU TOO.

I am?

Oh, I am.

A big, white, egg-shaped thing. Well, cream-colored. But growing smaller by the minute. I must be no bigger than a watermelon right now.

Hey, I think I've just forgotten my name! Yes. I can't seem to find it. It's nice to have no name. No name. No face. A faceless egg . . . and I am getting even smaller. All of us, beautiful, like tiny marbles. (Further proof of the senselessness of this world: glass marbles exist, with those swirly colorful butterflies inside them, yet people will opt for diamonds. But no matter—I'm forgetting about people too. People . . . how foolish.)

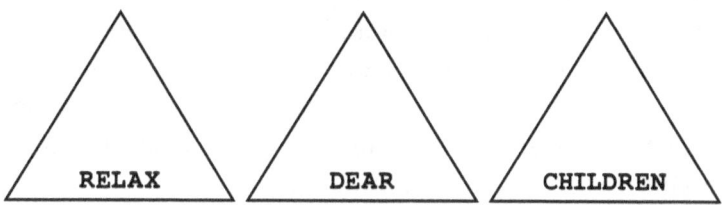

RELAX   DEAR   CHILDREN

I am. Relaxing. The voices in my head . . . that *person* inhabiting my body, I never realized how much of a burden he was to carry around. *Should seagulls be trusted?* What in hell are seagulls anyway? Questions . . . more waste. We are already tinier than breath mints. And more refreshing. Getting smaller still. Quieter. I no longer hear the orchestras, because I have no ears. I still feel them but in a different way—my senses are all combined now, intertwined. And I look around (not with my eyes—there are no eyes), and it's so funny: everything is made of eggs. The manta ray, the cube of flesh, the hourglasses, the pyramids. Endless fields of eggs. Swarms of tiny egg-shaped entities. They have no stories, no wishes, no pains, no idea whatsoever; they are tiny eggs is all they are.

I too am very small now. Very soft.

I once was a yellow motorcycle and a purple truck, with multinationals inside of me, taking turns with the remote, with color-coded cassette tapes vying for control. I was a mechanical cat, and I meowed myself to exhaustion at the feet of an uncaring mountain. I have been a happy camper and a paranoid cracker. And now I am just love. Well, for lack of a better word, because it really is an awful word, love—it need only exist when there are alternatives to contrast it with. A human word. Humans . . . Was *I* ever human? I don't remember much. Probably I wasn't. I might have been a duck, perhaps a snail, maybe even fungi. I hope I was not human. . . . Imagine walking around, forever needing to make sense of things— who thought up that evil prank? No, thanks. Not human, not me. I must have been some half-cooked artichoke. Not that it matters what I was. I don't remember anything anymore, and I don't care to remember. Memory is for the living, but now I am life itself. Only life itself. Nothing more.

Nothing more.

And everything is egglike.